For Lindsay,

A new frien

have connected with you

THE SKULL CHRONICLES III

DAUGHTER OF
THE GODS

D K Henderson

love & blessings

Dawn xxx

D. K. Henderson

Published by Lyra Publishing, 2014

Lyra Publishing
Wiltshire, England

Copyright © Dawn Henderson 2014

Cover design by Akira
http://www.createspacedesignz.com

Skull photograph by Philippe Ullens
www.soulfoodphotos.com

ISBN 978-0-9571952-9-5

www.dkhenderson.com

This book is dedicated to everyone who has a hunch that
maybe, just maybe,
there is more to our world than meets the eye.

.

Other books in The Skull Chronicles series

THE SKULL CHRONICLES

Book III

DAUGHTER OF THE GODS

GEMMA, 1

1.

So, here I am in Sedona. After Callum cleared off for Boston for goodness knew how long without a word of goodbye, leaving me completely in the lurch, Frankie offered to drive me down here so that I could take a few days chilling out after the tension of the previous week or so, and decide what to do next.

Maybe I need to explain briefly. Callum had brought me across to Arizona to take part in what I can only describe as a treasure hunt for the blue skull, Gal-Athiel. We had found her cave only to discover that the skull was missing, along with one of our party, Jack Milner, who had been sent along by Callum's sponsors. He had been a last minute addition to the group and a stranger to all of us. Everyone believed that Jack, skull firmly grasped in his hand, was now well on his way back to whoever had hired him in order to collect his pay-out.

Everyone but me. I knew differently. I knew that Jack had never left the maze of caves and tunnels, and that deep beneath the surface of the desert, his body now lay lifeless, the blue skull still with him. Had experienced with him his agonised last moments. And I couldn't tell anyone, least of all Callum. That message had been clearly spelled out to me by Gal-Athiel herself.

In his ignorance and fury, Callum had hightailed it from his motel room in Page back to his sponsors in an attempt to get some answers. Leaving me high and dry in the same motel, not knowing what to do next.

That was when Frankie, one of the other archaeologists of the expedition, had offered me a lift here where I had met up with Joe, an old and very dear friend. More importantly, Joe was someone I totally trusted and with whom maybe, just maybe, I could at some point share the whole story of Jack's fate. We hadn't spoken in several months after a stupid argument had escalated, as they often do. It had been good to put that to rest.

Joe and I were catching up big time, ensconced at a small table in a dark back corner of a coffee shop just off Sedona's main street. Outside, the autumn Arizona sun was blazing down, sending the temperature into meltdown, too hot at this time of the day to be sitting out in it. Inside though, it was pleasantly cool. A lively buzz of conversation filled what was obviously a popular and friendly cafe. We had met up about an hour and a half earlier to big smiles and mega-hugs and hadn't stopped talking since. It was as if our argument had never happened. We swapped stories – it seemed Joe hadn't stopped travelling for the last few months – and I had told him all about my adventures with Callum and his team.

Well, no. Not all. I left out the part about that searing intimate encounter with Callum under the desert stars. Partly because I still blushed when I remembered it, but mostly because a little voice in my head was warning me off. Our big row had been about Callum, as a result of which I had neither seen nor heard from Joe in several months. I had a suspicion that even a suggestion of what had gone on would cause an even bigger rift between us. Having just renewed our friendship, that wasn't something I wanted to bring about.

So far, I had kept my knowledge of Jack to myself too. I still wasn't sure I was ready to share it.

'Callum will be moving mountains to track down Jack. He's obsessed by the skulls, desperate to make a momentous discovery about them for himself. He'll be livid to have been so close to one of them only to have it stolen from under his nose.' Joe paused, thinking. 'If I know Callum, he won't stop until he's found Jack and got the skull back. Pride as much as anything, I suppose.' Joe had known Callum for some time. Knew his character well.

'He won't find him.' The words came out of my mouth before I had time to stop and think about it.

Joe stared at me closely. 'What do you mean, Gemma?'

The turmoil and tension that I had been pushing down ever since we had been down in the cave refused to stay hidden any longer. They couldn't. I was emotionally exhausted from keeping this horrible secret and needed to share it with someone. Tears filled my eyes and fell onto my face. Within seconds the strain was freeing itself, pouring out of me in a torrent. Huge, thankfully silent sobs shook me from head to foot as I bent my head to my knees, rocking my body to comfort myself. Unable to stem the avalanche of release that had been set off by that one simple sentence. Fortunately, this part of the coffee shop was empty except for the two of us, so I had no-one staring at my shivering distress.

Immediately Joe was beside me, holding me tight. It felt good, it felt safe, and I allowed my pent-up emotion to have its day. Joe's voice was murmuring in my ear, confused and concerned. 'Gemma. Gemma? What's wrong? What is it?' I couldn't answer him, couldn't speak. I was lost in a flood of releasing tension, fear and physical remembering of the pain I had felt. Lost in my own world. Joe just sat there, holding me.

Little by little the torrent eased until the it had spent itself and I returned, exhausted but cleansed. I became aware of Joe's arms around me, holding me firmly, his hand gently and reassuringly stroking my back as if I was a distressed child, words of comfort whispering from his lips, so close to my ear. It was a lovely warm place to come back to, a safe place, and I let myself linger there longer than I needed to, wrapped in an unaccustomed sense of being protected and cared for.

Eventually I pulled myself upright, sniffing. I must have looked a state. Some women may look fragile and beautiful after they have been crying. I am not one of them. I tend more to resemble a red Shrek with my snotty nose and puffy red eyes and blotchy face.

'Sorry, I mumbled, sniffing again. 'These last few days have been crap.'

Joe handed me a couple of the napkins that had come with our coffees. 'Here. I haven't got a hankie, I'm afraid.' I took them gratefully, wiped my face and blew my nose. 'Now,' he said firmly, 'what was all that about? Tell.'

So I did. Right from the so-real dream I had had back in England (the one I had told Cathy all about) to my noticing that Jack's horse was missing, to that last, horrific vision in the skull's cave when I had seen, and felt, Jack die. 'He's dead, Joe,' I sniffled, the tears threatening to relaunch their assault. 'Jack's dead, and I'm the only one who knows. And I can't tell anyone. His family...' I paused, fighting for control of my emotions once more. 'They'll never find out what happened to him. How can I live with that? Oh, what am I going to do, Joe? What am I going to do?' I fought against the rising onslaught, not sure I could keep it at bay. No, I would not start crying again. I would not!

Joe's arms came round my shoulders again, hugging me tightly. 'But you aren't the only one who knows, Gemma. Not any more. Now I know too. You don't have to carry this on your own any longer.' He broke off, thoughtful. 'I wouldn't bet on it being just the two of us either. That Navajo guy – Ches, was it? His father and grandfathers walked in both worlds?' I gave him a puzzled look. 'He told you they were medicine men?' I nodded. 'Then I'll bet you anything he knows too. His people never admit to anything but they are far more in the picture than they let on. You said he was acting strangely after you left the camp?' I nodded again. 'Well, my guess is that even if he isn't certain what happened to Jack, he has a pretty good idea.'

Suddenly it hit me. 'He said as much. In the camp, before we set off for the cave the second time. He said something then. I didn't pay any attention to it at the time, I don't think any of us did, but now... Callum said if Jack returned while we were gone, Ches was to keep him there. And Ches said... 'He will not return.' Those were his exact words. I suppose at the time we all thought he meant Jack would just do a runner, but what if it was more than that? That Jack wouldn't come out of the caves at all?'

'I believe that's exactly what he meant.'

'So what do I do now?'

'Nothing. What can you do? It's very obvious that Gal-Athiel mustn't be discovered, and equally obvious that

12

she'll do whatever it takes to ensure that. Ches won't talk. I reckon he understands all this better than anyone. Those caves are part of his sacred tribal lands. It wouldn't surprise me at all if his people have been watching over her for a very long time and consider themselves her guardians. He'll know that she'll only reveal herself at the right time to the right person.'

'What about Callum? He's on the warpath and he's not going to give up.'

'Just let him get on with it. Look, if you and Ches are the only two people on this Earth who know the truth of what really happened to Jack, which seems to be the case – OK, three now, if you include me – then all he'll do is keep coming up against blank walls. Eventually, he'll have to give up.'

I sagged back in the chair. Joe was making perfect sense. I had to put the whole horrendous incident behind me and move on. Only… I wasn't sure that I could.

MAAT-SU: The Lapis Skull

PART 1

THE ROCK TEMPLE

2.

The procession wound its way slowly along the sandy path that ran through the base of the rocky, steep-walled gorge. It was a colourful group. Their tunics and capes were woven from soft animal fleece, dyed to deep, vibrant hues from the plants and minerals that were abundant in the hills. Their hair was adorned with feathers of flashing crimson, emerald green, electric blue, and a deep, almost metallic black that shimmered with a rich violet hue when the sunlight caught it in just the right way. These treasures had been hard won, collected on perilous expeditions from the jewel-like birds that flocked in great numbers in the hot, humid forests that lay on the far distant side of this mountain range. The vivid brightness was in stark contrast to the solemn, subdued mood the procession carried around it like a cloud.

They numbered around three hundred in all; men, women, children. Grandfathers and babes in arms. The little ones were unnaturally quiet, sensing the sombre thoughts of the adults who surrounded them and walked slowly, wordlessly, lost in their despondency. Many times they had walked this route at dusk to celebrate the cycles of the year and the passage of the stars that continued, unerring and constant, above them. Never before so few though – once, long ago, thousands had made this journey – or with such heaviness in their hearts. And never before in the crippling heat of the day.

They passed along the narrow gulley, which in places here was only wide enough for them to proceed in single file, and never with enough space for more than two to walk side by side. Above their heads, the towering gorge widened out into a steep 'V', its walls barren and stark. No vegetation grew here. No moisture could withstand that assault of the sun at this altitude; the coarse brown rocks soaked up the heat and blasted it back out relentlessly. For those at the base of the gulley where no breeze could reach to ease the temperature, it was like being trapped in a furnace.

The group walked on, stoic, silent and uncomplaining. Although many here were suffering greatly, they would not give in. Their purpose was too important, the consequences of failure too unthinkable. Old men and women stumbled, and were helped back to their feet by those following on behind. Babies and children whimpered, to be hushed and comforted by anxious, weary parents.

At the head of this procession marched Halu, his head held high, seemingly unaffected by the heat. In his hands, held out before him, he bore a carved skull of the deepest blue lapis lazuli, flecked with gold and bearing a soft band of creamy white that swept across its crown, just as the great star river swept through the heavens above their heads when night fell. This was Maat-su, skull of Valkan. She was the reason they had come here today.

Behind Halu walked a young girl who had seen no more than thirteen sun cycles. She was Manua, the skull's handmaiden. While Halu communicated with Maat-su, learned her teachings and spoke her guidance, Manua

17

cared for the lapis skull on a daily basis, bathing her in the sacred spring, adorning her altar with flowers and fruit, placing there the offerings given by those who had come to ask for Maat-su's blessing. Manua's tenure was almost at an end. On the fourteenth anniversary of her birth she would be married and a new handmaiden take her place.

* * * * *

Manua had entered Maat-su's service at just eight years of age, nearly six sun cycles ago now. Over the last few moons she had grown increasingly excited and nervous. Her time was nearly at its completion and within four more moons she would be married. Most of her childhood friends already were. She had not yet met her future husband but did not doubt that Halu would match her with a good mate. Traditionally, this would be her father's responsibility, but as handmaiden to the lapis skull, the priest Halu had taken over the role. Manua loved him as she did her father and trusted him completely. Halu would choose a good, honest, kind husband who would give her numerous strong, healthy children and with whom she would be happy. He would also choose a man of status, as befitted her place in their society as former attendant to the sacred skull.

She had not met her successor. It was not the way. No-one other than Halu and the girl's parents knew her identity, and she would not be introduced until the change-over ceremony when Manua retired. The choice would have been made long ago, however, when the girl had been little more than a baby. As had always been the way. Singled out for her character and temperament. Maat-su's handmaiden must reflect the skull's own qualities of love, compassion, integrity and humility.

* * * * *

Manua glanced back at the trail of people following her along the narrow path. She felt uneasy, though she could not say why. Yes, the whole situation was fraught with anxiety – recent events could not have allowed it to be any other way – but this feeling was more than that. Deeper. She understood what was going on. Halu had explained the situation to her simply and clearly, and also shared with her what he had foreseen; all that she could feel as a sort of background noise. This unease was more immediate, as if something big and horrible was about to happen. Despite the powerful sense of foreboding, however, and the shivers that ran intermittently up and down her spine raising the hairs on her arms even in the suffocating heat, she was no nearer to establishing its cause.

The sensations were growing stronger. She had to distract her thoughts from them before they overwhelmed her. She allowed her mind to drift, smiling softly as she remembered how she had been required to rein in her natural fiery exuberance, which nonetheless still flickered through when she believed she was alone. Manua was unaware that this zest for life was one of the characteristics that had drawn Halu to choose her, for within Maat-su herself, though rarely revealed, flowed the same fiery energy. Halu would sit watching, unseen and smiling, as Manua sang and danced, or raced down a hillside overtaken by the sheer joy of living, rejoicing in the life force that flowed through her.

Manua loved Maat-su, loved the gentle yet powerful energy of the beautiful lapis lazuli skull and the fire that was held within her. The girl often sat with her charge long into the night, when she would be carried away into the far reaches of the cosmos, travelling to other worlds where she marvelled in their wonders and beauty, enthralled by the strangeness of these places and the beings that inhabited them. Even as Manua's body remained seated amongst the scented herbs of the hillside, her consciousness would be elsewhere. Yet however spellbinding these distant worlds were, in her eyes none could ever be more lovely than the one on whose surface she lived.

Absentmindedly, her thoughts now elsewhere, she followed Halu, reliving some of those magical moments. Her feet kicked up small clouds of brown dust that remained suspended in the still air. She no longer noticed the weight of the sun on her head and shoulders or the tiredness and lack of air that was taking its toll on many of those who followed.

Out of nowhere a wave of crippling blackness washed over the girl, fierce enough to stop her breath for a moment in the terror that gripped her heart. She stumbled, blind, and would have fallen had it not been for the strong arm and quick reactions of the man behind who caught her and lifted her back onto her feet. Just as quickly the darkness and dread vanished. Nodding her thanks, she took a deep breath to regain her composure. What had that been?

Halu sensed something going on behind him. Without breaking his stride he turned to look at Manua, a question in his eyes. She shrugged, then smiled her reassurance. Nevertheless, Halu looked troubled. Had he too felt this momentary shroud drop over them? He appeared to accept her reassurance and turned his attention back to the path. Had Manua not seen the anxiety in his eyes, she could have perhaps believed she had imagined it all. Halu's expression though had been unmistakeable. Manua had never seen that in him before; her unease returned more emphatically than ever, settling round her in a dense suffocating blanket. The nearer they drew to their destination, the heavier and more stifling it felt. She wondered what it meant.

3.

Halu was troubled, much more so than Manua suspected. The situation had become critical; the future of their entire civilisation was at stake.

The city was home to more than eight thousand inhabitants who had lived together in peace and harmony for nearly as long as this land and its people had existed. Until now. Over the last few years a threat had arisen unlike any they had faced for millennia. New and disruptive forces had arisen that sought to control and dominate through violence and fear. These forces were growing stronger by the day. Few dared to stand against them. Those who did paid the ultimate swift and brutal penalty.

Halu, and the three hundred who followed him into the mountains this day, were the only ones left who still held the courage, will and energy to resist. This was to be their final act of desperation and prayer, for their strength was at an end. They were making a pilgrimage to the sacred hall to call for help from Maat-su and those who had created her. Yet Halu had known, even as he had set out on this arduous trek, that it would be a fruitless plea. He was coming here with a different agenda, one he would not reveal until they had reached their destination. It tore at his soul to even consider what he was about to do, but there was no other way.

He glanced back at Manua as she stumbled, feeling true fear take hold of his heart for the first time, gripped by the recognition of the futility of his actions. For in that moment he had seen the black shadow surrounding her and hovering over those who walked behind. As he looked at his own hands, aching from carrying Maat-su for hour after hour, he saw them enveloped in the same darkness. Only the lapis skull, symbol of their last hopes, still glowed with her magical light. Was all truly lost? In leading his followers to their final act of prayer, was he also leading them to their deaths? He had a shivering premonition that it would be so.

What was Maat-su doing? She had always been there to guide and protect them. Was she now abandoning them in their time of greatest need? A rush of rage burst through him at the thought. All this time, had they been merely pawns in a game, whose rules and outcome were known only to her?

No. He shook himself mentally. No. He could not, would not, let himself believe that. He, more than anyone here, had to hold firm to his faith in the love and power of the sacred skull. For if he couldn't, who could? All would indeed be truly lost.

Nothing of this inner fury and confusion showed on Halu's face as he continued to lead the procession. To all outer appearances he was as calm, steady and impassive as always. Yet inside he was still fuming, his momentary rage at Maat-su now transferred to those who were steadily destroying all he held dear; the peace and harmony that had been held as sacred for thousands of years. Brutally corrupting all that was good and right. Turning it back against Maat-su who rested silent and tranquil in his hands.

She had not helped, had not used her power to counter this devastating tide of tyranny. Inwardly he wept, as he had outwardly wept during the many nights alone at her altar, for the future of his beloved people and the annihilation of a way of being that had nourished them for so long.

He forced his thoughts to a more positive train, knowing that dwelling on his fears would only strengthen their force. It was little use. The image of that black cloud stayed firmly imprinted in his mind. He could not shake off the certainty that the situation was hopeless and that he was powerless to change what would be.

4.

There was no time left to dwell on those painful feelings. They had arrived. The gorge ended in a natural amphitheatre, its only entrance the narrow pass through which they had entered. The walls here were almost sheer, towering high above them, the orange gold sandstone of the rim contrasting sharply with the dazzling blue of the mid-afternoon sky. All here knew this place well, most had made the pilgrimage on many occasions over their lifetime, yet still the spectacle and majesty of these surroundings did not fail to move them.

Breathtakingly beautiful though this place was, it was not just the natural wonder that held everyone spellbound. At some point, lost in the distant past, their ancestors had made their mark here. In the centre of the cliff that faced them, a massive rectangular doorway had been created standing the height of ten men and measuring a good dozen paces across. Flanking this entrance, two half pillars, carved in relief from the bedrock and skilfully decorated with lifelike leaves and vines, stood sentinel. The top lintel, again formed from the bedrock, was intricately carved with strange and exotic symbols, at the centre of which had been created a false keystone bearing the mark known to all down through the ages as the 'key to life'. On either side of the doorway, reaching to the same height, hundreds of tiny square openings, no wider than a man's hand span, had been cut through the rock face into the cavern beyond.

Halu paused, overwhelmed as always by the inherently sacred atmosphere that filled this place, a sacredness that had been intensified by thousands of years of ritual and reverence. Breathing in the spiritual essence it held, he allowed his heartbeat to calm, his unease to dissipate and his mind to fall still. He would not be able to communicate with Maat-su if he was distracted by his fears. With a theatrical flourish, perfected by years of execution, Halu lifted the skull high above his head and strode through the imposing entrance portal.

* * * * *

He had entered another world. On this side, all was cool and dark. On either flank, the painstakingly chiselled windows cast a trellis of soft light on a stone floor polished smooth by the feet of innumerable worshippers over the thousands of years this place had been used, but only a few paces into the chamber this light faded away and the remainder of this vast vault was steeped in darkness. So much so that for several moments those who entered found themselves blind after the glare of outside, their eyes taking that time to adjust. Once they had, the sight before them was humbling in its majesty.

Originally a natural cave of no meagre proportions, the interior had been enlarged many times over by the hands of countless willing workers, some of whom had laboured here for their entire lifetime. Over five thousand worshippers could have fitted in this gargantuan cathedral to Maat-su with room to spare, and in the not so distant past they had done so. The three hundred or so who now ventured inside stood lost in its vast emptiness.

26

Manua busied herself lighting the lamps that were spread unsparingly around the perimeter of the space and thickly dotted the wide, open expanse of the floor. As their light spread, the faint, barely distinguishable outline of the altar sharpened into clear focus. In the flickering light of a thousand tiny flames it was all overwhelmingly awe-inspiring and unreal.

Halu knelt before the altar, Maat-su still raised high in his hands.

* * * * *

For over five thousand years, Maat-su had been cared for by Manua's people, worshipped as both god and oracle. Where she had come from, no-one now remembered, although stories handed down through time spoke of magical beings, half-bird half-human, who had descended from the cloud covered peaks of the highest mountains on shimmering bronze wings. Cruel and cold, they had enslaved the populace and devastated the land around in their search for precious minerals.

The eerie, silent lake high up on one of the nearer ridges was held by everyone to be one of these scars. It was certainly menacing enough. Unlike all the other lakes in the area, the dense, inky depths did not reflect the blue of the summer sky or the sparkle of sunlight, instead sucking it in and imprisoning it so that no glimmer could escape. The icy waters were unforgiving and fatal. Anyone unlucky enough to fall in would perish with half a dozen breaths as their frigid grip pitilessly claimed its victim.

Then, one day, the bird-men were gone as suddenly as they had arrived, leaving the people to rebuild their broken, interrupted lives. All that remained were the scars of their occupation, a ravaged landscape… and a skull of the deepest, richest lapis lazuli, sprinkled with flecks of golden pyrite and washed through with a swathe of creamy white. Maat-su. They had left her in the main gathering place, held in a box of some strange metal that those who now held her in their guardianship had never encountered before.

And yet…. And yet? Manua could not believe that those old tales spoke the truth of what had taken place so long ago. There was so much that did not fit. Above and beyond anything else there was Maat-su herself. The lapis skull emanated a potent vibration of love, justice and harmony. The young handmaiden had spent the last five years of her life caring for Maat-su, surrounded by these blessings. Even if those ancient visitors had existed – and Maat-su had to have come from somewhere – surely a race as brutal and grasping as they had been portrayed would not have held in reverence an object whose energy and spirit was the complete opposite.

Why too, would her long dead ancestors have accepted, even welcomed, the skull if she had been a parting gift from such cruel and hated oppressors? Why would those oppressors have left her at all, have given such a precious gift to those whom they had despised and brutalised? And why would the ancestors then have spent generations of blood and sweat carving out this magnificent temple in the cliff so that they could worship her more nobly. No, Manua had long ago decided, the stories could not be true. She could not reconcile the legends of the past with the reality of her own experience.

Even at fourteen Manu held more wisdom than most of her seniors. She understood clearly that truth became distorted as it was passed from one person to another, even over the course of a single day. How much greater that distortion would become over a thousand and more lifetimes. Maat-su had been left for them, deliberately, a gift from the visitors to those whom they visited. What had really occurred all that time ago would never now be told, but Manua knew in the core of her being that it had not been at all as the legends portrayed it.

5.

Halu's thoughts were following a very different track as he knelt in silence before the altar of this majestic cathedral to Maat-su. As usual, and no matter how many times he had entered this sanctuary before, its effect on him remained equally and unremittingly intense. He was overwhelmed by its grandeur and sacred atmosphere, by the effort, sacrifice and sheer, bone-crunching labour that had gone into its creation. He remained motionless, rapt, oblivious to those filing in behind him, and to Manua who was busy flitting from lamp to lamp as she went about her allotted role of bringing light to this vast temple.

Suddenly anger, as unexpected and irresistible as it was ferocious, was flooding through him again. His attention had returned to his surroundings and reminded him of the reason for this pilgrimage today. It was an anger that had been simmering and strengthening for months but whose true force he had not recognised until this moment. He began to tremble as the emotion surged through his veins so violently that it was only with a monumental effort of will that he stopped himself screaming out his rage.

'Hush. It will not serve to allow it to gain mastery of you.' Maat-su was whispering softly, soothingly, in his head. 'Your anger is justified and yet you must control it. You cannot act effectively if you do not.' She was in his hands still, now pulsing gently; waves of calm washed through him from his head to his feet, a cooling, assuaging balm on the fiery fervour of his rage. He took a slow, full breath. Maat-su was right. He had to remain balanced, focussed and in control of his feelings. That was his role.

* * * * *

Maat-su had been their advisor, their god, for thousands of years. Halu had never believed it would be any other way. Why should it? She was the source of all that was good in their world. The people were healthy, well-fed and happy because of her guidance. Why would anyone seek anything else? And yet they had. It frightened and dismayed him.

The change had begun, as far as he could tell, around twenty years earlier, it had most definitely not been earlier than that, and had escalated rapidly. From somewhere, and to this day Halu had not been able to discover where, or through whom, and certainly not why, a new and altogether less benign influence had infiltrated their world. Amongst a minority of the population a hunger had begun to grow for power and dominance over their peers. A desire to stockpile wealth for its own sake, and to limit the supply of food and other essentials in order to push up their price and increase this wealth still further. To control how others lived, and even thought. To impose their own will and agenda, regardless of the consequences on the whole.

Very quickly this canker had spread. First, the more ambitious members of their society were enticed away from their former peaceful, cooperative lives. Those who watched this drift and feared losing out or being left behind followed in quick succession. Soon, Maat-su and all she stood for came to be viewed as weak, were scorned

31

and dismissed as irrelevant and unreal – a faint shadow of past times that had no meaning in the new order.

Halu closed his eyes, a deep, heavy sigh of sorrow escaping his lips. Why could they not see that love, compassion and justice carry a strength far beyond that which control, oppression and menace can wield? If only the people would understand. But by the time they saw clearly the true consequences of the path they were now treading, it would be too late. The new order would have established itself immovably in place. Those who held the reins of power, and those they favoured – the few – would hold the rest on a tight and harsh leash. Any transgression, including that of individuality and free self-expression, would be punished rigorously. Most of those who now excitedly sang the praises of the new way that was coming to them, lured by its promises, would find themselves living in abject fear and misery.

All this Halu could see. All this was yet to come. For now those who could not see beyond those false promises were being sucked willingly into the trap. The few who had followed Maat-su here today, perhaps only three hundred out of a population of thousands, were that tiny minority who would not be deceived.

Until now the new order had tolerated Maat-su and those who served her, but the situation was growing more difficult by the day. His future, and that of the skull, was dark. They were a symbol of the old ways. While on the surface the new leaders merely scorned and ridiculed Maat-su, beneath their words they saw her still as a very real threat to their ambitions. Fuelled by those who wished to see her influence eliminated completely, more and more she, and all who still held to her principles, were being held up as dangerous and subversive, a threat to society.

Even so, for the moment, Halu did not believe the incomers would act. They would not destroy Maat-su. They would not dare. In spite of their outward dismissal of her, they understood the true extent of her power and the consequences of such an action. They would not risk alienating those who, despite their eagerness for a new future, still held the skull and her guardians in their affection. As their dominance grew, however, and the speed of that change was accelerating at an alarming rate, there would come a time when he and Maat-su would have to be dealt with. As long as the skull existed, she posed a danger to their ambitions and was a magnet for unrest and rebellion. That end would not be long in coming. Would they go so far as to destroy the skull? Halu could not say. Of his own ultimate fate though he was in no doubt.

Halu had spent long hours with Maat-su, trying to understand why this was happening and why she would do nothing to prevent it. Pleading that she did something. He was no wiser. She told him only that he should not fight it, that it was a necessary step in the development cycle of humankind, which at each revolution had to sink to its lowest point before it could pull itself back up again, wiser and more perceptive than before. His pleas, his arguments for the well-being of the people she had watched over for so long, had no effect.

'I cannot change what must be, dear friend. You know that well.' He could hear the sorrow in her words. 'You, all of you, have free will. I cannot and I will not interfere with that. I have spoken many times, advising those who

33

would listen, asking them to reconsider, to think again. Few did. It is their choice. I cannot force them to do otherwise, if they are set in their decision. To do so would bring me to the level of those who stand against all I represent.'

6.

Halu was brought sharply back to the present by a heavy weight settling around his shoulders. Manua had completed her duties by laying the ceremonial robes – a full-length cloak, woven of soft fleece and heavily embroidered with fine gold thread that glistened in the lamplight – around his shoulders.

He lifted his head. Before him loomed the massive altar on which were set plates and bowls of embossed gold and other precious metals. In the centre, its dull grey a stark contrast to the rich colours that surrounded it, sat a square metal box engraved with strange, mystical symbols, each side measuring around two hand spans in length. This unassuming box was the casket in which Maat-su had been left by the bird people. Today, Halu would return her to its safe embrace for the first time in well over a hundred generations.

In front of it lay the key of gold, an object that had captivated Halu from the first moment he set eyes on it. Two curved arms, one of which was in the shape of a 'j', the other an 'f', flowed from a small central circle. It was the same symbol carved into the keystone of the great doorway.

Behind the priest feet shuffled and someone stifled a cough. Children whimpered, sensing the tension in the air. Everyone who had gathered today in this temple was afraid, and understandably so. Despite the smooth reassurances of the new order, they all recognised that their presence was tantamount to an act of treason, in defiance of the edicts nullifying Maat-su's status. They were risking everything, and were committed to doing so.

Halu sent a prayer that they would be protected, just for tonight. This would be the last time. In the morning, when the rituals were over, he would place Maat-su in her casket and flee with her into the highest mountains where he would drop her into the clutching waters of the black lake to remain undisturbed until the end of time. He would not let her fall into the hands of those who opposed her; his instinct was telling him that, far from ignoring or destroying her, they would seek to use her for their own dark purposes. He would not let that happen.

7.

The tiny lamp flames flickered. The sunlit chequerboard moved across the rock floor, stretching and slanting as the sun travelled its eternal path across the sky. Halu began to chant, low and steady, exactly as his predecessors had done back in the first days. He called on Maat-su and her creators to bless and protect them. The coming night would be filled with power, for the stars of Valkan would hang directly overhead in the clear velvety dark sky, their influence the strongest it had been in many years.

Hour upon hour he chanted, as afternoon turned to evening and the sun's light disappeared. His companions joined in at the appropriate places, their voices rising to a crescendo before fading away once more, leaving Halu's rich tones hauntingly alone in the twilight. Again and again, until it was time. The last notes died away, echoing in the high vaulted roof long after the voice had fallen silent. When the sound finally stilled, the hushed crowd watched as their priest rose to his feet and approached the altar, where once more he lifted the carved skull high above his head.

'Blessed Maat-su, goddess of truth, justice and harmony, daughter of the great gods who look down upon us from the glory of the skies, we thank you. You have graced us with your presence, your love and your wisdom since the beginning of our time. Now that time is at an end.' The deep, resonant voice rang out clearly to all who were gathered there. Gasps of disbelief met his words and tears fell from many eyes. 'It is with heavy heart and inexpressible sadness that we say farewell to you today. We wish it could be otherwise. We know it cannot. Blessed Maat-su, we ask that you continue to watch over us and protect us, to help us bear the hard days that lie ahead of us, even though you will no longer be amongst us. Guide us to live wisely always, with love and compassion for all. Though gone from our sight, you will forever stay in our hearts.'

Manua's cheeks were wet with tears. She had not expected this. Halu had not shared this with her. Like all who had come here, she had expected tonight to be a petition for help, not a goodbye. Maat-su, her beloved Maat-su, was leaving them. There would be no other girl coming along to take her place as handmaiden. It was all over. Judging from the low murmurs now rippling through the crowd, it had been a shock for everyone, though none would challenge the rightness of the action.

Even as the sorrow consumed Manua, Halu was laying the skull on the altar. He picked up the golden key and pressed it gently into a matching indentation on the side of the casket. With an almost inaudible click, the lid slid open to reveal an interior that was thickly padded with a soft silken fabric, untouched by its great age, that shimmered through the colours of the rainbow. With the greatest reverence, he placed Maat-su in the casket. Immediately, the fabric ballooned out to embrace her and hold her fast as the lid slid shut once more. It was done.

Everyone stood motionless, unsure what to do next, bereft and heartbroken. Halu stood like a statue in front of the altar, his eyes closed, trying to contain the emotions that were threatening to overwhelm him.

8.

In the space of a heartbeat, the grief-heavy silence was brutally shattered. Men were charging through the entrance to the rock cathedral – fifty, seventy, a hundred or more – yelling and cursing, wielding an arsenal of clubs, spears and long knives. Foot soldiers, loyal to the new order. Those inside fled from the onslaught, deeper into the cavern, until they were backed up against the altar, huddling in fear. Not one weapon blow had landed. It had not been necessary. The worshippers had not even attempted to put up a fight, knowing what the inevitable outcome would be. They waited, scared, angry and confused. Why had the soldiers come here? Permission for this ceremony had been granted by the highest authorities. What did it all mean? Parents did their best to comfort frightened children, themselves terrified and fearing for their lives.

The intruders fanned out around the edge of the cave temple. There was no means of escape for those inside; their only exit was blocked by the hard, cruel-looking men who eyed them menacingly. Although hunger for bloodshed gleamed in their cold gaze, the men were disciplined and well-trained, and they held themselves in restraint. Disobeying orders would result in the harshest punishment. And so they stood, and stared, and waited.

After what seemed a lifetime to those trapped inside this human barricade, yet in reality was barely a dozen breaths, a man strode through the entrance, between the sentries. Halu drew in a sharp breath. This was X'asazi, leader of the new order. He was immediately recognisable, standing at least a head taller than most of his men, proud and arrogant in his bearing, his features almost reptilian in their appearance. Eyes as cold and pale as polished aquamarine scanned his captives.

All hope drained from Halu. They had lied to him. All the promises had been given in order to draw out the few remaining citizens who opposed the new regime. If X'asazi was here, everything was lost, for only the most important matters merited his personal attendance.

X'asazi's harsh voice rang out, striking even greater fear into the small group who huddled, ashen faced, in the bowels of the cave temple. It was strident, grating and high pitched, ill-matched to the strong physique and imperious expression. It was all the more chilling for that.

'You all know who I am. I am X'asazi, ruler of this land.' Despite their terror, a low muttering broke out amongst some in the crowd at these words. Their land was not ruled by one man. It was ruled by the people, all working together for the common good.

'Silence!' The word hissed menacingly out into the gloom. Many of the lamps had by now burned out and darkness was returning by the heartbeat. 'I am ruler of this land and you will accept me as such. Should you choose to refuse…' He left the sentence hanging unfinished in the air, his threat unmistakeable. 'Every one of you has committed an act of treason by coming to this place today. You know that treason is punishable by death…' Again, a long pause. 'However,' a stomach-churning smile slid onto his face, a smile that deceived no-one, 'I am a merciful

41

man, and I extend that mercy to you now. Join me. Swear to me your allegiance and your obedience, and I will spare your lives. You will be free to return to the city and serve me.'

No-one moved. Anger and contempt, ill-concealed beneath X'asazi's oily exterior, exploded. 'I command that you pledge me your allegiance, or suffer the consequences.' Still no-one moved. Terrified though they all were, every one of them preferred death to slavery.

'It seems you have made your choice.' The sudden calm in the tyrant's words froze their blood, yet none faltered. 'So be it.'

Halu stepped forward, his heart pounding. Would X'asazi even let him speak before striking him down? It made no difference, he had to try. It was he who had called these people to come here, led them into this trap from which there was no escape. It was he who was Maat-su's guardian. It was he who must now speak up.

'This is not the way, X'asazi. You attempt, and will probably succeed, to force obedience through violence and fear, but you will never win the support and loyalty of anyone's heart and mind through such brutality. Can you not see? Why do you do this? What fear within you drives you to these actions?'

X'asazi's head turned slowly until those glittering eyes locked onto the priest's. Dead eyes. Inhuman eyes, even. Icy fingers, like a corpse's caress, wrapped around Halu's heart. It was futile. No spark of humanity hid anywhere within that man.

'Halu.' The name oozed from X'asazi's lips like pus from a wound. The corpse fingers gripped more tightly. 'I

42

was getting round to you. You have caused me a great deal of inconvenience. You have opposed me and my plans for the glorious future of our civilisation every step of the way. You have stubbornly refused to accept the birth of a bright new dawn. You insist on clinging on to the lies of the past and denying the revelation of a truth that has been concealed for far too long.'

'What truth is that, X'asazi?' Halu spoke quietly, swallowing the rage that was blazing within him. He had to challenge this man, but dared not risk pushing him off the knife-edge of his self-control.

'The truth of humankind.' X'asazi was frighteningly rational in his justification. 'The truth that most of humankind exists only to serve the purposes of the few who are destined to rule. It is a truth that has long been hidden by those who have wished to subvert the natural order of things, perhaps because they understood that they themselves were not of the chosen ones. No more. The time has come for the rightful heirs to take our place as leaders, and for those who serve to do our will as was always their destiny.'

'And yet,' Halu could not prevent his sharp retort, his fury heightened even further by the insanity of the words, 'for generation upon generation our civilisation has lived in peace, harmony and happiness because of these, what you call, lies. Maat-su has guided us wisely, and we have thrived.'

'Maat-su.' The name spat out. 'That demon. She has deceived you and betrayed the natural order. Well, no longer. From today she will no longer be able to spread her lies.'

'And you think that those who are to serve you will not object?'

'It matters not whether they object or not. They have no choice.' His patience ran out. 'Enough. Seize the box.' His last sentence was an order directed at the nearest soldier.

'Please. Don't take Maat-su from us.' Manua could hold back no longer, her despair stronger than her terror. She had darted forward and thrown herself at X'asazi's feet.

'Who are you?' The innocent question dripped menace. Manua's eyes dropped under his frigid gaze.

'M-M-Manua,' she stuttered. 'I am handmaiden to Maat-su.'

X'asazi looked down at the girl at his feet, no longer a child but not yet a woman. No emotion touched him other than a slight distaste at her plain features and stocky body. Had she been prettier, more physically enticing, he would have enjoyed taking her for himself whether she was willing or not. But he would not lower himself to deflower this one. Maybe he would let his soldiers have their fun with her... Even as this thought crossed his mind, another replaced it.

'Her handmaiden, are you? Well then, you shall accompany her on her last journey. Take the girl too.

As one soldier snatched the casket from the altar, a second wrenched Manua's arms behind her back and lifted her roughly to her feet. She yelped in pain, renewed terror darkening her features.

'No.' Halu leapt forward in a vain attempt to help her. It was the last thing he ever did. As he moved, a brief flicker in X'asazi's eyes sent a third man to step up behind the priest, throwing his left arm around Halu's chest in a vice-like hold. A blink later, the right had reached round to the other side of his jaw and with a swift, sharp movement wrenched it sideways. A soft, sickening crunch reached Manua's ears and Halu crumpled, his neck snapped.

The girl screamed as Halu took his last breath, the whole scene unfolding in ghastly slow motion in front of her. Then she collapsed, all fight gone, great sobs of heartbreak and fear bursting from her lungs.

'Take her.'

Manua was dragged, stumbling, across the floor towards the entrance. Through her daze, she heard X'asazi's voice ring out once again.

'Kill them.' He spoke as dispassionately as if he was ordering his supper.

* * * * *

His men needed no encouragement. Released at last from their restraint, they fell on the defenceless crowd like starving wolves on a herd of sheep. Blades and spears flashed, clubs rained down. Screams of pain, terror and death filled the temple within seconds, echoing like the wrath of hell in the vaulted heights. Surrounding Manua, seeping into her soul so that she could not escape it.

The soldier holding her was reluctant to leave, not wanting to miss out on the slaughter but not daring to disobey his orders. At the entrance he turned and looked back longingly, turning Manua with him so that she had a clear view of the bloodshed. In that moment she was embroiled in a nightmare that would remain vividly and sickeningly painted in her memory forever. All thought of her own fate, whatever that would be, evaporated in a split second as the horror unfolded.

Right before her eyes, an infant less than a full sun cycle old was torn from his mother's arms by one of the soldiers and tossed like a toy through the air. Manua's scream echoed that of the mother as the baby was caught by the shining blade of another murderer's knife, already gleaming crimson with the blood of its previous victims, and hung there like a monstrous ragdoll while the proud soldier waved his prize over his head like a flag. The mother's agonised howl fell to a pitiful soul-wrenching whimper that was itself cut short, and mercifully her life with it, as a club came down on her skull, shattering the bone to crumbs.

Manua doubled up and vomited violently, again and again. The man holding her simply laughed at her distress. He would not allow her the luxury of respite, yanking her fiercely upright so that once more she shrieked in pain at the abuse inflicted on her arms and shoulders. With a blow between her shoulder blades he shoved her roughly out through the doorway.

* * * * *

The morning sun was just rising, tipping the peaks of the mountain range with a rosy pink above which a creamy white sky drifted into the deep blue of a new day, painting a picture of indescribable beauty. The girl was oblivious to it all. Her vision was indelibly filled with the last moments of the slaughtered infant, the sequence playing itself over and over in her mind, unable to escape it.

They returned the way they had come – had it really only been the previous day? – trekking through the furnace gorge. Manua was aware of none of it, locked into an endless reliving of the nightmare that she had just experienced, its sounds and images consuming her, leaving no room for thoughts of her own fate.

9.

The city was a vast stone-built warren that clambered over the rocky slopes of the foothills, a foretaste of the towering mountain range that dominated the landscape here. Home to over eight thousand inhabitants, its narrow winding streets and low buildings provided the perfect protection against the extreme climate where baking, arid summers gave way to torrential autumn rains and snowbound winters. On the landward side of the mountain range, to the west, the foothills sloped down to a dank, humid rainforest. On the seaward side, where the city was situated, a bleak, barren plain ended in equally desolate windswept cliffs where treacherous river outflowings created unpredictable currents and tidal patterns.

The group accompanying Manua comprised four soldiers and X'asazi himself who had quickly caught up with them on that first morning, leaving his men to finish the massacre in the temple in the rocks. With them, safely cushioned in the casket, was Maat-su.

Manua had not spoken at all as hour after hour she stumbled unseeing along the path, her fire extinguished. She did not know her fate and she did not care. Halu was dead. The three hundred or so brave souls who had accompanied them to the temple were all dead. Maat-su was in the hands of the new order. What did it matter now what happened to her?

The city was in sight when they turned from the main route towards the sea. Manua noticed, and wondered a

48

little, before sinking back into her hell once more. She was hungry, exhausted and dehydrated. Her captors had treated her no better than an animal, and just as disposable, giving her the bare minimum of food and water to keep her on her feet. She had almost reached the end of her strength.

* * * * *

The beach stretched away on both sides, the only expanse of open shore in this rocky, cliff-backed coastline. A cold wind had sprung up from the north, an early foretaste of the winter lurking on the horizon, and Manua shivered in her thin summer tunic as she stumbled over the coarse sand.

A small craft was lying just above the waterline; a dug-out, hacked from one of the larger trees that grew outside the city. Everything had been carefully mapped out, the dug-out brought here in preparation for this moment. Manua was the only unanticipated addition to their plans. It was large enough for perhaps six to sit comfortably, one behind the other. As she set eyes on it, for the first time Manua was roused enough from her despair to feel scared.

She had no time to think further. She was pushed unceremoniously to the ground and within a moment her arms were retied firmly behind her back, her ankles bound with strips of coarse, tough leather. Rough hands lifted her and dropped her carelessly into the bottom of the crude canoe. Her head hit the side, hard, and for a while she knew nothing more.

10.

When Manua came to her senses, she was lying in the base of the boat, only now it was no longer still. It rocked and swayed, and she was feeling sick. Cautiously she opened her eyes, closing them again immediately as a wave of black dizziness flowed through her. The second attempt was more successful.

She was lying on her back, looking up at the sky. Painfully, she twisted her body to see more clearly. At her head, two of the men were paddling hard. At her feet lay Maat-su's casket, lashed with strips of the same leather that bound her own limbs, and behind that were the remaining two soldiers who had brought her from the temple, also paddling. In the very back sat X'asazi, smilingly smug and arrogant. He had won, and he was enjoying his victory.

They were at sea, but where were they going? And why? As she stared at X'asazi, whose attention was focussed firmly into the distance, she saw his expression change to one of concern. Something was wrong. Above her, Manua could see only deep blue sky dotted with white clouds, but she soon came to understand X'asazi's anxiety. Even as she watched, the blue turned swiftly to white and then to pale grey. What she couldn't yet see was the terrifying sight that had appeared on the horizon.

They were a long way from the main shore now, which had shrunk to a hazy shadow on the skyline. Ahead were a small group of islands, and it was over these that danger was stalking them. The skies were darkening quickly. A storm was approaching, and it was a big one.

It had come out of the blue. There had been no hint of bad weather when they had set out from shore in crystal clear skies and light winds. What was more, none of the men in the little craft was an experienced seafarer. Used only to negotiating the many inland rivers and waterways, they had little knowledge of the vagaries of the ocean.

* * * * *

The first breaths of the storm reached them in a chill breeze that picked up the waves and tossed the little boat around. The sickness in Manua's belly grew worse. Soon the paddles became all but useless against the rising seas. The lead oarsman turned to his leader with fear in his eyes. X'asazi came to a rapid decision.

'Here. This will do. It is not the place I had planned, but it will suffice. Dispose of them and get us back to shore as quickly as you can. If the full force of this storm catches us, we won't stand a chance.'

'No!' Manua had not immediately grasped the meaning of his words. The blow to her head and the unbearable nausea racking her body had slowed her thought processes. Now realisation struck with all the force of one of the waves that were battering the dug-out. She and Maat-su were to be thrown overboard. She would surely drown. In that same moment hands grabbed her ankles and lashed them to the casket. They were not going to take the risk that she might survive. Tied to the box, she would sink with it like a stone.

51

For the first time since X'asazi and his men had entered the temple, Manua fought for her life, struggling and bucking against the hands that held her. She didn't stand a chance against their strength. Still she screamed, wriggling and twisting, until one of her captors, fearful of being knocked overboard by her wild thrashing in the bottom of the already unstable craft, smashed his fist into the side of her head, stunning her.

They were finding it hard to keep their footing in the pitching canoe. It was inevitable. As they attempted to secure Manua to the casket in the cramped space, an unusually high wave hit the side of the little boat full on. The man at Manua's feet, suddenly unbalanced, was hurled into the water. A powerful current swept him rapidly away from the boat as he screamed for help.

'Leave him,' X'asazi ordered coldly. 'Just get on with it.'

Hardly had he spoken than a blinding finger of blue-white light split the sky in two. The air crackled with electricity. A deafening crash followed immediately behind. For a brief moment the world stopped, before a second bolt flashed to earth. This one found a perfect target. The man in the prow had only a moment earlier scrambled to his feet to help lift Manua and the casket. It was the worst, and final, decision of his life. The barely human screech of agony that issued from his lungs as his hair and clothes burst into flames was swallowed up by the subsequent thunderclap. He was dead before he hit the water. The stomach-churning smell of charred flesh reached Manua, still lying helpless in the bottom of the canoe.

'The gods are angry!' Abject terror was etched into the faces of the two surviving soldiers. They released Manua and seized up their paddles, turning the dug-out in the direction of the nearest island. X'asazi remained impassive in the stern.

'Carry out your orders. Throw the girl and that accursed skull overboard. Do it!' X'asazi's voice barely carried over the howl of the wind but its authority still held firm. Reluctantly, not daring to disobey, the two men laid down their paddles once more and turned to do as they had been commanded. Manua shrieked and struggled ferociously as they gripped her wrists and ankles.

Then they were gone and Manua found herself fighting for air. An enormous wave had crashed into the floundering craft, nearly capsizing it and catapulting the remaining men into the heaving sea. It was raging so violently that they stood no chance, sucked under by the powerful rip tides that surged around these islands like the gales that whirled and danced around the highest mountain peaks. That Manua did not get taken with them was nothing short of a miracle – or divine intervention.

She was still not safe, however. The wave had crashed down on the little boat, swamping it; her mouth and nose were barely above water level. With every movement of the canoe, water slopped and slapped her, washing over her face and into her mouth. She risked drowning at any moment. Moreover, as the seas continued their fury, she was also in real danger of being tipped overboard. Tied to Maat-su's casket as she was, there would be no hope that she would survive.

Manua's next hours were a hell on earth from which there was no escape. She resigned herself to an inevitable slow and painful death as the hurricane continued to rage and the dug-out was tossed around like a rat in the clutches of a wild cat. It would either sink, or fill with so much water that she would drown regardless. Though the severe seasickness she was suffering was so unbearable that many times over those hours she wished she would die to be free of its torment. She was sick, sick, until she thought her stomach would burst. She had managed to wriggle onto her side so that the waves crashing over her did not constantly strike her full in the face but it offered minimal respite, and the effort of keeping her head above water was exhausting. 'Please,' she prayed. 'Please Maat-su. Let it be over. If you are listening, please let me die now.'

Scarcely had the thought been sent than a particularly violent pitch threw Manua's head crashing against the side of the canoe and the welcoming dark embrace of unconsciousness mercifully engulfed her once more.

GEMMA, 2

11.

'Gemma!' I stopped dead in my tracks, not sure I had heard properly. Not sure I wanted to have heard properly. Slowly I turned to face in the direction of the voice that had called to me.

It was him. Callum. Coming out of a shop a few feet from where I was standing. He was the last person I had expected to see. Well, on reflection, I suppose that maybe it wasn't so strange after all. One thing though I was sure of; he was absolutely the last person I wanted to see. Anger rose up in me as he approached. He had effectively abandoned me in Page three weeks earlier, leaving me high and dry.

* * * * *

Three weeks. Three weeks I had spent in Sedona in Joe's company, having a wonderful time. Three weeks of easy laughing, joking in each other's company the way good friends do. No undercurrents. No tension. No pretence.

Joe had been here a couple of times before and knew his way around a little, so we had hired a car and he had taken me out to explore. We had walked the red rocks until our feet ached and our skin turned a deep bronze in the sun, and sat quietly amongst the majesty of its towering natural monuments, sensing the energies of its powerful vortex sites, stunned into silence by their beauty.

We had talked – about the skulls, about the information and messages they had gifted to me, about the book I had written as a result and the second one that was already half finished. At length about Jack and his disappearance. Sharing the burden with Joe had helped although there had been no resolution, probably because there was none to be found. But gradually, as the days passed and Joe's understanding and common sense approach seeped into my perspective, I was starting to come to terms with it.

* * * * *

One evening, as we sat drinking coffee and demolishing a huge box of squishy, creamy doughnuts on the balcony of Joe's motel room, I broached a question that had been troubling me since the incident in the cave, trickling subversively and uninvited into my mind.

'If these skulls are so positive and benevolent, if they're the epitome of love and light as we are being asked to believe, how come there's so much death and sadness around them wherever they turn up? I don't understand it at all. Surely if they're as powerful as they seem, they could come up with another solution?'

Joe looked thoughtful. 'Good question. It does seem a bit out of skew with what they stand for, doesn't it?' We sat for some time, not speaking, pondering the issue.

'I don't know.' Joe spoke slowly, gathering his thoughts as he went. 'It appears they need human guardians. Yes, they are powerful, but they are also vulnerable. They have no means of physically moving away from danger, only of deflecting it. And there will always be those, like the Shadow Chasers, who have learned to shield themselves against that protective energy. They don't have any way of moving towards to those they need to meet either. Not physically. They need to be in the hands of someone who understands and shares their purpose, who cherishes them and can communicate with them, and also act as their bridge to our world.' He fell quiet for a moment. 'And maybe,' he said at last, 'it's because when it comes to such an important cause, people are willing to give up their lives in its name. They willingly sacrifice themselves for the greater good.'

Self-sacrifice is a concept I have never been comfortable with.

'Jack wasn't willing! Gal-Athiel killed him. Surely she could have found another way. Led us off-course so that she wouldn't be found in the first place? But she didn't. She led him, and us, right to her chamber.' My voice rose as I remembered again. 'You didn't see that tangle of tunnels, Joe. We could have been wandering them, searching, for years and still not found the skull. So why did she let Jack find her, only to kill him?'

Joe sighed. 'I don't know, Gemma. I don't know. Perhaps the risk in not doing so was too great, too potentially catastrophic. Perhaps Jack was part of something that poses a real, serious threat to the skulls' safety, and as a result to our future on this planet, as human beings. There had to be a reason, and a crucial one, though what that reason is, we will probably never know.'

'A risk like the Shadow Chasers?' Could their dark legacy really still exist? The more I considered it, the more I saw how real the likelihood could be.

'Why not? There have always been secret societies with their own agendas for the world, above and beyond the reach of any government, or working hand in glove with them. Is it too much of a stretch to believe that the descendants of those Atlantean thugs could have carried their objective down through the ages?'

'Sounds like the plot of some crazy conspiracy thriller,' I objected, even though I was buying into the possibility. 'Way out there in fantasy land.'

'Isn't everything that's gone on? Is still going on?' Joe retorted. 'Try telling your readers that what you write is real. They'll think you're a lunatic.'

I dropped my head into my hands. He was right, of course. My whole life had been turned upside down over the last two years. The impossible had become a reality and was sitting there right in front of me, grinning up at me smugly. All at once I felt a fierce yearning to turn the clock back to before all this had started, to be living a normal life once again. And yet, even as the longing surged through me, I knew that I wouldn't go back even if I could. This new world was so much bigger than the one I had inhabited before. Scarier, yes, Uncertain, definitely. Dangerous? Possibly. But I had stepped willingly into it, and I would go on.

'You can connect with Gal-Athiel, Gemma. Why don't you ask her why Jack had to die?' Joe's voice brought me back to the balcony and the setting sun that was turning the sky a flaming pink over the towering red rocks.

'Sorry?' I hadn't really heard what he had said.

'The blue skull. Ask her directly.'

I was taken aback. It had never crossed my mind to reach out to her. When I was downloading the stories in my books it was always like I was watching them on a DVD in my head. I had never attempted to instigate any contact with the skulls that featured in them. I never thought I could. And yet, hadn't I heard Gal-Athiel's voice in the cave, speaking directly to me?

'I...I don't know, Joe. I don't know if I could, and to be honest, I'm not sure I want to.' I tried to turn Joe's focus away from the idea, afraid of what the consequences might be. 'Callum said he was going to dig deeper. See if he could find out why Jack wanted the skull and who was behind it all. He was suspicious of his backers. That's why he headed back to Boston. To have it out with them.'

'Did he discover anything?'

'I don't know. I haven't heard a word from him since he took off from Page. Why? What do you think is going on?'

'I'm not sure. Just rumours, all a bit vague and unsubstantiated.' He drifted off into his own thoughts, staring intently into nothingness. After a few minutes he shook himself and looked at me. 'Well? Are you up for it?'

'Up for what?'

'Linking into Gal-Athiel and finding out what she has to say?'

I shook my head. 'No, Joe. I really don't want to. She was the cause of Jack's death, and now you want me to poke my nose in? What if she sees me as a threat as well?'

'She won't.' I could feel the scepticism written all over my face. 'Look, I've been thinking about this a lot. One, she has already spoken to you. Two, you know where she is hidden. And you know what happened to Jack. Let's face it, if she saw you as a threat, don't you think you'd still be down in that cave system as well? Or somewhere else where you couldn't share what you know? But you are still here. She trusts you.' A long pause. 'And it seems she trusts me too, seeing as I'm still here. Gemma, I'm convinced that if she considered you a danger, you would have been stopped one way or another long before now.'

I didn't answer, weighing up my feelings.

'Gemma?' The question hung in the air. But I didn't know... And then I did. Certainty wrapped itself around me like a warm hug. That it was the right thing to do. That it was important for me to do it. More than important even. It was essential.

I nodded. 'Alright, yes. But I want you there with me.' Joe would be my substitute Cathy, my anchor and safety net. I may not have been new to receiving the skulls' messages but what I had just agreed to do was a leap into the unknown for me, and I wasn't ready to go there alone. Joe looked surprised and pleased. I think he had been sure I would refuse, knowing as he did my reluctance to delve into places I didn't completely understand.

'Great. I know the perfect spot, up behind Cathedral Rock. It's quiet, not many people go there, but the energy is strong and will help a lot.'

'When?' I was happy to leave this all in Joe's hands.

'Well, we fly home on Thursday. Today is Monday. I have to meet up with an old friend in Phoenix tomorrow, so let's say the day after. Wednesday. Early, before it gets too hot and there is anyone much else about.'

'Wednesday.' Having agreed, I was already starting to question the wisdom of my decision. Nevertheless the certainty remained that I had to go through with it.

12.

That was yesterday evening. Tomorrow was the day. And today I had to go and bump into Callum right in the middle of Sedona's busy uptown shopping area. It was the last thing I wanted. I was still furious that he had walked out without a word, furious at his insensitive behaviour after that intensely physical and intimate experience we had shared in the desert. Unsure too of how I would react at seeing him again and whether I could hide the turmoil I was still carrying over Jack.

He embraced me as if nothing had happened – well, perhaps for him nothing had – standing back with a frown as he felt me stiffen at his touch.

'What's wrong, Gemma?'

I was speechless. Not a word of apology for taking off without warning, leaving me high and dry in Page. Not a breath of understanding at why I might be feeling a little less than enamoured with him right now. Just those mesmerising slate grey eyes. All the tension I had been holding on to burst out of me in a boiling tirade, some of it justified, much of it totally unreasonable. I didn't give a hoot.

'What's up? You drag me halfway across the world on one of your treasure hunts, put me on a bloody horse to trek out in a furnace into the middle of nowhere, take me crawling round in some underground hell-hole looking for something that isn't there, seduce me in the middle of a damn desert, for god's sake, and then disappear without a word of explanation leaving me up the creek without even a crappy paddle! I've not heard a word from you in the three weeks since. Now I bump into you and you ask me what's wrong? What the bloody hell do you think might be wrong, Callum?'

People were looking at us – I wasn't exactly whispering. I didn't care. I was also being extremely unfair and I knew it. I didn't care about that either. As far as I was concerned, Callum deserved everything he got. I stood squaring up to his six feet plus frame, my eyes blazing, oblivious to the curious (and amused) glances of the other shoppers and tourists. I was pissed off at him, big time, and I wanted to make damn sure he knew it.

To my surprise he looked genuinely startled at my belligerence, as if it was something he had not considered. 'But you wanted to come, didn't you? Wanted to be part of it? To be there when we found the blue skull?' He stood in front of me looking confused, resembling nothing as much as a bewildered schoolboy who was unsure what he had done wrong. He reached out and touched my face gently. 'Gemma, if I upset you, or you felt I abandoned you, I'm sorry. I didn't intend to. I was just so angry that Jack had stolen the skull,' my heart contracted at those words, 'that I couldn't see anything else.'

Those irresistible slate grey eyes were gazing deep into mine with such an expression of concern and contrition that I felt my anger, and my resolve to have nothing more to do with him, melt away.

'I'm sorry too,' I conceded. 'I was being a bit harsh and unfair. I did want to come. But can you understand how I felt?'

'You had Frankie and Davey. I knew they would look after you. Please don't be cross with me, Gemma.'

He was charming and disarming. I knew it, and that by softening to him I was risking heading back into dangerous territory. Knew I should walk away right then. But I didn't.

His voice lowered. 'And the sex, Gemma. You wanted that too, didn't you? Just as much as me. I know you did.'

I couldn't deny that. I had wanted him, with an insatiable hunger. As his gaze continued to burn into me, I felt the heat rising within me again. I wanted him still, even if I was determined to keep him at arm's length. 'Yes Callum, I did. I was as much a part of that as you.'

'And it was good, wasn't it?' Again the eager schoolboy, desperate for approval.

Good? Good didn't even begin to describe how I had felt under that starry desert sky. It had been a storm of mind-blowing physical sensations, emotions and out of body experiences. 'It was better than good,' I conceded.

A smile spread across Callum's face and a gleam appeared in his eyes. Quickly I changed the subject. I wasn't going back there just now. However bewitching I found his presence, I had learned a few lessons about Callum and I wasn't going to get sucked back in by his charm quite so easily.

'Have you found Jack?' Of course he hadn't. He couldn't possibly have. I'd just said the first thing that had come into my head.

Callum glowered. 'Not a whisper. My backers are brushing me off pretending they haven't a clue what I'm talking about, playing the indignant innocents. How they can think I'll swallow that when they forced him on me in the first place...' He stopped and glanced around. 'Look, I don't want to discuss it out here on the street. Let me buy you a coffee.'

Relieved that his thoughts had switched from a repeat sexual encounter to the mystery of Jack's whereabouts and motives, which clearly ran in a constant loop in his mind, I felt on safer ground and accepted. I felt a complete fraud. I knew, perhaps was the only one other than Joe (and maybe Ches) who did, what had really happened to Jack, but I wanted to know what else Callum had uncovered.

Five minutes later, tucked into a quiet corner of the nearest bar, Callum plonked two iced cappuccinos down on the round glass-topped table, scowling. 'I haven't a clue what is going on, Gemma. The people who put up the money for the expedition are up to something. The mere fact that they are being so evasive gives the game away that they have something to hide. But at the same time, they are genuinely concerned and bewildered. I really don't think they have the slightest idea where Jack is either. Though I suspect they may believe that he's double-crossed them.'

'Who are they? These backers?' Images of Joe's secret societies flooded into my head.

'It's hard to say. The two men I deal with appear to be simply a couple of well-off businessmen with a fascination for the skulls who have gone into partnership to fund this sort of expedition. Or at least, that's what I used to think. Now I'm wondering if they are a front for something bigger.' Anxiety clouded his features.

'Like what? There's something you're not telling me.'

'Only because I'm not sure whether I'm seeing things that aren't really there.' Callum looked even more worried.

'Tell me anyway.'

'I got the feeling they suspected that I was involved in Jack's disappearance. That I'd struck a deal with him, or even got rid of him. Either way, they hinted that if it was me that had double-crossed them and was thinking of keeping the skull for myself, it would be a bad idea.'

Guilt surged in me. Was I putting Callum at risk by my silence? And yet I could not do otherwise. I would not. Gal-Athiel's words echoed through my mind: 'They must not know.' But what if Callum was really in danger? Once again my world plummeted into a maelstrom of conflicting emotions. Callum didn't notice my confusion.

'I think they believed me when I said I had nothing to do with it. I hope so. I lost my temper, and my reaction to their accusations was pretty full on, especially as I bust in on them without warning, clearly extremely pissed off.'

'So what now?' Callum's words had reassured me somewhat.

'They are going on about sending a party out to search the tunnels just in case he's still in there. You know, got himself lost underground.' I felt a fist grip my heart. 'They'll be hard pressed to get official permission. Ches told me ours was likely to be the last for some time. It won't stop them though. They'll go in anyway and run the gauntlet of the native people and their magic, which they'll dismiss at their peril. It's strong magic, whether they believe in it or not.'

The grip tightened. Would Gal-Athiel be found after all? Would Takuanaka's sacrifice and Jack's death all be for nothing? No. Even as the question formed it was answered. The blue skull would remain undiscovered. Forces were in motion that I could not begin to comprehend. Powerful ancient forces. Otherworldly forces. Jack had been allowed to find her so that he could take her deeper into the labyrinth. It was obvious to me now. That had always been the plan.

'When do you fly back to England?' I pulled my attention back to Callum. He was looking at me with an expression of concern that he was trying unsuccessfully to hide.

'The day after tomorrow. I'm flying back with Joe.'

'Joe?' In the tension of the Jack situation I hadn't mentioned Joe to Callum at all.

'Yes. He was in Oregon and flew down to meet up with me here after Frankie dropped me off. He's been taking me out exploring. Why?'

'It'll be better if you are out of the picture and safely back in England.'

'What do you mean?' He was beginning to worry me.

'It's probably nothing, but I'd be happier if you were at home. I don't know what's going on behind all this. They didn't know you were with us, I didn't tell them, but if they start digging they'll find out. It would be a good idea for you to put some distance between you and here, that's all.'

'Callum?' Worry was tipping over into real fear.

He smiled but was unable to hide his anxiety. 'Like I said, it's probably nothing at all to worry about but I would be happier if you were out of it.' He looked at his watch. 'I have to dash. I've got to meet with someone in a few minutes.' It was evident Callum didn't want to discuss the matter any further. 'I'm flying back to London in a couple of months. What do you say to meeting up then? I can update you on anything I've found out and we can catch up on things.'

He leaned over and kissed me full on the lips. His intention as to what those 'things' were couldn't have been clearer. Then he was gone, leaving me with a stomach that was churning with anxiety, confusion, and a most unwelcome excitement.

* * * * *

I returned to my hotel room unsettled by my unexpected meeting with Callum. My head was spinning with all that he had just shared, which tumbled together with unwelcome images of Jack and Gal-Athiel in a jumbled muddle.

I lay down on the bed trying to make sense of it all with little success, losing track of time as for what felt like the thousandth time I relived everything that had happened since I had arrived in Arizona. My thoughts wandered down every tangled path of possibility, only to double back on themselves each time and return to where they had started. The soft trill of the hotel phone eventually filtered into my consciousness, drawing me out of the eternal maze. It was Joe, back from his meeting in Phoenix.

'Breakfast at seven?'

'Hmmm?' For a moment I had no idea what he was on about. 'Oh, yes. OK.' Tomorrow was the day I would attempt to connect with Gal-Athiel. I was apprehensive still.

'Are you OK, Gemma? You sound a bit odd.'

'Yes, I'm fine. It's been a bit of a strange day, that's all. I bumped into Callum.' Even at the end of the phone I could sense Joe freezing momentarily. 'He hasn't got anywhere, though he did seem anxious about something. More than he was letting on. When I asked, he didn't really answer the question.'

'Well, that's Callum. Likes to keep things to himself.'

'Mmmm.' I yawned. 'I'm shattered, Joe. I'm heading for bed. See you in the morning. Goodnight.'

'Goodnight.'

I wandered across to the window. Night had fallen as I was lost in my mental meanderings, and I was gazing out at a heavy silver crescent moon that hung in a star-filled velvety sky of the deepest indigo over the looming black shadows of the bluffs across the valley. It was magical and beautiful, but tonight I wasn't in a mood to appreciate its otherworldly splendour.

13.

The next day dawned clear and bright, with a distinct chill in the air that bore the promise of the winter that was just around the corner. Even so, within a couple of hours the temperature would reach the high twenties Celsius and would stay there until late afternoon.

Joe had taken me to Cathedral Rock early in my visit to Sedona but this time we set out from a different trailhead, crossing a small river on stepping stones before following its course upstream for a mile or so. At weekends this beautiful place would be packed with visitors making the most of its delights. At eight o'clock on a mid-week morning it was deserted. We wandered along the idyllic trail, the chattering, burbling river, low now from the rainless summer months, keeping us company. It was paradise.

At our feet, insects scurried in search of breakfast, drawn from their night's shelter by the rising temperature as the sun lifted ever higher in the sky. Huge, barren, circular patches in the scrub showed themselves on closer (but not too close!) inspection to be the territory of colonies of uncomfortably large ants. On the unshaded east facing rocks, which were already receiving the early warmth as the first rays reached them, tiny lizards perched motionless, soaking up the heat.

Ahead of us, Cathedral Rock rose up like an ancient citadel, majestic and imposing, more than deserving of its name. Turrets and towers of brick red rock, carved more skilfully by the weather and the passage of time than any hand could have done, glowed brilliant orange in the low sunlight, thrusting into a soft blue sky that had not yet reached the deep intensity of midday.

After we had been walking for a mile or so, a side trail split off to the right. It was narrower and rougher, a sandy path that clambered between the towering bulk of Cathedral Rock to its left and a smaller craggy outcrop on the right. This was our route, rocky and unobvious, straggling up over the rough terrain, so different from the main trail we had been walking until now. We were heading away from the creek with its life-giving moisture. Here the trees and rich vegetation that lined the river's edge made way for mouse-ear cactus, stunted pines and desert scrub. We were still close to the main trail and only about a mile or so from the main road, but suddenly we had entered another world, a deserted world, far from any civilisation.

It was empty, arid, and at the same time stunningly, jaw-droppingly beautiful in its desolation. Joe, walking in front, raised a hand in warning and we stopped as a jet black snake slithered across the path ahead of us. In that moment I knew, without a shadow of a doubt, that I would come back here. It was so far removed from the lush, verdant English countryside that I adored and cherished. Nonetheless there was a pull, an ancient link to this primeval landscape that I could not deny or resist. I had come a long way since that first day at the ranch.

Only a few minutes later Joe pointed to a narrow opening between the rocks to our left, taking us off the trail. 'That way.' It led down into an elongated bowl-shaped depression in the land that looked for all the world as if someone had taken a giant spoon and scooped a section away. The floor of the hollow was covered with mini-cairns, tiny towers of stones and pebbles piled one on top of the other, none over a foot high. I had seen them all over in Arizona; they were built by visitors who had felt a particular spiritual connection to a place or sensed the energy and magic of it.

'Why here?' Though why not? But I was curious as to Joe's thought processes.

'This place is supposed to experience a high level of UFO activity,' he explained, watching me carefully to make sure I wasn't getting freaked out by his words. 'ET encounters. So I figured – these skulls are of off-world origin, right? Extra-terrestrial origin?'

'Y-e-s.' I was understanding his reasoning, though I wasn't sure I was liking it too much.

'So what better place than here to attempt to connect with one of them?'

I couldn't argue with his logic, even though part of me wanted to. I still wasn't completely sure I was ready for this. But I had said I would do it and I knew I had to, for my own peace of mind if nothing else. I would go through with it. That didn't stop my pre-skull-experience, scared little self trying to persuade me otherwise though.

I looked around. A flat lip of bedrock jutted out at the base of the bowl at its head. That would be the most comfortable option. As neither Joe nor I had any idea how long this experiment (I was still unable to consider it as anything else) would take, I could be sitting there a while.

'Have you got Tim?' Tim was my own little obsidian skull. I shook my head. I had left Tim at home in England. 'It doesn't matter. Here.' Joe reached out his hand. Sitting on his palm was a little carved skull maybe half an inch high made of crystal clear quartz. 'Ralph,' Joe stated. 'He may help.'

I closed my hand around the tiny object and immediately felt a tingling penetrate my palm, a sensation that quickly spread down to my fingertips and then, more slowly, up my arm. I took him over to the flat rock and sat down, crossing my legs, then looked up at Joe questioningly. 'How do I talk to Gal-Athiel?' I had no idea.

'Close your eyes and mentally call her, I suppose. Then just speak to her like you would to anyone. Ask her if she'll speak with you and answer your questions.'

'OK.' I gave him a nervous smile.

He leaned over and squeezed my hand. 'You'll be fine. You've done plenty of meditation; this isn't that different. Just let yourself move into that quiet space and see what happens. I'll be here watching out for you.'

I closed my eyes and took a couple of deep, slow breaths, the way I always did when I started to meditate, letting myself drop into that place of peace and stillness that is always there, just below the surface. Then, like Joe had suggested, I called to Gal-Athiel with my thoughts.

'Gal-Athiel, sacred skull of Theta, I call on you now.' I had no idea where the words were coming from, they simply flowed into my mind. 'Speak to me, Gal-Athiel. Help me to understand.' I wasn't sure what to expect – a voice from the ether? A scene playing through my dreams as it usually did? Whatever my expectations, they definitely weren't what did happen.

Within moments I felt my body go weightless, and I was lifting, drifting, gently upwards in a cloud of rainbow mist. Safe. Trusting. In front of me, Gal-Athiel's image floated in and out of view, the sweet sing-song voice that I remembered so clearly from Takuanaka's cave whispering to me, 'Welcome, precious child. Welcome.'

Lifting up higher and higher. Faces, strange faces. Appearing. Fading. And always the rainbow mist, translucent, glowing, magical. Dancing with colours and light. No words spoken. No words heard. Brief, too brief. Not wanting to return. Softly descending. Nothing different, yet everything changed. I was filled with peace, acceptance and an understanding of why that I wasn't sure I would be able to translate into words.

I opened my eyes to see Joe's worried face staring down at me. He was looking too anxious. I couldn't understand his concern. What had happened in those few short, achingly short, minutes?

'Oh, thank God. Gemma, are you OK?'

I nodded, puzzled. 'Yes, I'm fine.'

'What happened?'

'Well, not much really. I felt like I was rising up, surrounded in this glowing misty rainbow-coloured light.' I couldn't put into words how delicious the whole experience had been. 'I kept going higher and higher, and then Gal-Athiel came in and said hello, but she didn't say anything else.' I cast my mind back. It was all evaporating so quickly now that I was finding it hard to recall the experience. 'A whole load of faces kept fading in and out.

Strange faces, not all of them human looking. I floated around for a while, a few minutes perhaps, and then came back down. Joe, why on Earth are you looking like that?'

Because,' he exploded, his rattled emotions bursting through his defences, 'I have been worried sick. Because,' he knelt in front of me and seized my shoulders, 'you haven't been sitting there a few minutes, you have been sitting there for over two hours. I couldn't get through to you. You scared the living daylights out of me.' He sank to the ground.

Two hours? He was joking, right? Except that he wasn't. All at once I felt dizzy. I honestly believed I had been drifting around for what could have been no longer than ten minutes. Two hours? How?

'What happened, Joe?'

'You suddenly weren't there any more. It's hard to explain. Your body was there, but you weren't. It's like the bit of you that is you just went somewhere else. For the first ten or fifteen minutes I didn't think anything of it, but as time went on I got more and more worried. You never moved a muscle, Gemma. Not a twitch of an eyelid or a hint of a wriggle. That's when I tried to bring you back. I tried talking to you, I even shook you, but I couldn't get through.' He drew in a long, heavy breath. 'I was all out of ideas. I was beginning to think I'd lost you and would never get you out of it.'

As Joe was speaking, I became aware of the heat of the sun, which I saw was now high in the sky, burning down on my head and shoulders. In my 'absence' (for want of a better word) he had covered my scalp with my sunhat but it was still uncomfortably hot. I was also fiendishly thirsty

76

and becoming painfully conscious of the stiff ache in my legs and hips that was starting to shout for my attention. As for my numb backside...

'Here.' Joe handed me a water flask. I seized it gratefully and drew in a long, blissful mouthful. Clumsily, clinging on to Joe's arm, I stumbled to my feet – at nearly fifty years old, two hours of sitting motionless on a hard rock had taken its toll – and limped out of the heat into the shelter of an overhang where I massaged my painfully cramped limbs.

It was some minutes before Joe spoke again. 'Are you sure that was all, Gemma?'

'It's all I remember.' I hesitated. 'Something is different though. Me. I feel different. I still don't understand the whys of it all, but even not knowing the details I feel I can accept it now and let it go... Or maybe it's that on some level now I do understand, even if I can't get hold of that information... Oh, I don't know, Joe. All I do know is that at last I'm OK with what happened to Jack and the fact that I have to keep it a secret. I'm at peace with it. Maybe one day I'll be able to find out the whys.'

The sound of conversation and laughter reached us on the breeze. A group of hikers were making their way through the rocks to where we stood. It was time for us to leave.

Stiffly, awkwardly – my legs were still not moving all that freely – we picked our way back to the main trail. Tomorrow we would fly home to England. I was grateful to have been able to resolve my inner turmoil; taking it home with me would have been an unwelcome souvenir.

Nevertheless, I had an uncomfortable feeling that we had not heard the last of the business.

MAAT-SU: The Lapis Skull

PART 1

VANATU

14.

Manua blinked, opened her eyes, and quickly squeezed them shut again. The dark skies she remembered had vanished and bright sunlight now burned down on her. Its fierce glare, even filtered by the thin cloth canopy that shaded her, intensified the pounding ache in her skull. Something else was different too. Her defenceless body was no longer being shaken until her teeth rattled. And that foul sickness in her stomach had gone. Keeping her eyes tightly shut and her head still, Manua tried to make sense of where she was.

She was lying on her back, her wrists and ankles now free, and beneath her fingers she could feel soft, thick cloth. Her arms and shoulders ached brutally from where they had been forced behind her back and bound, taking the brunt of the storm's abuse, but they appeared uninjured. She was being rocked very softly, tenderly even, and the sun was pleasingly warm on her body. Tentatively Manua reached up to touch her scalp and winced as her fingers made contact with an enormous bump on her forehead. There was a second, equally impressive bump at the back of her skull, cushioned by a thick soft pad of folded woollen cloth.

A shadow fell across her face – she could see the sun's brightness dim through her closed eyelids – and a man's voice, low and reassuring, spoke to her.

'So, the sea goddess awakens.'

Manua could hear the smile in his words. Reluctantly, she forced her eyelids open. At first she was unable to make out his features, silhouetted as he was against the light. Slowly though he came into focus. Smiling down at her was a kindly, lined face, from which eyes the colour of amber looked at her with concern. She struggled to sit up until a firm hand on her shoulder gently pushed her back down.

'No, you must rest. You have been through a ferocious ordeal and it is nothing short of a miracle that you survived it.'

A strong arm at her shoulders supported her as he lifted a scoop to her lips. Manua drank the pure fresh water greedily but her rescuer would not let her take too much. She had swallowed so much salt-laden sea water that her body was dangerously dehydrated.

'No, no. That is enough. Little and often, or you will make yourself ill.' His voice, soothing and reassuring, was lulling her back to sleep. Manua lay back gratefully. She was safe. The nightmare was over. Her heavy lids closed once more, only to open again with a start.

How could she have forgotten? Maat-su? Where was Maat-su?

'She is here. Do not worry.' He patted the casket which sat only a short distance from Manua's shoulder. 'She is safe. Sleep now.'

*　*　*　*　*

When Manua awoke her headache had dulled to a distant background thudding, only really making its presence felt when she made too sudden a movement. Other than a raging thirst – she had been aware of her rescuer trickling water between her lips from time to time, but it hadn't been enough – and the pain in her tortured shoulder muscles, she felt almost her usual self. The sky was at that in-between stage, neither light nor dark, and there was a sliver of paler sky on the horizon, though whether it was dawn or dusk she had no way of telling.

Tentatively, aware of the fragility of her head, Manua sat up and looked around properly for the first time. She was still at sea, although this boat was unlike any she had ever seen before. The crude dug-outs and rafts of her own land bore no resemblance to this wonderful craft. It measured a good six paces from side to side and at least double that from prow to stern. She was lying on a raised platform just forward of centre and above her fluttered a canopy of finely woven cloth. The shelter appeared to have been erected in a hurry. Had her rescuer put it up solely for her benefit?

In the centre of the boat a slender upright post held a sail that was fixed at the top to a cross pole and fastened in place with rough rope. The prow itself stood tall and proud, like a warrior going into battle. At the rear, a small, low cabin crouched, scarcely higher than the gunwales, maybe her height or a little less, and behind it a tall thin silhouette stood motionless, staring up at the sky. Her rescuer. The whole craft appeared to be built of tightly interwoven reeds and whip-slender branches, skilfully shaped, sealed with a thick black substance that gave off an acrid odour under the warm sun. Who could have built such a thing, and how? Surely a vessel as grand as this must belong to a great king. Manua felt suddenly shy as

82

her adolescent imagination ran wild. Had she indeed been rescued by a king?

A low chuckle reached her from the rear of the craft. The figure was moving towards her.

'No, Manua. Not a king. An ordinary person, just like yourself.' She gaped. How had he known her name? How had he known what she had been thinking?

He smiled. 'It is a gift I possess. I can read your thoughts if I choose, as easily as I hear your words.'

'Is that how you knew about Maat-su?' She indicated the box, which had not been moved.

The man chuckled again. 'No. The skull of Valkan and I have been friends for a very long time. I sensed the danger she was in and came to rescue her. It seems I was meant to rescue you as well.' He moved to the cabin and returned with bread, cheese and fruit which he set in front of her along with a full flask of water. 'Now eat. You must be ravenous. You have slept for two full days.'

Even before the words had left his lips, Manua felt the gnawing hunger in her belly. She was weak too, swaying a little as she sat on the gently moving deck. Two days? She had scarcely eaten for another two days before that. No wonder she was so light-headed. The girl fell on the simple food with delight. Once her initial appetite had been appeased, she looked across at the tall thin man who had been watching her with a kind, if gently amused, expression.

'Better?' he asked.

Manua nodded vigorously. 'Much better, thank you.' Her initial hunger relieved, her curiosity was returning. 'Who are you?'

'I am Vanatu. It was my people who brought the sacred skull to your land so many years ago.'

'Are you one of the bird people?' Manua stared closely at him. Surely that was just a legend? This kindly soul did not match the description of those strange beings from the old stories. Then again, she had never really believed the tales anyway, had she?

'I am a descendant of those people, yes. Their sole surviving descendant. When my time to pass comes, there will be no more.' She could hear the sadness in his voice, a sadness that stayed for only a brief moment before he brushed it aside. 'But that is yet to come. For now, I have the task of taking up my legacy as Maat-su's guardian.'

The sky behind him was lightening quickly now. Day was coming. As Manua finished eating he leaned towards her.

'Tell me what happened.'

'Don't you know? Can't you read my mind?' She was teasing him, already comfortable in his reassuring presence.

He laughed. 'I could, but I won't. Before, I had little choice, but now... Well, it isn't really very polite is it? That one time was enough. I promise I will never do it again without your permission.'

So Manua told her story, from the time they had all left the city for the cave-temple – had it really only been a few days ago? – to the moment she had lost consciousness in the dug-out in mortal danger of her life. When she had finished speaking, the sun was high in the sky. Her companion nodded solemnly.

'I suspected as much. The new phase is beginning. One by one the sacred skulls have been returning to their hiding places until the time comes for them to be reunited. The others have long been secured. Maat-su is the last. Now she has come home to me, her true guardian.' He looked at Manua questioningly, sure of her answer even before he asked. 'Would you assist me in caring for her?'

Of course she would. Maat-su was all she had left of her former life. She had nowhere else to go, no-one else to be with. She nodded. 'Yes please.'

'Then let's go home.' Vanatu turned to adjust the sail.

'Where is home?'

'A beautiful land. A place of peace and sunlight. In times to come, a great and lasting civilisation will flourish there, one founded on the principles of those who created Maat-su and the others like her: those of peace, love, co-operation and harmony.'

'It sounds like the city,' Manua breathed, remembering sadly.

'It is the essence of the way your people lived for millennia until these darker days that have so recently come upon you.' Vanatu too appeared sorrowful. 'One day in the midst of this new civilisation, in a great temple of light, Maat-su will take her place alongside her brothers and sisters as the thirteen skulls of truth are united once more.' Light shone in his eyes as he spoke and he seemed to have gone a long way away. Then he shook himself mentally and grinned at Manua. 'But that is for the future, Manua, the far distant future. For now, it is just home.'

15.

It was indeed the beautiful land that Vanatu had promised. They made landfall on a shallow beach whose sand was soft and white and made Manua's toes curl in pleasure as she wriggled them into its warmth. It was edged with lush vegetation, clusters of sweet scented shrubs and trees that swayed in the breeze, whose vibrant blossoms gave shelter to a myriad of exotic birds and colourful insects. In a clearing, just a short walk from the water's edge, stood Vanatu's home, a simple but large and comfortable cabin built of wood and roofed in huge palm leaves.

* * * * *

Manua was happy here, more than she had ever been. Happier even than during the time she had been with Halu as Maat-su's handmaiden. With Vanatu she had no set duties to perform, no rigid demands on her time. She could simply do as she wished, spending time with the skull whenever she chose. She loved to wake in the morning to the song of the birds in the forest, which seemed so much sweeter than that of the birds that fluttered around the city of her birth, and to step outside into the clear salty air to watch the world awaken. She loved the beach and the sea, which was always there, unchanging, and yet at the same time was never the same from one moment to the next. She contentedly collected food and firewood, and did

86

whatever was necessary for their relaxed day to day existence.

Food was plentiful. A wide variety of sweet fruit, tender green shoots, nuts and juicy berries grew in abundance here. Vanatu would catch fish; often Manua would sit and watch, marvelling at the skill of this tall, scarecrow-like figure standing motionless, waist deep in the ocean, until the moment he darted his arm into the water with unnatural speed to seize one as it swam around his legs. There was shellfish from the rock pools and sometimes, when Vanatu was feeling daring, honey from the nests that hung high up on the inland cliffs.

From time to time they visited the settlements inland. There Manua and Vanatu would trade – shells she had collected from the shore, his exquisitely carved flutes, fish and other coastal treasures – exchanging them for cooking pots, soft skins and meat. The essentials of life.

The settlements were populated by people of all races, living together in friendship and peace. Golden haired and black, light-skinned and dark, tall and slender, short and stocky. A mixing pot of genes. It was so different from the city of her birth, where everyone's skin was the colour of seasoned walnut and, other than X'asazi, Manua had thought with a shudder, almost identical in stature.

Vanatu was a caring and kindly man. He taught her much about the world that she had become part of. In the future she learned, it would come to be known as Atlantis, a name that would endure in the minds of men long after its disappearance. One that would inspire intrigue, mystery and many legends which, Manua learned, would be as far from the truth as the stories told of the bird people in her own land. He shared with her visions of how it would be, far ahead in the future, when the great city of Yo'tlàn stood proud, crowned by its magnificent pyramid temple. The thirteen sacred skulls, Maat-su amongst them, would be reunited in this temple, guiding the priests and people for millennia, just as Maat-su had done in Manua's land. Once, with tears in his eyes, Vanatu also related how, on a sad, sad day even further into those times, an element would arise who would overthrow this benevolent society, seeking power and domination.

'Just like in the city,' Manua had broken in. Even now, when it was long behind her, she was unable to keep the catch from her voice.

Vanatu had nodded slowly. 'Yes, just like in the city. When that time comes there will be other brave souls, just like your priest Halu, who understand and who will risk their lives to protect these skulls. Men and women who will spirit them away and hide them until the time of the final reunion.'

'Will they succeed? Will the skulls be kept safe?' There was an urgency in Manua's words.

'I do not know. I am not permitted to know the ending. We must hope so.' Vanatu's face was solemn. 'Humankind's future will depend on it.' But he would not tell her how he knew all this, despite her constant questioning.

* * * * *

As sun cycle followed sun cycle, Manua grew from a child into a woman. Many of the young men she met on their trading expeditions sought to win her heart, for despite her plain features and stocky build she possessed an inner light and beauty that far overshadowed any pretty face or shapely limb. Yet to all of them she responded with a gentle but firm 'No'.

Deep in her heart Manua carried a secret. In the time since her arrival here she had fallen deeply in love with the tall, gangly man who had saved her life. That he was so much older than her (she would only find out later just how much older) did not matter. Her heart belonged only to him. Yet she kept her feelings hidden away, for she knew that for all his kindness and care he did not return her love. She was a daughter to him. He rejoiced in her presence in his hitherto solitary life, but she would never be anything more. So she settled for his company and his fatherly affection, happy to be spending her days in nearness to him, and got on with the business of living.

Vanatu was not as blind to Manua's feelings as she believed him to be and he regretted them, sad that she would not seek elsewhere a love that would be returned and a husband, children, to bless her life. Despite his constant encouragement, she would not. On the day she turned down her tenth suitor, he decided it was time to speak.

'Manua, do you not desire to know the touch of a man? The warmth of his love? The joy in hearing your own child's laughter? Do not be so determined to deny yourself such delights.'

'I am happy here with you, Vanatu.' She turned her head to the fire so that he would not see the love in her eyes.

'Oh Manua, my precious child. Do you really believe I am unaware of your feelings?' She glanced at him sharply. 'No, I have not intruded on your thoughts. I gave you my word that I would never do so, and I have honoured that promise. You do not pretend well. You are as transparent as the stream that flows from the mountain slopes. It is one of the countless qualities that endear you to so many. I know too that you understand that it will never be.' He fell silent for a moment and when he spoke next his words carried in them a heaviness that would never be erased.

'I fell in love once. Her name was Kia. She was kind and gentle, with a way that would charm the universe to answer her wishes.' He smiled. 'Much like you Manua, but tall and long-limbed with hair the colour of young mahogany and eyes like the sea.' His voice took on a faraway quality as he remembered his love. 'I was young then, naïve, and I thought I could make it right. Change what could not be changed. We spent all her life together, but the inevitable happened. It had to. I could not do the impossible. I could not stop time.' A single teardrop ran down his nose and hung from the end, shining in the firelight. It never fell.

Manua did not understand. What was Vanatu telling her? He saw her puzzlement. 'I watched her grow old and frail, Manua. I watched her age and die before my eyes when I did not. I never stopped loving her, or loved her less through all that time. She was as beautiful to me in those later years, when her hair was white and her eyes clouded and she walked with bent back and stiff knees, as she was in those first days when she was young and strong and vital. I had to watch her leave me.' His voice faltered for a moment before he continued.

'You cannot imagine how that feels, Manua. No-one could, unless they had lived through it. I swore then that I would never put myself through such a torment again. I would never fall in love again.' He looked directly at her, at last wiping the solitary teardrop away and smiled sadly. 'It was a very long time ago, and yet it is still as near to me as this moment.'

'How long?'

'Well over five hundred sun cycles. I don't know exactly. I stopped counting.'

'Five hundred? But...' Manua fell silent as confusion and doubt jostled with her. That was impossible.

Vanatu spoke softly. 'I do not age as you age, Manua. The lifespan of my people is many times greater than yours, perhaps twenty five hundred sun cycles, often more.'

'So how old are you?' Manua spoke slowly, still filled with disbelief, her eyes firmly fixed on the thin man's face. Fear was rising up in her heart and she was battling to keep it under control.

'Honestly? I'm not sure. I no longer count the passing of time. About twelve hundred, perhaps a few more or less. Now do you understand, Manua? Now will you allow yourself to love another?'

Without saying anything Manua scrambled to her feet and ran out into the night. Had Vanatu told her the truth? If so, he wasn't human...

He let her go. He had spoken the truth, and Manua had found it frightening. She needed time alone to come to terms with his words and accept them. And him too, for he was not what she had believed him to be. She would, in time, and he would give her all the time she needed.

16.

'Hello? Vanatu?' Manua poked her head into the cabin. It was empty. Where was he today? There. Standing on the shoreline, gazing out on the ocean as he had always loved to do. As usual he sensed her presence before he saw her, turning to wave cheerfully and loping across the sand to meet her.

'Manua.' He didn't hide the delight in his voice. 'How are you, my child?' My child. It made her laugh as it always did. It sounded so incongruous now that her hair was silver-grey with age and her face lined.

'I am well, Vanatu.' She gazed back at him affectionately. It was true. She was well, strong and healthy still if from time to time a little weary and achy in her joints. He, on the other hand, had not changed in the least and looked not a day older than when he had plucked her and Maat-su from the sea all those years ago. Impossible as it was, he was evidencing the truth of his long ago words.

'And Lipu?' Manua grinned as she thought of her beloved husband, a loyal and honest man who loved her as deeply as she loved him but could never be anything other than grumpily tender and affectionate. 'He is well too, Vanatu, though to hear him speak you would believe him on his deathbed. Until of course there is a boar to hunt or a tree to fell or a celebration to dance at.' She settled on the sand at Vanatu's side and their easy conversation drifted on.

* * * * *

After Vanatu had spoken on that distant night, Manua had thought long and hard about her life. In the early days she had made a promise to herself that if she could not be his wife, she would be his ever present friend and companion, looking after him when he grew old. In that moment, however, something had changed. Vanatu would never need her to care for him. It would be the other way around.

Then there was the pain that had darkened his eyes and caught in his voice as he spoke about his dead love. Didn't she want someone to feel that way about her too? To experience the gentle caress and hot belly of a lover? Kisses exchanged and tender words whispered? The thought crept up on her unexpectedly, sneaking into her mind out of nowhere. She had never even entertained those notions before; now they had made themselves known, they would not go away again.

It took a little while, but eventually Manua came to a place where she was ready to open to the possibility of a new love. He appeared in the form of Lipu, a previous suitor who had been too stubborn to give up on her and refused to take her original rejection as a final answer. Lipu was honest, strong and forthright, matching Manua's own fire, and within a very short time she returned his affections. Less than three moon cycles after Lipu renewed his pursuit of Manua, Vanatu presided over the ceremony that sealed their union.

* * * * *

Vanatu missed Manua's constant presence in his life but it was a loss far more compensated for by his joy in her happiness. Manua blossomed as a wife and mother, her warm heart, caring nature and ready smile always available to all. As time passed, he fell back into his solitary, though far from lonely, existence. Manua visited him often, initially alone but soon accompanied by her children, and in time her grandchildren. And he had Maat-su. Though she remained dormant, never communicating with him in any way, her warm, protective energy encompassed him in everything he did.

The skull still rested in the cabin on a shelf of honey-coloured pine that was lavishly decorated with delicate shells gathered from the beach and fresh flowers from the forest. The custom had been started by Manua far back in those early days and was one Vanatu gladly kept going after she left, in celebration of Maat-su's gifts. Her essence of harmony and peace had spread far beyond the small confines of his home, bringing peace and unceasing abundance to the community for far around. The people of this idyllic region thrived.

17.

As sun cycle followed sun cycle in the endless dance of the cosmos, Manua grew old and died. Lipu followed her soon to the grave as did, in time, their children and their children's children. Vanatu grieved their passing, one by one, comforted only in his knowing that, while their physical form no longer existed, their souls lived on. He allowed himself to feel the sadness at their absence from his life, and the unfillable hole it left but took comfort that, even if he could no longer see or speak to them, they were still around him. Indeed, from time to time he believed he heard Manua's sweet voice on the wind, the joyful songs she had always sung tickling his ears once more.

His life continued, unchanging, as everything around him flowed through its eternal spiral of birth, growth, death and rebirth. Tens of years became hundreds, and still Vanatu carried on his simple life. Nothing out of the ordinary happened. Nothing particularly good, nothing particularly bad. Life just went on, as it always had, watching his friends born, age and pass on, as he remained. He took a great deal of comfort in the constant, steady presence of Maat-su. She had not spoken to him once, he wished she would, but there was really no rush. He still had much of his life ahead of him.

Time passed and passed until eventually Vanatu could not ignore the changes in his body. He was growing old. His eyesight, still keener than a falcon's, was not as sharp as it had been only a few years earlier. His joints had begun to protest when he rose in the morning and it was taking longer and longer to shake off their stiffness. Memories had crumbled into the dust of time and he could no longer recall why Maat-su had come to him, although always they were there, fluttering at the edges of his thoughts, an elusive ghost calling to him. Maat-su had come to him for a purpose other than that he should take care of her and keep her safe, he was certain of it, but what that purpose was had dissolved into the shadows of his past. If she didn't remind him soon, he pondered, it would be too late. His life was nearing its end. Still there was no hint of communication. No unusual thoughts creeping into his mind. No whispers as he slept.

When Vanatu had drawn breath on the Earth for nearly three thousand cycles of her sun, Maat-su spoke. Not as a subtle murmur in his head or a fleeting image in a dream, but in a clear, bell-like voice that he could have sworn his physical ears had heard.

'Vanatu, my oldest and dearest friend and loyal guardian, it is time. Time for you to remember who you are and why I am with you.' Vanatu's hands were being drawn to the skull, settling around her. Suddenly he was no longer in his cabin by the sea but in a small settlement, surrounded by people who resembled his dear, long passed Manua. They paid him no attention, as if he wasn't there.

Maat-su reminded him then of the story of his people, as he had so long ago related it to Manua. Told him once more how they had travelled in giant winged craft across the galaxy from the star system of Valkan to the land where Manua's first ancestors had lived, arriving in friendship and with a desire to be of service to those who lived in that place. They had come seeking a rare mineral for their ships, one found only deep in the bedrock of the mountain range and had asked that the people extract for them what they needed in return for knowledge that would help the people thrive and advance. They had asked only to be accepted as friends and welcomed by those they visited, taking nothing that was not freely given. It did not unfold as they had wished.

The newcomers looked unlike anyone the people had ever encountered before, half-human half-bird, with hooked beak and feathered skin. They arrived in flying craft that resembled an eagle in flight. Gods come down from the highest mountain peaks. Some had been suspicious of them, but the Valkani never acted in any way that did not show the deepest kindness, consideration and respect for their hosts. They stayed only a short while, promising to return with riches beyond measure to pay for the minerals they required, which they would collect upon their return.

* * * * *

They were gone for a very long time and in their absence myths grew strong about them. They came to be considered as gods, omnipotent and eternal, worshipped for their strength and abilities. Some of the stronger, more dominant members of the society sought to win special favour from the bird people on their return and forced those in weaker positions into slave labour to mine the minerals day and night, going even so far as to sacrifice the innocent in the mistaken belief that this would ingratiate them with their new masters.

When the Valkani did return, many moon cycles later, they were horrified. The actions of those who now held a firm grip on the land were against everything these gentle bird people held precious. They requested, and then demanded, that such atrocities stop immediately but by that time those who ruled were enjoying too much power to let it go. No matter what the Valkani said, their pleas were rejected. Instead, the rulers demanded the priceless treasure they had been promised as payment. It was not forthcoming.

One morning, the visitors were gone. Of the tyrants who had ruled the land, none was to be found. In their place was left a life-size skull carved skilfully from the deepest blue lapis lazuli, sprinkled with golden flecks and brushed through with a creamy swathe that mirrored the Milky Way in the night sky overhead. This was the treasure that the Valkani had promised in return for their minerals. Maat-su.

She was indeed a treasure beyond price. Her influence and energy spread quickly through the shattered community, healing and restoring peace and balance where there had for so long been pain and suffering. She opened hearts and healed wounds, and soon the sound of laughter and song was heard again throughout the settlement. None doubted that this was her work and they swore to follow her guidance always. They created a place of worship where they could give thanks to Maat-su for her assistance, a labour of love that occupied over five generations of the people, and those who were able to communicate with her most clearly became her guardians, and later the priests and priestesses, of the great temple in the rock.

The new society that was born from these events flourished in its new found freedom and harmony. Until Manua's time.

Maat-su reminded Vanatu that his ancestors had been these same bird people. When they left the settlement, taking the tyrants with them, some of them decided to stay and make their future on this beautiful world of blue seas and skies, and rich, verdant green, settling far from Manua's land to avoid reviving old memories and lust for power. They built their new homes on a vast, empty continent, quickly adapting their physiology to Earth's environment, so alien to their own. Becoming more human. It was easy for them; they knew how simple it was to change their physical form through the power of their minds.

Those who left this world never returned or made contact with those who had stayed behind. As founder members of the Galactic Council however, the group who had created the plan to bring the thirteen sacred skulls to Earth, they continued to watch over this world, and the development of the human race, from afar.

*　*　*　*　*

Maat-su then showed Vanatu how there were another twelve skulls, all of which had been created, as she had been, by races of highly advanced beings from across the universe under a plan by the Galactic Council, the benevolent watch-keepers of the universe. The thirteen skulls had been brought to Earth by their creators and spread across the surface of this planet, cared for by guardians such as himself or hidden under the watchful eye of the star races. Soon now, the time would be upon them when these sacred and powerful objects would be brought together for the first time. They were being collected from their current guardians by the star races that had created them, and taken to a specially chosen land. There, they would launch humankind into a Golden Age of understanding and peace from which its development would accelerate in huge and rapid leaps. This land was Vanatu's home, the continent that would, in times to come, be known as Atlantis. Recollection began to stir in the long-sealed vaults of Vanatu's mind.

Already many were gathering here from across the globe. They were the ones who would give birth to this new civilisation, who understood its purpose and ethos, and were aligned to it. Maybe they didn't know why they had been drawn here but all had a role to play. More and more of them were landing on these shores by the day: visionaries, seers, healers, builders, artists, farmers and so much more. Some, a few, were of pure Earth origin. Many more were descendants of those star people who long, long ago had come, and stayed, just as Vanatu's own had done.

'You, Vanatu, as sole descendant of the Valkani, are tasked with delivering me to this place. Those who came before and returned to their home world have now moved into a higher dimensional existence, one from which they cannot return to the physical world in which you live in order to deliver me themselves.

'A great temple is being built in the centre of a city that will be named Yo'tlàn, which itself will be the apex of this great civilisation. The temple is in the form of a pyramid, the form of power, built of golden stone that gleams in the sunlight as if on fire, reminding all those who see it of the sun that burns within each of them, and it carries a capstone of pure gold. In this temple we, the Skulls of Light, will be united to share our power, knowledge and energy of love with your world. We will be watched over by our guardians, as we have always been, and the peace that lives here will exist throughout the world.

'It is time, Vanatu. Make your preparations, for your destination is many moons' walk distant and you are no longer as young and strong as when I first came to you.'

* * * * *

She showed him then his journey across this vast unpopulated land until at last he arrived in a great city filled with gracious buildings and wide avenues that stretched out in all directions. It was a city still under construction. He saw massive blocks hovering in the air as if by magic, drifting slowly to settle exactly where they were needed, guided by the outstretched fingers of those who commanded them. Great silver discs, gossamer-delicate vessels like gigantic spiders' webs, spiky sea-urchin spheres and oblong pods filled the sky or rested on the ground outside the city, which itself was thronging with people of every shape, size and design, both earthly and unearthly, all living and working together in harmony.

Dominating the whole scene was the great golden pyramid temple, gleaming fire under the clear blue sky. It was mighty, imposing, and at the same time welcoming, offering a sense of stability, security and benevolence.

He saw the skull chamber, completely circular, empty for now. Twelve opaque white quartz pillars stood equidistant around the circumference, waiting for the arrival of the skulls. In the centre a massive pedestal, also of pure white quartz. This was where the Master would rest.

And he saw too, that once his task was complete and he had safely delivered Maat-su to the temple priests, his work would be done. He would be able to sleep at last, rejoining all those who had gone before. His eyes were wet as he saw his beloved Kia, as youthful and lovely as she had been when he first met her, holding her hand out to him.

* * * * *

Two days later, his few preparations complete, Vanatu walked out of the cabin that had been his home for over two thousand years. He would not return.

GEMMA, 3

18.

I walked out of the green tunnel into the Arrivals lounge at Heathrow airport, weary and drained. It felt like a lifetime ago that I had left here. Had it really only been, what, five weeks? It felt so good to be back in a normality I recognised, safe in the comfort zone of my usual world. Already, Arizona and all that had gone on there was becoming less real. Like a vivid dream, so real and concrete at the time but when you wake up and draw further away, it takes on the hazy edges of another dimension.

'Gemma.' Cathy hurled herself out of the crowd at me, bundling me into a huge bear-hug. It was good to see her. Cathy's earthy common-sense and sharp gift for looking beyond the veil of this world into others to find answers was just what I needed right now. I was hoping she would be able to help me make sense of some of the things that had happened, even if I couldn't tell her everything.

'Joe.' She peeled herself off me and flung her arms around his neck instead. 'It's good to see you too. Where did you disappear, taking off without a word for so long?'

She took a pace back and looked at each of us in turn. 'So, you two met up then?' I couldn't mistake the question in her voice.

'Cathy.' There was a gentle warning in the word. I know Cathy, know that when she gets an idea, it's almost impossible to distract her from it. This time she took sympathy on me. She shrugged, winked at me, which Joe thankfully didn't notice, and let it go. 'I can't wait to hear all about it. Your emails were a bit sketchy.'

Chattering away she led us out to where her car was parked. After ten sleepless hours on a plane I wasn't taking any of it in. Joe, on the other hand, had dozed for much of the flight – I so envied him that ability – and was happy to talk. Cathy sensed my fuzziness and turned with a sympathetic smile. 'Sorry, Gemma. I'll shut up. I'm yabbering away here and you're done in.'

I let Joe take the front seat and crawled in the back where I could sprawl, letting the weariness wash over me. Before Cathy had driven out of the terminal area, my eyelids were closing.

On the edge of my consciousness I was aware of Joe and Cathy talking, general chit-chat that had no real importance, but I wasn't able to join in. I was lost in my own twilight world, somewhere between sleeping and waking, that was simultaneously neither and was both. I heard their voices and the purr of the engine. At the same time I was enveloped in a dark, warm, cosy blanket from which I couldn't emerge. Not that I wanted to. It was such a delicious place to be.

They came then, drifting in and out of this place, hazy at first, like the edges of a dream. The skulls, each in turn emerging softly in front of me, calling my name, crystallising and then fading, to be replaced by the next... and the next. Thirteen in all. The thirteen sacred skulls. Followed by fleeting images, like individual frames on a roll of film. Opulent palaces and creeper-bound temples. Dark caves and empty plains that stretched into infinity. Faces: Joe, Duncan. My own, reflected in a sparkling pool.

Callum, reaching out his arms as if calling for help. And others, so many others, that I did not recognise.

'Gemma. Gemma. We're here.' Cathy was gently shaking my shoulder, pulling me out of this strange and mysterious world. I must have fallen properly asleep at some point. The ninety minute drive had flashed by in seconds. I looked out of the window with a deep sense of peace. I was home. As Joe lifted my luggage from the car, Cathy hugged me again. 'Give me a call when you wake up. And don't forget about Norway.'

Norway? What did she mean? My head was too fuzzy to think straight. Before I formed the words to ask her, Joe was hugging me goodbye and they were back in the car and heading down the lane. Norway? Try as I might, I couldn't remember Cathy saying anything about it. Maybe it would come back to me – after I'd slept for a week.

Well, eighteen hours straight, as it turned out.

* * * * *

More strangeness. When I did finally wake, something had yet again changed. Something inside me. I didn't know what. I couldn't put my finger on it. A sort of certainty maybe? Strength? An even deeper comprehension? I couldn't name it, but it was there. As if the shift in my perception that I had experienced on one level while I was connecting with Gal-Athiel in the desert – was that really only three days ago? – had finally settled, sunk down so that it was no longer just a mental knowing but had become an integral part of me.

108

Yes, it sounds crazy. It sounded crazy to me even as I was thinking it. Crazy or not though, at the same time I knew it to be true. Luckily, I had people around me who would accept it completely. Neither Cathy nor Joe would think me crazy in the least.

19.

The next day I met up with Cathy, knowing full well she wouldn't be satisfied with anything less than a full debriefing.

It was one of those glorious autumn days that you only get in England, and even then rarely, when the sun, low in the sky, sets the turning leaves to flame and the barely-there mist dampens the ground just enough so that the rich smell of earth and leaf mould tantalises your senses with each footfall. We had decided to make the most of the weather and head out for a walk in the woods.

Cathy was late but for once I didn't mind. No one else was around. In soul-soothing solitude I sat on a fallen tree stump and drank in the magic of the morning. I had fallen in love with Arizona with its sun-scorched primeval landscape but this was where my soul belonged. Squirrels darted around my feet, playing in what might be the final day's warmth of the year, taking the chance to gather more food for the cold months to come. In the still leaf-heavy branches above my head, those birds that had not flown off to warmer climates whistled and fluttered and chirped. It was a magical setting that morning that drew me in so that I didn't hear Cathy's car pull up, only stirring as the door banged shut.

What was going on? Cathy was always bubbly and bright; this morning she'd taken it up a good few notches and was buzzing like an over-excited ten year old.

'Morning, Gemma.' She breathed deeply. 'Oh, it is so lovely here. I can't wait to hear all about your adventures. Come on. Spill.' She linked her arm in mine and we set off down the track.

'Uh uh. Not until you tell me why you are bouncing about like a wallaby on speed.'

'I'm not. I'm just dying to find out what you got up to in the good old US of A.'

'Rubbish!' I wasn't in the least fooled by Cathy's indignant expression. Cathy and I had been friends for years. There was more to it than that. I let it go. It would be useless to try and wheedle it out of her. She would tell me soon enough in any case. Cathy could never keep anything secret from me for very long.

So we wandered the peaceful, sun-dappled woodland tracks and I shared my adventures with her. She doubled up with laughter, unable to speak, as I regaled her with the story of my first close encounter with a horse and my embarrassing saddle-sore backside. Gazed wistfully into the distance as I described the stark beauty of the blistering desert landscape, its deep shadowy canyons and psychedelic sunsets. Blinked in unbridled admiration as I described our expedition into the caves. I skirted around Callum, just mentioning him casually here and there. Cathy was not going to let that one go.

'What about Callum? I mean, you were besotted with him, and he clearly fancied you. Did anything happen?'

Even now, a month afterwards, I flushed crimson at the memory of our torrid union under the desert stars. Cathy stopped dead, open-mouthed, at my reaction.

'My GOD! It DID! And from the look of you it was something else. You have got to tell me.'

'I can't really explain it, Cathy. It was… It was like nothing I've ever experienced before. Primeval? Elemental? Like all the forces of nature in that place were moving, expressing themselves, through us… As if we were simply the conduits for something much greater than either of us. It was incredibly passionate, uninhibited and utterly mind-blowing, but it was nothing to do with love.'

'Sometimes things happen that we will never find an explanation for. Perhaps you were just in the right place at the right time?'

'That's true.' I grinned, still blushing. 'Whatever the reason, I won't forget it in a hurry.'

'So are you two an item?'

I shook my head. 'I may have been a bit infatuated with him…' I caught sight of her raised eyebrows. 'OK, OK, so I was totally besotted with him, and if I'm honest those eyes still turn me into a pile of putty, but I've dropped the blinkers. I've come face to face with a few aspects of Callum that aren't so appealing.'

'Does Joe know about it?'

Again I shook my head. 'No, and I don't want him to. We've only just got back to normal after that last row and I don't want it all to blow up again.' I sighed. 'I don't know what it is with Joe. He's Callum's friend after all but every time I mention Callum's name he goes all distant.'

'And you don't know why? Have you asked him?'

'I haven't the least idea. And yes, I have asked him. He just says I'm imagining it.'

'Mmmm.' Cathy said no more, though I could sense she wanted to. We walked in silence for a while before she turned to me again. She had picked up that I was keeping something hidden. Cathy was deeply intuitive and a powerful psychic.

'There is more, isn't there? Something else that happened out there?'

I nodded. 'But I can't tell you. I want to, but I can't.'

And I did want to tell her. I wanted to share the whole ghastly Jack incident with her – after all, it had been Cathy I had shared that initial warning dream with – but I couldn't. It wasn't that I didn't trust Cathy. I did. Implicitly. Other than Joe she was the only person I would have trusted with this. Even so I couldn't ignore the persistent 'No' that tugged at my gut. So it remained unsaid.

Cathy would not push further. Despite her apparent (and misleading) scattiness, she held a rock-solid integrity. She would not pry into places I didn't want her to go, understanding that if there was something I wasn't telling her, I had my good reasons why. If and when the time was right I would share my secrets with her.

She squeezed my hand. 'I know you can't. It's OK.'

I smiled gratefully and changed the subject.

'What's all this about Norway?'

'I told you at the airport.'

'Well it didn't register.'

'No. I thought as much because you didn't react. You were pretty wiped out. OK.' Cathy looked a bit sheepish and apologetic all of a sudden. What had she done? She took a deep breath. 'You remember that article I read out to you? The one about the discovery of an ancient gold artefact on the Norway – Sweden border?'

'Yes.' I did remember, although I hadn't thought about it much since I'd left for America.

'And you remember how you said no-one would take you seriously even if you did contact the research team?'

'Y-e-e-s.' I had an idea what was coming next but wasn't sure I wanted to hear it.

'Well,' Cathy hesitated before plunging in again, 'I did a bit of research and then emailed the archaeology team involved, told them about your book, and sent them a copy of the manuscript.' The confession poured out in a rush of words.

'Cathy.' I was furious. No, actually that was wrong. I wasn't furious. I wasn't even angry. I HAD changed. Before, I would have freaked out, got upset and scared, and allowed my imagination full rein to torture me with all sorts of unsavoury scenarios. But now... Now what I was feeling was more like I was being pushed off the edge of a cliff. It was terrifying, not knowing if anything would break my fall, and at the same time exhilarating. A rush of excitement and anticipation was born within me.

Pretending to be afraid, Cathy shrank back and squeezed her eyes shut, then opened one and peeked at me with a grin on her face. 'Are you angry at me?'

'Angry? I'm furious.' I lobbed a toffee at her, an equally broad grin on my face. 'No, I'm not really.' I wasn't going to let her off the hook quite so easily though. 'I should be though. Going behind my back.'

114

'You weren't here to ask,' she pouted, her eyes twinkling with mischief. 'Well? Aren't you going to ask me what happened?'

Of course I was. I couldn't wait to hear. 'Tell me!' I demanded. 'Did they reply?'

'Yes, they did. I got a really snotty letter from the head archaeologist telling me I was talking nonsense, that I should do my research on the history of human civilisation blah di blah di blah. It was clear he wasn't interested in the least. So I thought OK, I've tried, and I've come up against the traditional scientific establishment that refuses to accept the possibility of anything that doesn't fit into their conventional narrow-minded viewpoint of how it was. It really pissed me off I tell you Gemma, but I didn't think there was much else I could do. I mean, they point blank won't consider other possibilities even when all the evidence points there.'

I stood back and let Cathy vent her irritation. This was one of her chief soap-box subjects, one on which we were in complete agreement.

'I mean, just look at all the ludicrous stories they come up with to explain the glaring anomalies that make a mockery of their beloved 'truth'.' She paused to draw breath. 'Anyway, I thought that was that, so I gave it up as a bad job.'

It had turned out pretty much as I had expected. The tingle of anticipation evaporated, excitement turning to a leaden lump of disappointment.

I glanced up at her, expecting to see her looking despondent too. To my surprise, she wasn't. Of course.

She wouldn't have been so excited about telling me if that had been it. There was more.

'Come on, Cathy. Out with it. Stop teasing and TELL ME.'

'Oh, OK. Like I said, after that first crappy email, I thought that was the end of it.' She looked like a child that has found herself alone with the cookie jar. '…Then I got another. It came this morning. That's why I was late getting here.'

'Same person?'

'No. This was one of the other archaeologists. Name of Olina Something that I can't pronounce.'

'And? What did he say?' Cathy was having fun, keeping me dangling.

'She. And… She's fascinated. Thinks you might be onto something of huge importance and wants to meet you to talk about it all.'

I gave out a huge whoop and did a little happy dance in the fallen leaves.

Cathy gave me a hard stare, grabbed my arms and peered into my eyes. 'Come on, out with it. Where is she? What have you done with the real Gemma?'

I pulled away, laughing.

She became serious. 'You've changed, Gemma. In a good way. You seem, oh I don't know, more confident? Stronger. Certainly less scared of everything. And more determined maybe?' She paused, searching for the right word to describe what she was sensing. 'Yes. All that. But there's something else… Certain. I think that's it. More certain about everything that you are doing and seeing.'

I nodded 'I know. I can feel it. It's as if everything that has happened suddenly makes sense, even if I don't know what that sense is yet. Just a sort of gut knowing I suppose.'

Cathy grinned. 'Fantastic. Welcome to my world.' Thanks to her years of metaphysical and energy practice, she understood exactly where I was coming from. I was grateful not to have to explain further – I wasn't sure I could have in any case. 'Now, about that email…'

My thoughts flew back to our original conversation. 'Where? When?'

'Hang on.' Cathy pulled her phone from her pocket, squinted at it and pulled a face. 'No signal. And I can't remember the exact details. It'll have to wait until we get one.'

We couldn't pick up a signal anywhere in the woods. Eager to see for myself what the email said we headed back to our cars and then on to the nearest pub with wi-fi. Once we had settled into a corner of the cosy bar, Cathy pulled up the email for me to read. It was lengthy.

'*Dear Mrs Lockley* (that was Cathy*), I have just come across your recent email and wanted to send you my reply, which does not correspond at all with that of Dr Winterson.*'

'He's the head archaeologist, the one who can't see past the end of his nose,' Cathy piped in.

'*From the moment I saw this object glinting on the stream bed, I knew it to be something of supreme importance. Its age alone, as evidenced by its position, could make it no less. However, there was more to it than that. Something intangible but very real.*

'As a scientist, I have been trained to view every discovery through the eyes of evidence and verifiable fact. As a human being, I understand that not everything in our world can be explained solely in this way. We have senses far beyond our five acknowledged physical ones and we must pay attention to them. It is my firm conviction that it was only in looking past the evidence of his physical senses that Howard Carter found the tomb of Tutankhamen.

'I'm going off the subject. My point is that I have always believed that this artefact, which has been called the 'key' since its appearance, bears witness to an ancient world we as yet know nothing of. One that disappeared so completely without trace that we no longer even consider its possibility. One, moreover, that is so beyond the realms of everything we know that it is impossible to envisage it as ever existing.

The key is more than a simple gold artefact. The energy emanating from it is palpable, and initial scientific tests have established it to be of an alloy of gold and an unknown metallic substance. The gold is of a natural purity not yet recorded on Earth. The other element has got everyone scratching their heads.

'Much of what I have just told you has not been released to the public, and is unlikely ever to be so. Due to the contents of Mrs Mason's book however, and the fact that it was written before the key was found, I feel it is important to share it with you.

'Unless you and she are part of a very clever hoax, a scenario which I dismiss completely, I believe she holds a crucial piece of this puzzle. One that we, as scientists –

and I, from a deep personal interest – cannot afford to ignore.

'The artefact will be put on public display for four weeks from January of next year at the Museum of Natural History & Technology in Trondheim, the museum attached to the Norwegian University of Science & Technology where the key is undergoing examination. Would it be possible for Mrs Mason to visit at this time? I would very much like for her to see and hold it for herself, and will find a way to make this happen. I cannot see any other opportunity in the near future as the university has put in place some very tight restrictions on access to the artefact.

'In the meantime, would you please be kind enough to forward this email to Mrs Mason? I would very much like to arrange a Skype call with her in the next few weeks as there is a great deal more I would like to discuss.

Kind regards

Olina Gjerde
Assistant head archaeologist
Norwegian University of Science & Technology'

MAAT-SU: The Lapis Skull

PART 2

DENDARAK

20.

Kua'tzal rummaged anxiously through the folds of his heavy travelling cloak. It was here somewhere. In his mind he knew that earlier that day he had tucked it safely away in a pocket but his nerves were so taut that he couldn't stop himself checking it was still there.

The focus of his search was a high-level permit, granted over a moon's cycle earlier, which would allow him to travel unchallenged and unimpeded to and around the city of Dendarak. The permit had been authorised by Xy-barian, head of the Shadow Chasers, himself. In this time when free movement was being eroded daily by the ever-growing frequency of random checks and searches by the Shadow Chasers, scrutiny from which even the Priests of the Light were no longer immune, it was worth a king's ransom. To Kua'tzal, it was priceless. He was carrying with him to Dendarak a secret, one that, if it was to be discovered, would cost him his life and threaten the future of humankind. His fingers closed around a slim sheaf of papers. He breathed again. It was there, as he had known it would be.

It had been a long and unusually tense journey. Kua'tzal had made this trip many times in the past, always for the same reason. Never before though had so much rested on his shoulders. Two days he had been in this shuttle, thankfully for the most part alone; these days few people travelled willingly to Dendarak without good cause. Mindful that he would arrive in the city before nightfall, Kua'tzal forced the tension from his shoulders and cleared his mind. He would need to be sharp and watchful, having his full wits about him, from the moment he stepped down onto the street. He was no longer a young man. The events of the last couple of days had tired him more than he had allowed himself to feel until this moment. He needed to rest. Kua'tzal allowed his eyes to close. Sooner than he expected he drifted into a light, restorative sleep.

*   *   *   *   *

As the rooftops of Dendarak came into view, dark silhouettes against a deepening indigo sky, Kua'tzal's eyes fluttered open. The feeling of relaxation his sleep had created evaporated in a moment. This was it, the moment of perhaps his greatest, though by no means final, test. His paperwork was inviolable, which ensured his meagre baggage would pass without scrutiny; nonetheless carrying its precious and dangerous contents into the city right under the noses of the Shadow Chasers was a test of his nerves he was not relishing. One sniff of suspicion and it would all be over: the years of planning, the yet-to-be-enacted climax, all that Atlantis had ever stood for.

The shuttle passed through the city gates and pulled up a short while later in a wide, open square. Kua'tzal waited patiently for it to come to a complete stop. To his great fortune, the guards who waited to inspect his documents were bored, at the end of their shift, and not particularly interested in the lone passenger who disembarked. One cursory glance at the weighty signature on his permit was enough for them to wave him through without a second glance. Kua'tzal strolled away as innocently and casually as he was able, holding in a small cheer of victory as he walked unchallenged into the streets of the Shadow Chasers' stronghold that was Dendarak. At the same time, he was deeply aware that this was only the beginning. The task that lay ahead would demand as much of him as he had to give, and perhaps more.

* * * * *

Kua'tzal was the appointed representative of the Priesthood of the Temple of Light in Yo'tlàn, first city of Atlantis. His role, one he had been charged with for many years now, was to negotiate with the upper hierarchy of the Shadow Chasers in an ongoing attempt to temper their ever-tightening grip on the personal freedom of the people of the land. This was the role that had brought him the valued and valuable permit.

It was a treasure hard-won, however, one that had required Kua'tzal to nurture a certain level of trust with the usurpers. He had carefully cultivated a wary friendship – no, that was too strong, an acquaintanceship? relationship? – with some of their senior commanders which had eased their acceptance of him in these talks. He had even gone so far as to hint at a fundamental sympathy with their aims, which thankfully they had never yet put to the test. It was a persona Kua'tzal had carefully and painstakingly constructed over many years, and all in anticipation of this moment. He had not known when it would come, only that it would come, and that he had to be in place when it did.

The deception had cost him dearly on a personal level, for he had never been able to let his mask slip. No-one –

not the Shadow Chasers, not the other priests and priestesses of the Temple, not the ordinary people he met in his day to day life – could suspect it to be anything but the truth of who he was. It resulted in a lonely life. His colleagues in the Temple, while refusing to allow the destructive grip of outright hatred to enter their hearts, disliked him intensely, ignorant of the truth behind the man and his actions. Only the four most senior priests, those who had asked him to take on this task to buy them time, knew that. Only they knew too the sacrifice and pain it caused this most kind-hearted and tolerant of men. It had taken its toll physically as well as mentally. He was gaunt, stony-faced, his forbidding appearance in stark contrast to the open smiles and hearts of those who shared his life within the corridors and chambers of the great Pyramid Temple.

At the same time, Kua'tzal recognised that it was all a game, that despite their honeyed words and platitudes the Shadow Chasers were merely humouring the priests for as long as it suited their purposes to do so. Behind their oily smiles and empty promises, they merely tolerated his diplomatic overtures, no more, to keep the Priesthood from open rebellion until the time came to crush them. This the Dark Ones would do easily, leaving them free to impose their will unopposed.

Kua'tzal and his fellow conspirators had sensed it would come soon. The Shadow Chasers had been hesitating, fearing that any premature move against the Temple would create open revolt in the general population. Cowed the people of Atlantis might be, crushed as yet they were not. The time for pretence had come to an end

125

however. Tonight, all would change. Kua'tzal had played his hand, was still playing it. Tonight others would do the same. It was a hand they would be called to play until the very end, one that would take them all away from their homeland forever. His life, and the lives of eleven others like him, would never be the same again. Kua'tzal was afraid, but he would not fail.

* * * * *

There was no going back now. The previous night Kua'tzal had committed an inconceivable act of sacrilege, and he had done it with the full blessing of the four senior priests. He had entered the Skull Chamber in the Pyramid Temple and taken one of the sacred skulls, replacing it with a lifeless replica. The treasure that now bounced along in the bag he carried slung over his shoulder was no less than this skull – Maat-su, skull of Valkan. Tonight, the eleven other men and women, all priests and priestesses of the Temple, would enter the chamber one by one and switch the remaining skulls, as he had done with Maat-su. They would vanish like shadows in the night, each of them the new guardian of a skull, spiriting it away far from Atlantis to keep it from the clutches of those who wish to use its power for their own aims. It was a dangerous act. None who were involved underestimated the risks, or the consequences of failure.

It had been a plan long in the making but in the end hasty in execution as the need to move quickly was thrust upon them. The Shadow Chasers had long coveted the Skulls of Light, sources of immeasurable power, knowledge and consciousness, held safely under the

126

guardianship of the priests. They had become impatient, hungry for complete control of the people, the land – and the skulls. The priests had learned from the skulls themselves that the takeover was imminent. Plans long since made for this event, not anticipated to occur for some time, were hastily brought forward and the final details put in place.

21.

Kua'tzal made his way to his usual lodging house, walking briskly to shake off the day and a half of enforced inactivity from his legs. His destination was an unremarkable, plain-fronted building set a little way off one of the seven wide tree-lined avenues that fanned out from Dendarak's main square. Inside, the inn was comfortable, if simply furnished. More importantly, the owner, a bearded, taciturn man named Perek, was a staunch and trusted ally of the Temple. Despite his ill-concealed distaste for Kua'tzal and the priest's apparent sympathy to the Shadow Chasers' cause, Perek's loyalty to the Priests of the Light and therefore, however reluctantly, to Kua'tzal, was unshakeable. This loyalty did not temper a profound dislike for the priest, however.

'Oh, it's you.' Perek jerked his head to the left. 'Two flights up, end of the corridor. One night again, is it?'

Kua'tzal nodded. His escape route had been carefully planned. Tomorrow evening, long after the sun had set, he would board a ship that would carry him far from the shores of Atlantis forever. 'I'll leave my bags and pick them up later tomorrow after my meeting, as usual.' Even as he spoke, Perek was already disappearing back into his personal quarters, banging the door behind him.

* * * * *

A comfortable bed was pushed against one wall of the small room, a small table set beside it. On the opposite side stood a low, wide dresser above which a large window let in the warm, hazy rays of the afternoon sun. Weariness gripped Kua'tzal unexpectedly; the desire to stretch out on the bed and sleep was almost too much to resist. He fought the demands of his body. Rest would have to wait a while longer. There was a lot he had to do. But first...

Kua'tzal sat on the edge of the bed, reached into his bag and withdrew a heavy bundle. His hands were trembling with excitement. Unwrapping the soft fabric covers, he brought Maat-su out into the light of day. It was the first chance he had had to look at her since he had entered the Skull Chamber early the previous morning. As always, he was awestruck by the presence and power of this sacred object, even as she was now, sleeping and inert.

He was not surprised that she had dropped into a state of dormancy. Dendarak was the main centre of Shadow Chaser activity. Their headquarters were here, as was the main garrison. Maat-su could not risk discovery. Every Shadow Chaser was well trained in the subtle arts. Even the tiniest expression of her active energy would alert them to her presence.

The priest was not one of the skull's usual guardians. His work had led him along a different path. Nevertheless, like all who worked in the Temple, he had frequently had contact with Maat-su during his years there. This familiarity did not lessen his appreciation. Always, when he gazed on the lifelike skulls, he marvelled at their beauty and at the skill of those craftsmen from all corners of the universe who had created them.

Throughout Atlantis, a handful of highly-skilled craftsmen had been carving skulls for generations, were still carving them. In spite of their experience and artistry however, none had ever created one as perfect and powerful as the thirteen that had come from the stars. The techniques used in their creation were a mystery that the skulls would not reveal. Kua'tzal recognised too that even if anyone did succeed in replicating their perfection, they would be incapable of creating the life, the living, intelligent, individual and yet one consciousness, that was the force of these sacred treasures.

Reluctantly, Kua'tzal rewrapped Maat-su gently in her coverings and placed her back in the bag. He had work to do, urgent business that he could not ignore. Maat-su would be safe here. Perek kept his premises secure, and crime in Dendarak was rare in any case. Still, he was loath to let her out of his sight. He had no choice. It would be irresponsible to take her with him and far too risky. For the first time ever though he added his own protective field around his room, focussing his mind to build an invisible energy barrier around its walls. It could not be seen or felt, and it would not stop the Dark Ones, but it would be enough to keep any curious intruder away. Satisfied that he had done all he could to keep Maat-su safe, Kua'tzal stepped out onto the city streets once more.

* * * * *

Dendarak was a city whose beautiful architecture of golden domes and pyramids, wide airy avenues and

130

fountain-filled squares was reminiscent of Yo'tlàn. But whereas that city was still vibrant and alive, the choice of the Shadow Chasers in making Dendarak their headquarters had brought an air of heavy lifelessness to its avenues and squares. Even though it was only mid-afternoon, the streets were almost empty and the few people who were out and about scurried past with their heads down. The key to an easy life here was to obey the rules, keep your head down, and stay as invisible as possible.

That was not an option for Kua'tzal. He was scouting out the route he would need to take the following day to the port. Moreover, he would be taking it after dark. He needed to be sure of his way, to walk with confidence and assurance, acting like he knew where he was going; any hesitation and uncertainty would draw the attention of the Shadow Chaser patrols who constantly roamed these streets. Tomorrow he could not risk being challenged. His papers would not help him if he was found roaming the dark in a place he had no purpose to be. Today, in broad daylight, with Maat-su safely tucked away in his room, it was a different matter. He had had a long journey, needed to get some air and to stretch his legs. He had a meeting with General Nagual and his commanders in the morning, and a sly name drop, together with a bit of bluster and indignation (and a few carefully veiled threats if necessary) would do the trick. The signature on his papers was not to one to be argued with.

22.

The sun had not long risen the following morning when Kua'tzal left the lodging house and set out for the Shadow Chaser's headquarters. He had been here numerous times, at least four times a year for as many years as he cared to remember. In the beginning, when the power and influence of the Shadow Chasers was still limited, they had needed the compliance of the Temple and were willing to compromise their demands to get it. In those days, these meetings had been genuinely useful. For too long now, however, they had been a waste of time, a sop to the powerful Priests, and one which paid only lip-service to any co-operation.

His hosts were always polite. Too polite, with their empty promises, cold eyes and crocodile smiles that, in spite of his apparent sympathies, would tear him to shreds at the first opportunity. Ignoring the requests Kua'tzal brought to the table, always with a smile, always with an excuse. Throwing the occasional consolation titbit to keep him sweet and coming back.

He was not fooled and neither were his colleagues. They had seen the direction events would take, seen the inevitable outcome, and set their own plans in motion. The Temple elders had gone along with the charade, portraying themselves as ingenuous and gullibly eager for a resolution, feigning a certain level of trust, buying themselves as much time as possible before the inevitable devastation fell. As much time as they could to complete their preparations.

It was a charade that would not have fooled anyone who cared to delve deeper, but in their arrogance the Shadow Chasers, intelligent though they were, had allowed themselves to believe too much in their own cleverness and superiority. Their egos massaged by the seeming compliance and eagerness of the priests, few thought to look deeper. Those more insightful who did more often than not had their doubts dismissed by their seniors. It was an organisation of egos, power struggles and self-enhancement. As he sat with them in the midst of this, it never ceased to astound Kua'tzal that they had managed to achieve such power and control.

One way or another, whatever happens from here on, this will be the final time, Kua'tzal thought with a shiver as he approached the compound gates. The final time he would pretend compliance and agreement, acceptance and friendship. The final time that he would allow himself to be mocked and belittled. From tonight, everything would change.

* * * * *

The grim compound and headquarters stood in stark contrast to the elegant beauty that graced the rest of Dendarak, however faded and chilled the city had become. It was a chill brought about not by its climate but through the presence in its midst of the Shadow Chasers, the Dark Ones as the people called them, with their constant threat of subjugation and violence. These fortress-like buildings were grey, forbidding and utilitarian. Though nothing had

133

ever been proved, Kua'tzal knew that behind those high, blank, sinister walls suspected sympathisers were brutally and cruelly interrogated. No physical violence was ever involved. It was not necessary. The Shadow Chasers were masters at extracting information through other, more subtle and effective techniques, long since honed and perfected. Raping the minds of their victims in ways equally as cruel and devastating as any physical mistreatment could be. The mental resilience and strength needed to withstand such torture was beyond almost all who entered, and never left, this place.

Kua'tzal shook off his dark thoughts as he passed through the gate. His mind shields were up and unshakeable. They would not be breached today by the mental probing of the Shadow Chasers. It would not raise suspicion. They would expect no less, and would have set up their own impenetrable barriers. He approached the door to the meeting chamber, squaring his shoulders both physically and mentally. After so many meetings he knew exactly what to expect. It would not be a pleasant experience. His hand reached out and turned the ornate handle, pushing open the heavy door.

It was as it always was. Five of the Shadow Chasers' High Command sat facing him on the far side of a dark, highly polished wooden table. In an unspoken but clear display of superiority and intimidation, a small, uncomfortable, hard wooden chair had been set at the other side of this table, some distance away. It was a deliberate move to instil an immediate feeling of being at a disadvantage. He was the defendant facing – what?

The man in the centre of the five was tall and thick set, with cold, intelligent eyes. This was Nagual, an ambitious general who had risen to his power by means of clever scheming and a ruthless elimination of his competition. He was flanked by two men and two women, all loyal and ardent supporters, carefully chosen because they did not seek further advancement themselves but were happy to bask in the reflected glory of their leader. Nagual rose.

'Good morning, Kua'tzal. What a pleasure to have you with us once more.' Nagual's voice was oily and insincere and he did not try to hide it. He brought his right palm to his heart in a crude parody of the priests' gesture of greeting, one of open hearted welcome. Coming from this man, who was the polar opposite to all it represented, the gesture was obscene and sacrilegious. The general was obviously seeking to provoke the man standing before him, and Kua'tzal found himself responding, his pulse racing and his blood pounding. With an almost superhuman effort, he succeeded in concealing his emotions, swallowing the bitter anger that was rising up within him and burning his throat with its bile.

He returned the gesture, his voice level as he replied. 'Greetings, General Nagual.'

23.

Many hours later, his face set in an expression of amiability and acceptance that he was far from feeling, Kua'tzal left the meeting. It had gone exactly as he had anticipated. His proposals and questions had been ignored, his words twisted beyond any semblance of their true meaning. He had been treated as a mindless, worthless nobody. All couched in the most civil and reasonable words of course. Nagual had been playing with him, letting him know in no uncertain terms that it was he who held the power. The general had tried to provoke him, and as usual he had failed. It had been so for a long time now, but today's meeting had taken the baiting up several notches. Through his general, the arrogant Xy-barian was letting the priests know that he was blatantly confident and ready to make his move. Kua'tzal could feel it. Well, the Shadow Chasers may be about to take control of Atlantis, he thought grimly, he could see no way in which they could be stopped, but they would be denied possession of that which they most coveted - the thirteen crystal skulls of the Pyramid Temple.

With a hot, barely concealed fury churning in his guts, Kua'tzal's already steadfast determination to fulfil his mission ignited to a level that until then he did not know was possible. He forced himself to calm the tumult of emotions that were threatening to cloud his focus, which in this moment needed to be as sharp as it had ever been.

He was to be at the dock just after nightfall. Before leaving the temple in Yo'tlàn Kua'tzal had committed to memory every detail, which was etched in his mind as clearly as if it was right in front of his eyes. The Edrus was leaving tonight on the tide, ostensibly with a hold filled with goods to trade with distant lands to the west.

It was later than he had anticipated. Nagual had kept him much longer than usual. Puffed up with his own importance and position he had at length proudly extolled the glories of the brave new world they were creating. Kua'tzal must be at the dockside an hour after sunset, but first he had to return to his room to collect Maat-su and the remainder of his pitifully few belongings. He had had to maintain an appearance of complete normality, bringing with him to Dendarak only what he needed for the few days of his planned trip.

All at once, the reality of his position hit him like a hammer blow to the chest. This was it. This was really it. After so many years of planning and subterfuge, the daring plot to spirit away the skulls and thwart the ambitions of the Dark Ones had come to a head. The previous night, the twelve remaining skulls had been taken silently from the Skull Chamber and inert duplicates left in their place. Last night twelve priests, men and women of all ages and from all backgrounds, had said goodbye to their lives forever to embark into a perilous journey into the unknown. Tonight, in only a few short hours, he would do the same.

Kua'tzal quickened his pace. He had no time to lose. He could not miss his only passage out of Atlantis. The exertion calmed him, burning away the anger, fear and grief that was churning inside him. By the time he reached the door of his lodgings he felt balanced and clear-headed again. It did not last. As he pushed the door open, Perek materialised, an odd look on his face.

'Kua'tzal?' What now? He had paid his bill and could ill-afford the time to stop and share small-talk with the innkeeper.

'I'm in a hurry.' He pushed passed, heading for the stairs.

'Kua'tzal.' Something in Perek's voice caused the priest to stop and turn to face him. 'I have a message for you. From Yo'tlàn. It was delivered a couple of hours ago.'

'Well, what is it?' Impatience, and the seeds of anxiety, shortened Kua'tzal's manner.

'The dove will not fly tonight. She must roost quietly until the morning when the moon turns.'

Kua'tzal looked at him in dismay. He knew exactly what it meant. The Edrus had been delayed for some reason and would not sail tonight. He and Maat-su would have to lie low until the next full moon when the tide would be high enough for her to enter the port.

His face must have betrayed his dismay for Perek spoke up. 'Is everything alright, Kua'tzal?'

Kua'tzal thought quickly. 'Yes. Yes. Everything is fine. But it seems I will have to extend my stay here in Dendarak for several days. Will that cause you a problem?'

Perek shook his head. He was obviously puzzled and wanted to ask more but kept his questions to himself. 'No. We have precious few visitors in Dendarak these days. The room is yours for as long as you need it.'

The priest nodded his thanks. 'I would appreciate it if you would tell no-one I am still here.' He trusted

138

completely the innkeeper's loyalty to the Temple, it had been tested and proven on many occasions, but Kua'tzal would not risk sharing more information than was absolutely necessary. If Perek were ever questioned, and as a known supporter of the Temple it was always a possibility, he would tell the Dark Ones all they wanted to know. He would not be able to resist. The less he knew, the better.

'Of course. But won't questions be raised if you don't board the shuttle to Yo'tlàn this evening?'

'No. I have an open permit. My arrival and departure will not be recorded.'

'Well then, if you go to your room I will bring your supper up shortly. There are no other guests here tonight so you do not have to concern yourself about being seen.'

Kua'tzal turned and trudged wearily up the stairs, wave after wave of unwelcome thoughts filling his head, a hundred questions clamouring for answers. His life had suddenly become even more uncertain and a great deal more perilous. Last night the remaining skulls had all been taken from the Temple. How long would it be before the Shadow Chasers discovered the switch? Probably not until the energy began to weaken, which gave the fugitives four, five days at most? Then what? Retribution would be swift and merciless, the hunt for them relentless. And he would be here, trapped in the lions' den with no possibility of escape for at least another week after that. Could he really avoid their clutches for all that time and be on the Edrus when she finally sailed? He had no doubt of the message's validity. Perek would have checked its source carefully.

What had happened to delay the Edrus? What was going on?

Meanwhile, two floors below, the same question assailed Perek. What was going on? Perek had never liked the priest, found his sly sympathies for the Dark Ones repellent; now he was beginning to question his assumptions. Had he got him wrong all these years? There was clearly much more to him than met the eye. Of one thing Perek was certain: Kua'tzal was carrying a heavy secret.

24.

For five long days Kua'tzal stayed closeted away in his room. It was too risky to head out into the city. His only contact was Perek, who had little news to bring him. With every day that passed, the time when the Shadow Chasers would discover the deception in the Temple grew nearer. With every day that passed, the likelihood of a relentless, full-scale man-hunt increased. Five days, and all was disconcertingly quiet still.

* * * * *

The knocking inside Kua'tzal's head grew louder and louder, more and more insistent, trickling down through the layers of his unconscious mind until finally it nudged him towards wakefulness. As he fought his way back up through the layers, the sound became increasingly clear…

Kua'tzal's eyes flew open. Someone was banging forcefully on the door.

'Kua'tzal. Kua'tzal!' It was Perek, calling to him in a low but urgent voice. Kua'tzal staggered out of his bed, sleep still hovering around the edges of his consciousness, and pulled open the door. The innkeeper burst in, shutting it quickly behind him. 'Dark Ones. In the street and coming this way. They're searching every property. If you don't want them to find you I suggest you get out of here now.'

Kua'tzal was already pulling on his clothes, all lingering drowsiness evaporating under the threat of discovery. His energy shields would not keep the Shadow Chasers at bay. He had grabbed his bags and was heading out of the door towards the stairs when Perek seized his arm.

'Not that way. They're in the main street. The back entrance.' He pulled Kua'tzal along the corridor to where a small door was half-hidden behind a curtain. 'Emergency exit.' Perek opened the door and led the way along a rooftop walkway to where a flimsy rope ladder snaked down the rear wall of the building into a narrow, dark alleyway. 'Down there.'

'What's going on?' The situation was critical but Kua'tzal had to take the time to find out all he could.

'You tell me.' Perek fixed him with a cold stare.

'What has happened, Perek? You keep your ear to the ground. You must have some idea.'

The innkeeper relented. 'I don't know for certain. There is a rumour that the Skulls of Light have been stolen from the Temple. That the Dark Ones have gone berserk and smashed up the Skull Chamber. Apparently they have sworn to get the skulls back no matter what the cost, and are offering all kinds of reward for the capture of the perpetrators.' The penny had not yet dropped. 'If you don't want to get caught up in all of that, you need to go. Now!'

Kua'tzal's heart contracted painfully as he heard Perek's words. This was it then. There was no time to lose. He swung his leg over the parapet onto the first rung of the ladder, feeling it swing disconcertingly under his weight.

Perek reached for the bag to hand it to the priest but Kua'tzal stopped him with an explosive 'No!'

The innkeeper stopped, at first confused, then with a suspicion of understanding mingled with disbelief and astonishment washing over his features. 'You?'

A faint flicker of a smile brushed across Kua'tzal's face. 'My friend, it is never wise to believe what your eyes see and your ears hear. They can be deceived. Listen to what your heart tells you. Your heart will never lie.'

'I don't know what is going on,' Perek replied slowly, 'and I don't want to, but if it's what I suspect then you need to go. Now!' He passed a small sack across to the fleeing priest. 'It's not much, just some bread and cheese and a flask of water, but it will keep you going for a while.'

In an unaccustomed gesture, Kua'tzal seized his host's hand in a clasp of farewell and gratitude, then took the sack and leant over to where the pouch containing Maat-su was lying against the parapet. He slung both bags over his shoulder and started to descend the ladder. A whispered 'May the light go with you' followed him. He took a last glance up; Perek's head and upper body were just visible against the night sky. With a confidence he was a long way from feeling, Kua'tzal gave a final wave. The moment his feet touched the ground, the ladder was hauled up concealing, at least for a short time, his escape.

25.

He was on his own now in an unfamiliar city with nowhere to hide and at least eight more days before the Edrus would sail. He did not even have Maat-su's help. She was dormant and would remain so until they were far from the shores of Atlantis. That was, of course, assuming the ship would be at the dockside on the given date. Now that he had left the lodging house, he was out of touch with anyone. All he could do was turn up on the night and pray all would unfold as planned.

He put a safe distance between himself and the lodging house before stopping in the shadows of a doorway to take his bearings and consider his options. They were few. He could trust no-one. Some in Atlantis, like Perek, were committed to working against the Dark Ones and all they stood for, prepared to risk their lives for the cause if it came to it. Most people however were too afraid. They would not hesitate to save their lives and those of their families by handing him over to Xy-barian and his thugs. Kua'tzal did not feel resentment towards them for that, self-preservation was a natural instinct, but it meant he had nowhere to turn for help.

He could not return to Yo'tlàn. There was nothing to return to. If the Shadow Chasers had discovered the deception, as Perek had told him, and it was surely inevitable that they had, they would have taken control of the Skull Chamber and the entire Temple. Moreover, they would be scouring the land searching for the fleeing guardians and the skulls they carried. He slumped, allowing for a moment his fear and despondency to get the better of him.

Distant shouts and the loud banging of fists on doors roused him from his dark thoughts. Shadow Chasers, not that far away and by the sound of it heading towards him. He had to move.

The imminent danger restored his courage and determination. He would not give up Maat-su. That was beyond question. He would find somewhere to hide out and head for the dock on the stated evening. If the ship was not there, only then would he reconsider his options. Maybe he could find somewhere to hide Maat-su in Atlantis itself? He didn't know, but he would find the answer.

The shouts were even closer. Were they at the inn already? He thought he recognised Perek's indignant voice carrying through the dark silence of the night time streets. Move, Kua'tzal. Move. He drew his cloak more tightly around his body, pulling the collar up around his ears to hide his pale face from the moonlight. At a fast pace, he set off as quickly as he could in the direction of the port. If he could find somewhere to hide there it would be less distance to travel later. He would have to trust that his next step would become clear, that he would know it when the time came, and that maybe, in some subtle way, Maat-su could help him.

He kept to the back alleyways as far as possible, digging deep into his memories to stay on course. It all looked so different from that first afternoon when he had reconnoitred these streets. Now it was dark, he was dodging the Dark Ones who were out in force, and he was searching for somewhere to hide. Street lighting was scant off the main thoroughfares and he merged easily into the shadows of these empty side streets. The major arteries were a different story. There the lamps had been turned to full power, bathing the entire expanse in an inescapable spotlight. The Shadow Chasers had been clearing the streets; anyone foolish or desperate enough to still be there would stand out in full view.

In crossing these avenues and squares Kua'tzal relied entirely on his inherent extrasensory skills, scanning subtly for the presence of hidden eyes that would pounce as soon as they spotted him. Waiting for anyone in the vicinity to move away before darting across the no-man's-land to the safety of the shadows beyond. By some miracle – or was Maat-su even in her sleeping state still watching over him? – no potential threat loomed.

He still had no idea of what he was going to do and was simply allowing his feet to carry him intuitively. His luck held. He met no-one… Until he turned a corner out of a narrow back alley into a wider, residential street, and almost walked right into a group of Shadow Chasers. By some miracle, they didn't spot him. They were too busy, their attention distracted as they bullied and intimidated an innocent householder a little further up the street, demanding her papers and threatening a search of her premises for no other real reason than their pleasure in wielding this power and their ability to create fear. A quick scan would have told them she had nothing to hide.

Kua'tzal darted back into the alleyway, flattening against the wall before peeking back out around the corner.

146

The Dark Ones had grown bored of tormenting their victim and were coming in his direction, scanning all the side openings as they passed by. They would not miss him this time. What could he do? There was nowhere to go. His heart was pounding, his pulse racing. Again though, it appeared he was being helped. Just visible at ground floor level of the dark, unlit building behind him, a shutter was ajar. He had missed it as he had hurried past, his attention focussed on watching for Shadow Chasers and avoiding capture. Kua'tzal tentatively reached out a hand to investigate; the window behind it was open too.

Trying not to make a sound, Kua'tzal hoisted himself over the windowsill and tumbled painfully into the room behind. The thud of his body hitting the hard wooden floor echoed excruciatingly loudly. Surely the Shadow Chasers must have heard it and would come to investigate? He got up unsteadily, wincing as pain shot through his shoulder – there was no time for that now, he would allow himself to feel the effects when he was sure he was safe – and pulled the shutter closed, fastening it securely, then doing the same with the window. He slumped down against the wall beneath it, breathing hard. He had done all he could do. Would it be enough? Fear enveloped him as he sat and waited.

The seconds ticked on. Footsteps passed by, right outside the window, so close that Kua'tzal swore he could hear the Dark Ones' heartbeats. They must have sensed something, for the steps stopped right next to the wall where he was crouched. He held his breath, not daring to breathe for fear they would hear him. Shouts. Fists pounding hard on the door, as if to break it down.

147

Another door opened, further along the street. A sleepy bad-tempered voice, suddenly wide awake and compliant at the sight of the Dark Ones.

'Who lives there?' Kua'tzal imagined a gloved fist brandished at his hiding place.

'Na'tik and his wife. They have gone to Cangura, two days west of here, for his brother's funeral. They left yesterday morning and won't return for several days. He asked me to keep an eye on the place for him.'

'Is anyone left there?'

'No. It's just the two of them. I went in earlier to check everything was alright. It was empty.'

A muttered discussion followed. Kua'tzal's heart was in his throat, his palms sweating. Was this the end? Was he about to be discovered, and Maat-su with him?

'If you see anyone hanging around, let us know immediately.' To the fugitive's relief, there came the sound of footsteps moving away. He uttered a silent thank you to the heavens.

* * * * *

For the next few days, Kua'tzal led a miserable existence. He was hungry, cold and scared. He ate sparingly of the little bread and cheese. He had to eke it out; he could not risk heading out to find more. There were a couple of positive aspects however. The man who had proclaimed so loudly his responsibility to his neighbours did not put in an appearance, his commitment an empty promise. There was sanitation, and fresh, clean water piped to the house, which was itself clean and comfortably furnished. Despite it being summer it was cold though, and it was dark. The shutters had to stay locked closed day and night. Kua'tzal could not risk lighting a fire or a lamp, in case it was seen from outside. Only the tiniest glimmer of light shining in through the chinks in the shutters told showed him when the sun had risen.

Would the ship come? Where was it? What had delayed its arrival? Day and night rolled together in this gloomy, tedious world he was inhabiting. He slept when he was tired, woke when he was not. The time of day, even the days themselves, would soon lose any meaning. Kua'tzal had to stay alert; he could not risk missing his one escape route out of Atlantis. Each day he marked the sunrise with a line in the dust on the old dresser that stood in the main living room.

Eight marks in the dust. Finally the day had arrived when he must leave his hiding place and make his way to the dockside. Time dragged as he waited for the hours to pass and the sun to set. When at last the hour came, hunger growling in his belly and lightening his head, Kua'tzal gathered up Maat-su and slipped out of the house. Like a shadow he ghosted through the darkened streets to meet his future. He pushed all anxiety from his mind, knowing that they would increase the likelihood of failure. In their place, he focussed firmly on seeing himself standing on the ship's deck, far out to sea on a calm sparkling ocean, safely away from Atlantis and the reach of the Dark Ones.

26.

Kua'tzal paused at the last corner. He had negotiated the silent streets without incident. They had been empty, devoid of life, without sign even of a patrol. In front of him now stretched the wide, empty expanse of the dockside, the final obstacle he would have to face in Dendarak. Beyond that... Kua'tzal's breath caught in his throat. He had not been expecting a ship like this.

The Edrus was a beautiful craft, especially so tonight with her pale hull silhouetted clearly against the deep blue-black of the night sky and the full moon glittering silver on her masts. She was sleek and elegant, her looks and her speed more those of a thoroughbred than the workhorse that she was. The ship was riding low in the water, her holds already full of finely crafted Atlantean goods to be traded overseas. Nowhere on her cargo manifest, however, were registered the thirty or so passengers – men, women and children – who would be leaving with her when she sailed. All of them were refugees, willing to risk their lives and their freedom to flee the ever tightening fist of the Shadow Chasers' regime.

Like him, they would have made their way to the docks under cover of darkness to be smuggled on board in ones and twos. It was not the best of nights for such a perilous clandestine activity. The sky was clear and the moon illuminated the dockside almost as brightly as afternoon. It could not be helped. There could be no more delay. It was a miracle that the Edrus was sailing at all. How had she gained permission? Throughout Atlantis, the Shadow Chasers would have been on full alert since the switch in the Skull Chamber had been discovered. Every port in the land would have been shut down immediately. Surely it had to be divine intervention that was allowing her to sail tonight?

Peering out over the cobbled dock, he could see no-one. Even the ship appeared abandoned. Would they all make it? During his days of enforced inactivity, Kua'tzal had wondered often about his fellow passengers. How were they dealing with the delay? Were they holing up secretly, as he was? Had some decided it was too dangerous or difficult? Or had no option but to give up and return home?

There was no time to think about that now. On the far side of the quay, a squat black shape huddled in the lee of a taller building. The store house. The meeting point and his objective. Kua'tzal glanced round once more to make certain there was no-one around, then darted across the open ground that separated him from the small building and slipped inside. It was empty. He was puzzled. Had all the other passengers already been taken on board? There was plenty of time still, wasn't there? He'd assumed the Edrus would be leaving on the high tide, just before dawn. Cautiously he peeked through the doorway. The dock was still deserted, the ship too, no sign of activity heralding her imminent departure as she rocked peacefully at her moorings.

He was the only one in the small shed. He had to be the next, and possibly the last, to board. As he continued to watch through the gap in the doorway, however, he spotted another dark figure zigzagging his way through the shadows, darting from one point of cover to the next. Then he was gone, vanished from view. To where?

Kua'tzal's head whipped around, startled at the rustle of a soft footstep behind him. He had not noticed a second doorway at the back of the shed and the newcomer had taken him by surprise. He could just make out a bulky silhouette before the door closed, shutting off the weak light. Invisible against the wall, Kua'tzal remained silent, not wishing to reveal himself. Was this another passenger, or a more sinister visitor? Surely not the latter; he had been too furtive and stealthy in his approach. A Shadow Chaser would not have hesitated to show his hand.

'Is anyone in here?' The whispered enquiry reached Kua'tzal's ears and he started in astonishment. He recognised the voice.

'Jar-Kan? What are you doing here?' An unpleasant thud followed by a quickly stifled oath answered him as the man he recognised as Jar-Kan cracked his head against an unseen low beam, the result of the newcomer's own surprise... and dismay.

Then, a second or so later, 'Kua'tzal? What in the name of all that's sacred are you doing here?' After the astonishment came slow understanding. 'Oh no. Oh no, no, no. Not you. This I don't believe.' The tone of his voice told Kua'tzal that Jar-Kan was less than overjoyed at the discovery.

Kua'tzal felt his own heart sinking. Jar-Kan? Why was he here? He should have been far away, travelling his own separate course. Everything had been so carefully planned, every minute detail mapped out, to keep the skull guardians' paths from crossing. It had to be so, to safeguard the skulls. Separately if one guardian was captured and the skull seized, then tragedy though it would be, it was one skull alone. But once they came together...

'Kua'tzal?' Kua'tzal pressed a finger to his lips, commanding silence. Someone was approaching the shed.

A low voice from the doorway interrupted both men's unspoken thoughts. 'Come with me, keep your heads down and keep up.' He paused, taking in both men. 'Who are you?' His voice carried the weight of suspicion as he eyed up Jar-Kan.

'Lumi.' Jar-Kan avoided Kua'tzal's unspoken question at the lie. 'I seek passage.'

The sailor stared closely at him for a moment. He was scanning the big man's energy, tuning in to his mind. The crew of the Edrus were obviously not the standard rough and ready mariners. Judging by the crewman's actions he was as well-trained in mind scanning and energy reading skills as any priest of the light. Or any Shadow Chaser.

It was a minute or two before he spoke. 'Well, I don't sense any dark energy around you. There is something unusual going on but...' He paused, frowning, as he contemplated the big man. Eventually he nodded. 'OK, you're in. But the first sign that you aren't what you claim and you'll be feeding the sharks. Come on. We'll be casting off within minutes.'

Without waiting to see if they followed him, the crewman turned back to the ship. The two priests scrambled through the doorway after him, staying as low to the ground as possible in the bright moonlight, and followed him the short distance across the paved dock to

153

the gangway. It may have been only a few paces, but both men felt as exposed and vulnerable as if they had been crossing the main square in Dendarak at midday, the skulls in their hands.

It was with undisguised relief that they scrambled on board and, at the crewman's indication, ducked down behind a towering pile of crates and sacks – cargo that would not be stowed now until they were at sea. Even as they were stepping on board, the gangplank was being pulled up behind them. The ship was alive with busy, but silent, activity.

'A few minutes? I thought we weren't sailing until just before dawn.' Kua'tzal was puzzled.

The sailor grinned. 'That's what our papers say too. Apparently, we can't leave until high tide because our draught is too deep, which is why the Dark Ones have scheduled their inspection for an hour before dawn.' He winked. 'We lied. We're ready to raise anchor and sail out any minute now. As if we are going to let them check out our cargo this time around. There's no guarantee they'll let us sail at all, so we're taking that decision into our own hands. We have no intention of letting them stop us.'

Distant snarling shouts and a clattering of boots interrupted the sailor's explanation. His demeanour changed immediately; he stiffened, his easy smile transformed into a grim scowl. 'Shadow Chasers. Heading this way.' The words spat out in disgust. 'Obviously, they didn't believe us...'

He had not been the only one to react to the approaching figures.

'Cast off and make way.' The command barked out like an explosion from a deck above and to the left of their heads.

'Stay out of sight.' The last sentence was cast behind as the sailor leapt into action.

The deck suddenly burst alive with activity. Docking ropes were released and sails readied. The Edrus began to move, slipping away from the dockside at a speed that took the rapidly closing Shadow Chasers by surprise. The crystal-powered engines quickly carried the ship clear of the harbour.

'Ahead, full.'

'STOP!'

The rest of the words were lost in the clatter of the huge sails unfurling, and as the wind filled them the ship leapt forward, her lean prow cutting through the water with all the grace and elegance of the dolphins that later would accompany them for much of their journey. Cargo ship she may have been by description, but the Edrus had been built for speed and she was revelling in her freedom.

Far behind, growing smaller with every second that passed, the group of furious red-faced figures on the dockside shook their fists impotently. A peal of laughter rang from the upper deck. 'By the time they set sail we'll be well out of their range. The Edrus is the fastest ship on Earth. They won't catch us now.'

Kua'tzal knew it to be true. The Shadow Chasers had few ships, preferring to place their energies on controlling the populace. Their interest did not (yet) stretch to the world beyond Atlantis. They may make a token effort at a chase, he mused, but were more than likely to just let the ship go. Of course, they did not know what she was carrying. If they had...

Huddled behind the pile of crates and sacks, his companion turned to him. 'It will be wiser to act as if we are strangers,' he whispered. 'It will avoid suspicion and difficult questions. I know all on board are supposed to be sympathisers but we cannot take the risk.'

Kua'tzal read the underlying implication in Jar-Kan's voice. He did not trust him, Kua'tzal, and Kua'tzal understood the other priest's position. He had for so long played the part of holding sympathy for the Dark Ones' position that his companion was unable to view him in any other way.

'Agreed.' He fell silent as the crewman appeared once more, his grin back in place, relaxed now that they were putting an ever increasing distance between themselves and the land.

'Come on,' he said to the two fugitive priests, 'I'll show you to your bunks.'

GEMMA, 4

27.

Only a few weeks later I stepped onto the tarmac at Værnes, the international airport that serves Norway's third city, Trondheim. After the artificial warmth of the plane's interior it was, to put it bluntly, bloody freezing! Several degrees below zero with a bitterly cold wind blasting straight down form the Arctic Circle and a light sprinkling of snow on the ground. Not as much as I'd expected; the location, right on the Trondheimsfjord, was keeping the worst ravages of the winter at bay. Even so, as I hurried across the exposed apron to the Arrivals lounge, the cold seeped through my thick coat and set my teeth chattering.

It was late evening. The plane had been delayed at Amsterdam and the scheduled five hour flight from Bristol had turned into a nine and a half hour marathon. Olina had said she would come to meet me and drive me to a hotel near the University. I had phoned her from Schipol and left a message. I could only hope she had picked it up in time.

The airport concourse was empty other than the exiting passengers and those who had come to meet them. I had already spoken with Olina on a couple of occasions by Skype and felt confident I would recognise her. On the concourse however, no-one looked remotely like her or appeared to be waiting for a lone traveller from England. One by one my fellow passengers drifted away. Where was she? I was struck briefly by a sense of déjà-vu. It was so like my arrival in Phoenix not so many months earlier when Callum had been so late in materialising.

Well, not quite. There was one big difference this time – me. I was no longer that unconfident, uncertain woman who had sat and bawled in Arizona on a hot, early autumn evening. How it had happened I wasn't sure, but it had. Then I had despaired. Now I was simply tired and a little stumped. What to do? Chances were that Olina had simply been delayed for some reason, but that didn't help me. The airport was shutting up for the night. I couldn't stay here. I walked across to the information desk in case she had sent through a message. Nothing.

OK. Think, Gemma. What were my options? They weren't many. As I saw it, I had two choices: either find a hotel here for the night, or travel into Trondheim and find one there. I chose the former. It was late and cold, and I was tired. The last bus had already left and the thought of hiring a car and driving the thirty kilometres or so – and then looking for somewhere to stay – didn't hold much appeal. Olina had booked me a room but hadn't left me the hotel details. She had been going to drive me there, so I suppose she hadn't thought it necessary.

The man at the information desk couldn't have been more helpful. He quickly found me a room at a decent rate and within a very short time I was cosily ensconced in a taxi for the five minute drive to the hotel. I was anxious to ring Olina but as I still hadn't upgraded my dinosaur of a phone I couldn't do it until I got to my room. When I did call there was no answer. That was a bit odd. There was no point really in phoning the university, it would be closed and the staff gone home by now. Maybe she had lost track

159

of time and was still working in her laboratory. I tried the university number anyway, just in case. As I was expecting, no-one answered.

Where was she? There wasn't a lot I could do but wait for her to get in touch. I ordered supper through room service and went to bed, wondering where she was and why she hadn't contacted me.

By the time I went down to breakfast the next morning, I still hadn't heard from Olina. Had something happened? Had she been in an accident or something? Little did I suspect. I called her cellphone again – again no response – so at eight thirty I called the archaeology department at the university. A very shaken sounding woman picked up the phone. When I asked to speak to Olina she stifled a sob, fighting to retain her composure.

'I... I'm sorry, but you can't. Dr Gjerde is seriously ill in the hospital. She was attacked yesterday evening.'

I sat down heavily onto the bed. 'What happened?' My voice was flat, dead, as her words sank in.

'No-one knows. The cleaners found them this morning.'

'Them?'

'Dr Gjerde and Dr Mackintosh. They had been badly beaten. Dr Gjerde was alive, just, but Dr Mackintosh...' Her fragile self-control crumbled completely.

'Do they know who did it, or why?' I was speaking just for something to say.

'No. But the artefact, the key, was gone. Stolen.' The woman stopped speaking, realising she had probably said too much. She had pulled herself together a little and her voice now held a trace of suspicion. 'Who are you? Why do you want to speak to Dr Gjerde?'

Numbly, not really registering my actions, I hung up without answering. I was deeply in shock. That's why Olina hadn't been at the airport. She couldn't be. She was lying in her lab, left for dead. My mind was churning sickeningly. Who would do this? Why? Not wanting to take in the implications. Because this hadn't been some random act, some opportunist theft. Someone had wanted the key strongly enough to kill for it.

Again, why? Why was it so important? Oh, I don't mean in the historical or archaeological sense. Not even because of its association with the crystal skulls. I mean, why? What possible use could it be to anyone unless... Unless they were in possession of one of the ancient caskets and needed the key to open it. Or anticipated that they soon would be...

No. Surely that wasn't possible. Even if the skulls still existed, and it was beyond all doubt for me now that at least some of them did, what was the likelihood of their original caskets surviving? They would be close on a quarter of a million years old by now and it was unlikely they would have been treated as reverently or guarded as carefully as their contents. Would they?

For a long time I lay on my bed staring at the ceiling, unseeing, trembling and scared. The world was going mad and I was sitting right in the middle of it. The adventure had in this moment become a nightmare, and it was one I couldn't wake up from.

It was several hours later that I roused myself from my dark thoughts. There was no point in going into the city; I had lost all taste for exploring the beautiful old streets and churches of Trondheim, an attraction I had been so excited about just the day before. I called through to the airline to bring my return flight forward. I didn't want to stay here a minute longer than necessary. It was too late to catch a plane back to Bristol that day but I could fly out the following morning. There was no other real option. I would just have to kill time until then.

Putting the phone down, I wandered across to the window. It was only early afternoon but the sun had already sunk to the horizon. At this latitude and at this time of year daylight lasted barely five hours before the night descended once more. Dusk was falling and in the deepening blue sky, today clear of clouds, the first stars were already sparkling.

Just like at home, I didn't draw the curtains. The hotel faced the fjord and I was on the third floor, so there would be no-one to look into my room. I love to lie in bed at night and see the night sky outside. Gaze at the moon and stars or watch the clouds scuttering across the darkness. I switched on the TV and wasted the rest of the day watching old movies, badly dubbed into English. I could have called Cathy or Joe but right now I didn't want to speak to anyone. I was still dealing with the day's fall-out. There would be time enough to fill them in on what had been going on when I got back.

I went to bed early again. At just after two in the morning I woke from a deeply unsettling dream in which I was being chased across a frozen landscape by giant figures dressed in black leather armour and wielding black swords. It took a few moments for me to realise it had been just a dream and for my racing pulse to slow and my breathing to even out. Out of habit I glanced out of the window. Across the water of the fjord, high above the ridges opposite, the sky, which should have been a deep inky black, was a pulsing curtain of vivid green light that swept across my view, dancing and swirling like ghostly spirits playing in the heavens. The aurora borealis! I grabbed my dressing gown and hurried to the window to see more clearly. This was something I hadn't been expecting.

Below me, at the front of the hotel, several guests had bundled themselves up in layers of warm clothing to come outside and were standing staring skywards at this supernatural light show. I hurried to join them, pulling jeans and several jumpers on over my pyjamas before dragging on my hat, coat and gloves, and stuffing my thickly socked feet into my boots.

As I stepped out of the hotel the cold took my breath away, crystallising it into soft white clouds that drifted off into the night. It had to be at least minus ten Celsius and my nose was already freezing. I pulled my scarf up to protect it – frostbite was a real risk in this damp iciness – and stood in wonder at the magical display unfolding before my eyes. After the unpleasant events of the day I found it soothing. It was hypnotic, otherworldly. My tension drained away. Nature was displaying her magnificence and I was oddly reassured by it.

It was far too cold for any of us to remain outside for very long though. One by one we gave in to the bitter iciness and returned to our rooms. Even so, I didn't go back to bed for a very long time. The Northern Lights had cast their spell on me and, curled up on the floor wrapped in the duvet, I sat watching their spectacle until at last it faded and dissolved back into the night's blackness.

The following day I flew home, subdued and in a thoughtful frame of mind. What was going on, and where would it lead next?

28.

As soon as I had dumped my case on the kitchen table, I tried calling Joe to let him know what had happened. He wasn't answering so I left him a brief voicemail asking him to ring me back as soon as he could. Then I called Cathy.

'I had a hunch you might be back.' I could hear her puzzlement. 'What's up?' I related the whole saga. When I finished there was silence at the other end of the line.

'Cathy?'

'I'm here. I'm letting it all sink in, that's all.'

'Well what do you make of it?'

'Honestly? I don't know. It seems someone is prepared to go to an awful lot of trouble to get their hands on that key.'

'That's what I thought, but what I don't get is why. What possible use would it be to anyone? Or is it simply because of what it is? You know, its uniqueness. Some crazy, stop-at-nothing collector who collects rare and precious objects just for the sake of owning them wants to add it to his own personal treasure trove.'

'Badly enough to kill for it?'

'Maybe.' I sighed. 'Whatever the reason, Olina is in the hospital in intensive care and the doctors don't know if she'll pull through. I wish I'd never heard of the bloody thing. Don't you pick up anything?' I was pleading with Cathy's psychic side now. I could almost hear her shaking her head as she replied.

'Sorry, not a thing. If I do, I'll call you straight away, you know that.' She paused, her voice anxious. 'Be careful, Gemma. This is no coincidence. It isn't just a game any more.' I held back from telling Cathy I hadn't ever considered it a game in the first place, it was all far too real for that. 'Look, I'll come round tomorrow morning and we can go over it again, see if we can't make some sense of it all.'

* * * * *

The doorbell rang early the next day. Not Cathy, but the postman, was standing on the doorstep holding out a parcel to me. Odd. I wasn't expecting anything. I nearly dropped it when he handed it to me, surprised by its weight. I carried the heavily taped box into the kitchen turning it over curiously in my hands. It was quite small, perhaps eight inches by five, by about an inch and a half deep, and heavy for its size. I couldn't see anything else until I'd found my glasses.

Specs firmly perched on my nose, I peered at the writing. My name and address had been written in black felt tip in simple but elegant handwriting. I looked more closely at the stamps and smudged postmark. My nerves began to buzz, and tingly bursts of energy surged up and down my spine. Norwegian stamps, postmarked Trondheim. I looked carefully. No return address so I turned my attention back to the postmark. 14th January 2014, 11.30am. The morning of the attack on the research lab. The energy bursts erupted into full-blown explosions. It couldn't be, could it?

My hands were shaking so much I could hardly grip the scissors as I cut into the layers of tape that sealed the parcel, opened the box and drew out an equally well-sealed bundle of cotton wool and bubble-wrap. Wrapped around it was a folded sheet of paper, on the outside of which, in the same handwriting as the address, was written one solitary word: *'Gemma'*. A letter?

With hands that no longer seemed to belong to me, my breath coming in quick gasps and my heart fluttering like a captured butterfly I peeled back the layers of padding…

It lay on my palm, heavy, unusually warm, glowing in an aura of its own light which was suddenly enhanced by a shaft of winter sunshine that fell directly onto it from the window behind me. The key. Magical, mystical, come from a different world to this one. And I was holding it. I stared down at it in wonder. It was beautiful. No, it was more than beautiful. It was breath-taking. And it was exactly as I had seen it in my mind so many months before. Captivated by its spell, I lost all sense of time.

29.

That was where Joe and Cathy found me, over an hour and a half later. Laughing at some joke or other they burst into my living room, as usual not needing to knock, and stopped in their tracks, mouths open, eyes wide, as they saw the shining object in my hand.

'Is that…? Is…? NO!!!' I nodded wordlessly as Cathy dropped to her knees in front of me, unable to pull her eyes away from the key I still held. Joe slowly, disbelievingly, lowered himself onto the sofa next to me, likewise transfixed.

Cathy reached out a hand, her finger tips first cautious and light, then stroking it reverently. 'It's beautiful. So ancient. Magical.' Her psychic senses were drawing in feelings and memories from the key. 'Not of this world, but we know that. Lavender skies, two suns. Wisdom.' She pulled her hand away sharply. 'Ewww. Not nice. Pain, lots of pain. Sadness. Sorrow.'

'May I?' Joe held out his hand and I placed it flat on his palm. He turned it over and over, gazing at it in wonder and amazement. No words would come. They weren't necessary. We could all sense the power emanating from this small and oh so mysterious object. It was a power that reached in and touched us all on the deepest level. When he looked up, his eyes were wet.

'All my life I have been fascinated by the ancient mysteries of Earth,' he said slowly, 'and now I'm holding one of them in my hand. It's crazy, it's unbelievable, and,' he grinned widely, 'God it feels fantastic.' Rationality getting a toehold at last he looked at me hard, a question in his eyes. 'This is the Norway key, yes?'

I nodded.

'Well, what the hell are you doing with it? I don't understand. Did they lend it to you?'

'Not exactly.' I hesitated. Of course Joe didn't know. I'd told Cathy but not him. Once again I related the story, from Olina's non-appearance to my arrival home and then added on the morning's events for both their benefit.

'Okay, I get that, but it still doesn't explain how or why you have this key.'

Joe was right. It didn't. I remembered the letter. I picked it up from the floor where it had fallen and waved it excitedly. 'Maybe this will tell us. It was wrapped around it.' I unfolded it. It was actually two sheets of paper – a pretty lengthy letter – dated the day before it was sent. Handwritten. That was a little odd too. My voice husky with a mix of apprehension and anticipation, I began to read it out loud.

'Dear Gemma,

Please excuse my assumption in involving you in what may prove to be a risky situation. We have only spoken a couple of times, but I honestly don't know who else I can trust. You know about the key, about its origins. You understand its importance.

Strange things have been happening here that have left me wary and frightened. I can't be clear, because it isn't clear. It's more of a gut instinct. I'm certain I am being watched and followed every time I leave the university, and I have spotted several men hovering suspiciously around the museum over the last two weeks. The same men, just standing there. Then a week ago we had a request for a 'special private viewing' of the key, which the department refused. As I say, nothing concrete, just an uncomfortable feeling that won't go away and that is growing stronger daily.

I do know, simply from being around this beautiful artefact, that it is a powerful object. To be honest, it has us all baffled. We cannot trace the source of its power. We can't even begin to understand where it is coming from. But it has a tangible energy that everyone who gets close to it can feel. When you hold it, it is like a strong electrical current running through you, and when we place the key too close to our instruments, it sends them haywire, which means we have made little progress in examining it. This energy seems able to switch on and off at will, which is a bizarre way to explain an inanimate object, especially coming from a scientist, but it is the only way I can describe it.

You may wonder why I am telling you all this. Please bear with me a while longer. This evening, while I was holding it and examining it, a clear and irresistible feeling flooded through me. The key was in danger, and so were we (my colleagues and I). Someone wanted this key very badly and would stop at nothing to acquire it. It had to be hidden in a safe and undiscoverable place.

As a scientist I have been trained to deal in facts. As an archaeologist I have also learned to listen to and trust my gut instincts. This one I could not ignore. But who, and where? I spoke to Jim Mackintosh, my colleague in this *research, and he agreed with me that the key should be safeguarded. I did not mention it to the other members of the team, knowing they would dismiss my fears as irrational anxieties. They are unable to recognise the importance of this discovery, and the possibility that it could change everything we know about the history of humankind on Earth.*

When I sat and thought about who could help, you were the obvious choice. In truth, you were the only choice. You already know about this treasure. I told Jim I would take care of it, but I didn't tell him what I was going to do.

Here it is. Take it, keep it safe. Keep its whereabouts a secret. Tell no-one.

There is already a replica in existence, made for the museum display so that we could continue our work uninterrupted. Only a few of us were party to this as it would cause an outcry if the public found out they were being duped. I have made the switch and will stall for as long as possible. My fear is that we do not have much time.

With kindest regards
Olina Gjerde

'No-one must find out about this, Gemma.' Joe's voice was hard, determined. 'Whoever is after it has already killed, and would certainly do so again. Can it be traced to you?'

'I don't think so, no. Olina was very thorough. She sent it standard post so it's not a tracked parcel. I didn't have to sign for it. I suppose if someone got hold of Olina's emails they might put two and two together though…'

'OK, well let's assume you're in the clear, for now. What are you going to do with it?'

I shrugged. My mind was working on a different track. 'Do you think whoever was behind this attack has realised yet they've got a dummy?'

'If they haven't, they soon will. You can't fake the energy coming off that thing. And when they do, they'll be savage.' He glanced around, grabbed the packaging and threw it onto the fire. 'We have to get rid of any evidence it was here.' As the flames caught it, the plastic bubble-wrap blistered and melted, momentarily sending thick, stinking black smoke billowing into the room. 'No-one knows you've got it. Let's make sure it stays that way. Now we just have to find somewhere secure to keep it.'

'Safety deposit box?' Cathy spoke up for the first time in several minutes. 'At the bank.'

'Would that work?' I looked at them both hopefully.

'Why not? If I've got it right, they're extremely secure, short of a major heist. Plus you can say what you like about the contents, you don't have to prove what is in them, and your identity is held securely in the bank's records.'

It seemed a perfect solution. I called my branch only to discover that safety deposit boxes were no longer freely available. However, the customer service advisor said that, if I could give her an hour or so, she would contact all the vaults and see if they had anything. I spent the next hour fidgeting and generally being irritable. Beautiful and magical though the key was, I didn't feel safe having it and I wanted it gone. A long ninety minutes later she called me back. There was just one box available in Bristol if I wanted it; I could access it in the morning. Without hesitating, I reserved it. I would have to keep the key in the house with me overnight, but that couldn't be helped.

Cathy still wasn't picking up anything from it other than the pulsing warmth and electric tingling that Joe and I could also feel. We sat with it on the floor between us for several hours, speculating on the whole question. The black skull, Gileada, to whose casket this key belonged, had been sealed into an icy Arctic prison. Was it still inaccessible? And was whoever wanted this golden key so badly also after Gileada? Did they already possess the casket and if so, where on Earth (literally) had they found it? Or were they hoping that the key itself would lead them to the skull? We came up with no answers, only a whole lot more questions.

Of course. I slapped my palm to my forehead in exasperation. 'God, I'm so stupid! Don't you remember? The entrance to the cave where Gileada was left bears the indentation of this key. If they really are looking for the cave, this will show them when they've found it.'

'But they know what the key looks like. It was plastered all over the news when it was found. They don't need the key for that; they've just got to look for a mark that matches it.'

'But they may need it to unseal the entrance. Don't you remember, it was the key that sealed it up in the first place?'

'I think you're right, but if that is the case, then there is another, bigger question,' Cathy said slowly. 'How do they

173

know about it? Your book isn't going to be released for another six months. No-one can have read it yet. So, how would they know?'

She was right. OK, so we were still speculating, but the more I considered it, the more I was sure that was the reason for the attempted theft. In which case, Cathy's question remained: how did anyone know about it? Unless... I had given Callum a copy of the manuscript a year or so ago. Could he have shown it to anyone? His sponsors maybe? I was even less comfortable with that thought, knowing Callum's suspicions about them. Would they link it to me? Only time would tell.

One thing was for sure, I couldn't wait to get that key out of my possession. I fetched some fresh bubble-wrap and a thick brown envelope, wrapped it up and stuck it under the mattress in the spare room. By lunchtime tomorrow it would be safely tucked away in an anonymous bank vault.

The following morning I drove into Bristol with Joe riding shotgun. I didn't need him but I felt much safer having him there. Several hours later I returned home with a weight lifted off my shoulders. Joe was taking the safety deposit box key to Duncan's for safekeeping, so there would be no physical link to me at all. What would happen next – and I was certain the story was far from over – only time would tell.

* * * * *

I called the hospital in Norway a couple of times asking after Olina, claiming to be a close friend of hers, always careful not to give my name. The first was the day after I had stashed the artefact in the bank's vaults. There was no change, the helpful nurse told me. Olina was still on life support but stable, and there were some faint but positive signs she may be rallying.

The second time was a week later, when the woman on the end of the phone was much less accommodating. She refused to release any information to me, without giving any reason. I called the university instead and found out why. It was now also a murder. Olina had not survived. Only two days previously her condition had deteriorated badly and the difficult decision had been taken to switch off her life support. The receptionist had then become a little suspicious, asking who I was. I simply hung up.

I sat and wept. I had barely known Olina Gjerde. This deep sorrow had a much deeper source. There had been three deaths now in just over the same number of months, and those were only the ones I knew of: Jack, lost in the caves beneath the Arizonian desert; Dr Mackintosh in the initial attack at the university in Trondheim, and now Olina Gjerde. How many more lives were being sacrificed for these skulls that I didn't know about? Was mine going to be added to this list?

The only morsel of light was that with Olina's death only Joe, Cathy and I knew the whereabouts of the key. There was nothing left to trace it to me.

30.

Weeks and then months passed. Nothing unusual or untoward happened and my fears gradually eased as I drifted back into the normal pattern of my life. My first book was going through the lengthy process that is publication, due to be released in early August, and I was well on track with the sequel. The dreams were still occurring with clockwork regularity and I was loving the process of bringing them to life, creating images with words in the same way that an artist does with his brushes and paints.

I was spending a lot of time with Joe and Cathy, but our conversations these days were less on the skulls, Arizona and the key, and embracing more general topics instead. Tim, my own little black obsidian skull, sat forgotten on the mantelpiece. I had no pull to sit with him, despite my earlier promises to myself to do so.

Callum had disappeared again. I'd not heard a word from him since our chance meeting in Sedona. No doubt he was off on one of his expeditions, or chasing up some lead or other he hoped would guide him to Jack and Gal-Athiel. I'd kept in touch with Frankie, another member of that fruitless Arizona expedition, but even her emails had become sporadic. She was working on a project on Easter Island, where communication, even in the twenty-first century, was unreliable. One thing I had learned from her was that she had not had any contact with Callum either.

When I wasn't writing, I went for long, lazy walks, and pottered in my garden, enjoying its blossoming throughout the spring and early summer. The pace of life was gentle and calm, a respite after all the previous dramas. I was being lulled into a security that could not, and did not, last.

* * * * *

In early July, out of the blue, Callum called. He would be in town the following day and it was crucial he saw me. As usual it was all very vague. I agreed to meet him for lunch in Bath.

Bath, with its Georgian streets of honey-coloured stone was packed with visitors. It was a gorgeous summer's day, the weather continuing to bless us with warm sunshine and clear blue skies. I picked my way through the crowds, bombarded by a global mix of languages, parties of excited French and Spanish schoolchildren jostling alongside coachloads of chattering Japanese, camera-hung American tourists and laid back Australian backpackers. On a day like this, the city was so busy it was hard to move.

The cool of the hotel foyer was a world away from the hustle and bustle outside. As I walked into the restaurant, Callum stood up and waved. He had chosen a booth at the far end where we could talk without being overheard. I wasn't quite sure how I'd react; it had been close on a year since our night of sexual intimacy in the desert but the memory was still vividly alive for me. I was determined to keep my boundaries strong this time. Callum was too good at pushing them aside.

He stood and greeted me with a kiss on the cheek. Even so, my heart lurched. The warmth of his hand on my shoulder and his charismatic grey eyes locking onto mine momentarily risked wrecking my aplomb. But only momentarily. A fleeting reaction, born of what? Because as I looked at him more closely I realised that I was seeing the real man for the first time instead of the illusion I had built up around him. The schoolgirl crush had gone. Yes, his eyes still held that fierce magnetism but in front of me now was an averagely attractive but fairly ordinary middle-aged man.

'Hello, stranger,' I joked. 'I thought you'd disappeared off the face of the planet. What have you been up to?'

Callum rested wearily back against the padded seat. 'Looking for answers. Diving deep into places I probably shouldn't be going and finding nothing but more questions.' He closed his eyes for a couple of seconds. 'I don't care. I'm not going to stop digging until I get what I'm after.'

'Get what? The blue skull?'

'No. I told you. Answers.' He leaned forward lowering his voice, even though we were the only people in this section of the restaurant. 'Something big is going on, Gemma. Something that someone is going to any lengths to keep hidden. I don't know what or who yet, but I'm going to find out.'

'What do you mean?' All these 'somethings' and 'someones' seemed very vague and Callum had piqued my curiosity. I waited for him to explain more.

'Like I say, I still don't know very much, even after all these months of digging. From the little I have found out I

178

believe that a group of very powerful people is looking for the thirteen skulls with the aim of bringing them back together.' Again he glanced around. 'I have a couple of really promising leads. Could be about to make a big breakthrough. It's best if you don't know any more though. It might be dangerous. From what I've uncovered, these guys don't mess around.'

In a flash the unpleasant events of January flooded into my head. 'Norway? Dr Gjerde and Dr Mackintosh?'

'You know about that?'

'I was in Trondheim to meet Dr Gjerde when it happened. I arrived the night of the attack.' A hefty intuitive nudge was telling me not to go into details, and to keep the subsequent events surrounding the key to myself. 'I never got to see her,' I finished lamely.

'So you got mixed up in that.'

'No, not really.' I made light of it. 'I flew in, phoned from the hotel, heard the news, and flew home again. No-one even knew I was there.'

'That's good. I suspect that the people involved in that are the same group involved in a whole raft of other unpleasant incidents. They don't mess around, though it appears they don't want to draw unnecessary attention to their activities either. They only act when they are sure.'

I drew in a long, slow breath. 'Why are you telling me this, Callum?'

'Just so that you'll be careful. I don't honestly believe you are in danger, but better safe than sorry. As soon as your book is published, you'll be out in the open. You'll need to watch what you say, not give anything away that might arouse any suspicions that you know more than you are letting on.'

'Like what? I haven't a clue what you've been up to. The cave in Arizona was empty so it's not like I've even glimpsed one of these skulls, and as far as anyone else is concerned, I write fantasy fiction.' Another thought bounced back into my mind. 'Callum, did you show anyone my draft manuscript?'

'Yes, the guys that financed the blue skull expedition. I needed something to persuade them it wasn't a total wild goose chase. Why?'

'I was wondering why anyone would go to such lengths to get their hands on an old artefact. If they knew of the skulls' existence and were searching for them, and then learned about the cave, it could explain a lot.'

'Those guys are definitely involved, even if I can't pin down how yet.' Callum looked thoughtful. 'Which makes it even more essential that you don't give anything away.'

I had lost my appetite. The vibrant salad in front of me suddenly tasted of sawdust as all the fears that had evaporated over the past few months flooded in, drowning me again. The day, that glorious sunny summer day, lost its sparkle. We ate the rest of our meal in sombre mood, deliberately steering the conversation to trivia. When we finally stood up to leave, Callum took my hand.

'I'm sorry, Gemma. I didn't want to scare you but in this case forewarned is definitely forearmed. Do I think you are in danger? Probably not. I'm the one that's being a real pain in the arse for them, poking and prodding where they don't want anyone to go. Even so, you do need to be careful.'

'What are you going to do next?'

'Oh, I've a good few things to follow up, people to speak to. More than that, I'm not going to tell you.'

'Will you come to my book launch next month?'

Callum shook his head. 'No, it's best if you didn't get linked to me at all. I've rattled far too many cages and if I'm right, it's going to get rough soon. I don't want you involved.'

* * * * *

My feet carried me to Victoria Park, that wide expanse of green that overlooks the ancient Roman city of Bath. In the afternoon sun its golden stone was glowing as if on fire. I saw none of it. My mind was filled with a procession of less enticing images: the black skull, Gileada, nestled in an icy tomb; Gal-Athiel lying next to Jack's lifeless body in the darkness of a subterranean labyrinth; two bodies lying crumpled and bloodied on a laboratory floor; a pulsing key of gold floating in blackness. And in a momentary flash, Callum, bruised and beaten, lashed to a wooden chair in a bleak, empty room. Foreboding, a premonition of further tragedy to come, swept through me and I shivered violently, oblivious to the heat of the day.

181

MAAT-SU: The Lapis Skull

PART 2

EXODUS

31.

The details of that sea voyage have since been chronicled elsewhere, but will stand a retelling.

They had left Dendarak in fine weather, and for the first day or so made good headway as the fresh breeze filled the Edrus' sails, slicing her sleek hull swiftly through a deep blue-green sea. Two days out the wind dropped. Not a breath disturbed the smooth glassy surface of an ocean that reflected the sun like a mirror, dazzling anyone who gazed on it for more than a moment. The Edrus was now back under the power of her crystal engines, which ran as silent as the sea beneath her hull, the only sound the swish of the water as it slipped past her prow.

For the passengers, it was a time to relax. Many of them spent their days lounging on her polished wooden decks, ooh-ing and aah-ing in delight at the antics of the dolphins that arced and somersaulted in the clear waters alongside. After the danger of their recent flight and taut nerves stretched to breaking point by the unforeseen delay in sailing and the enforced confinement this delay had created, everyone was in sore need of this pleasant respite. Little by little the passengers relaxed. They did not waste their energy speculating on what would greet them when they disembarked; there would be time enough for that later. For now, they were enjoying each moment for what it was.

It was not easy for the two skull guardians, who had more or less grown up together in the Temple complex, to act as strangers meeting for the first time. In every conversation, certainly at the beginning of this journey, there was the ever-present risk that they would give themselves away with a careless word or shared reference. They created fictional backgrounds, histories that the other passengers accepted without question, and Jar-Kan retained his alias, introducing himself as Lumi. Their greatest ally was Jar-Kan's continuing suspicion of Kua'tzal, whom all the Temple priests considered a pariah. It was a long-held mistrust that the big man was finding hard to release, though his instinct was constantly urging him to do so.

In truth though, every passenger on board was in a similarly precarious situation, each running from the Dark Ones, each with his or her own secrets and reasons, none yet comfortable enough with the strangers they travelled with to reveal their stories. Questions into each other's backgrounds were not encouraged. Suspicion born of experience would not be healed overnight. With time and familiarity though, trust would grow, even between Kua'tzal and Jar-Kan.

* * * * *

To avoid all risk of being detected by those who travelled with her, Maat-su remained dormant throughout the voyage. Untrained though her travelling companions were, there was a chance that someone could have retained the ancient natural openness and sensitivity that would connect with the skull's unique energies.

185

Despite her sleeping state, however, she subtly communicated with Kua'tzal. Deep in the night, when the star-hung sky watched over the sleeping ship, she would influence his dreams, showing him visions of the future. Showing him the place where he would build a new Atlantis, far from the polluted energies of the old.

It was a hot, fertile land of powerful energy points and vortices. A land where a great river flowed through lush forests and rocky plateaus, bringing life to its banks, and where the crops grew strong and healthy. A land of jewel-like birds and fragrant flowers, of laughing people – and magic. The people who already lived there, she reassured him, would welcome the Atlanteans warmly into their midst, for their arrival would fulfil an ancient prophecy foretold.

In this land Kua'tzal and his companions would set the foundations of what would be, in times to come, a great and enduring civilisation, using the knowledge of the skulls and of the great continent of Atlantis he had so recently left behind. The star races, regular visitors to Yo'tlàn's Pyramid Temple, would help him, sharing their technology and knowledge to add to that which Kua'tzal had brought with him. This was a land these same people from the stars had been visiting for thousands of years, drawn by the energies and the welcome of those who inhabited this place.

Another from Atlantis would join him here. Together they would be the architects of great monuments and temples that, with the help of their off-world friends, they would construct along the banks of this Great River, not just for their splendour and majesty, though their appearance would be one of breath-taking beauty and elegance, but for their practical uses. They would build pyramids to harness the energy flows of the land and the power of the sun, balancing, enhancing and amplifying them. In addition, the structures would act as knowledge stores and libraries, the information imprinted within the stones of the monuments. Kua'tzal was overwhelmed by the pictures she painted for him. Was this really to be his destiny?

He could not ask her. She would not reply.

32.

It was on one of these pleasant, easy afternoons, eight days after they had sailed from Atlantis, that all hell broke loose.

Kua'tzal had been below deck, stretched out on his bunk, when he heard the warning shout. Something in the sailor's voice, an unmistakeable terror, chilled the priest to the bone. He glanced out of the small window, one of many that ran along this side of the ship, and froze. On the horizon, a wall of water was tearing towards them, a gigantic wave perhaps twenty times taller than the Edrus stood to her top mast.

Feet pounded on the deck boards as those outside ran for shelter, slamming doorways and hatches behind them. There was barely time to grab a handhold before it hit. A few of the first in had managed to tie themselves to their bunks; others had no choice but to simply hang on. Murmured prayers and soft sobs came from men and women alike as they waited for it to hit. Not one believed they would come through this alive.

Through the window Kua'tzal watched as the wave hurtled closer at terrifying speed. Perhaps the most chilling aspect of all was the silence. No roar. No rush. Not a sound. Kua'tzal was unable to tear his eyes away from the window, staring hypnotised and frozen at the ghastly spectacle. Until it vanished. The captain had turned the Edrus' bow to face the oncoming nightmare.

It was upon them. Up and up the ship's bow rose, until she was standing on her stern. How could the Edrus take such punishment? Gasps of horror and panicked screams echoed through the cabin as the world turned through ninety degrees. Walls became floors and ceilings became walls. Everything that wasn't fastened down, and much that had been, flew through the cabins. Miraculously, no-one was hit.

Outside the window now the light had gone, replaced by a dark opaque blueness. The ocean had swallowed the ship whole. Water streamed through every gap, cascading through its interior like a waterfall. A moment later the sea released the Edrus from its watery grip and sunlight streamed into the dripping vessel as she righted herself. A collective gasp of relief proved premature; immediately it began again, the ship turning nearly vertical, this time in the opposite direction, bow down, stern open to the sky, her rudder thrashing uselessly in the air.

Twice more the Edrus was subjected to this brutal treatment, each time those aboard believing it would be their last moment. Twice more she came though unscathed, thanks in no small measure to the craftsmanship of those who had built her, and the skill and courage of her captain and crew.

When it was over, it was as if it had never been. The instant the final wall of water had released them the sea regained its mirror-like calm, sparkling innocently in the sunlight. No sign remained anywhere of its latent ferocity or of the deadly assault it had just launched. The passengers and crew limped onto the deck, licking their wounds and thanking the stars that they had survived. The captain, a surprisingly petite woman, descended from the bridge to an extended and heart-felt round of applause. There was no doubt in anyone's mind that it was her expertise, bravery, and experience, together with the courage and seamanship of her crew, that had saved them.

Every person on board, though battered and bruised, was alive, and an air of celebration and determination rapidly established itself. With a will they worked together to put the ship to rights. Those with practical skills helped the crew carry out repairs to the structure of the ship. Others busied themselves mopping out swamped cabins, restoring order to the devastated interior and dragging sodden beds and clothing into the sunshine. Soon a pale mist hovered over the ship's decks as the waterlogged ship began to steam and dry. With the necessary work done, someone pulled out a flute. Soon everyone, including the captain and crew, were celebrating their survival.

All on board the Edrus believed that it was over, that whatever event had created the giant waves had run its course. They could not have been more mistaken. It was only just beginning.

* * * * *

Deep below the surface of the Earth, a chain of events had been set in motion that would, in times yet far in the future, bring the gravest of consequences to the land of Atlantis, and devastation to the world beyond its shores. It had begun the night the Shadow Chasers had taken control of the Pyramid Temple intending to seize the thirteen Skulls of Light. Their hand had been forced; something was wrong. Power levels from the skulls had dropped drastically over the previous few days. If the priests were planning a rebellion, they would not be allowed to succeed.

The Shadow Chasers were too late. By the time they had recognised the danger, the skulls were already far from Yo'tlàn, being carried to safety to the distant reaches of the Earth. When Xy-barian strode arrogantly into the skull chamber on that fateful summer morning, the smirk of victory on his face evaporated in a blink. In front of him stood the great central plinth and its cluster… Empty. The Master skull had gone.

In a growing frenzy, he had examined the twelve skulls that watched him blankly from the outer circle, flinging each useless object to the ground in a white hot fury that intensified with each glance. From the centre of the chamber he screamed his rage. Lifeless, inert copies, all of them.

His vengeance was ferocious. Everyone unlucky enough to be inside the Temple complex was seized and taken away for the most brutal questioning. Men and women, priest and layperson alike, it did not matter. Any priest or priestess not present was hunted down and arrested. None were spared Xy-barian's wrath.

The Temple too paid a heavy price. Xy-barian ordered it to be destroyed so completely that it could never be rebuilt. He himself wielded the first mighty blow, shattering to glittering white splinters the central pedestal and cluster on which the Master skull had rested for thousands of years. Blow followed blow, until the twelve other plinths also lay broken and useless on the floor, the duplicate skulls smashed beyond recognition. The once glass-smooth amethyst panels that lined the walls of the circular chamber fared no better.

Xy-barian could have no concept of the repercussions of his actions. They would demand a heavy price that would be paid by the whole world. For the centre plinth and the huge cluster that surmounted it had held the Master skull for thousands of years. During that time they had absorbed and stored a colossal amount of energy from the skull. Energy that was still held within their structure. The moment they had been shattered by his hand, that energy had been released in a tidal wave of vibration and taken the path of least resistance. That path was downwards into the energy vortex that existed deep in the Earth's crust beneath the Pyramid Temple.

These vortices acted as pathways that channelled energy across the planet. The one below Atlantis was one of the largest and most powerful. It absorbed the vibrations emanating from the destroyed Skull Chamber and magnified them, as was its nature, as they sank through its core into the rock below. The more fragile of the fault lines could not resist its power and tore apart. The tidal wave that had so nearly been the end of the Edrus and all on board her was only the first agonised scream of a wounded Earth. One day, far in the future, the writhing throes of her healing would rip the great continent of Atlantis apart and carry it to the ocean floor.

33.

The cold, windswept beach on which they landed was a far cry from the warm days of late summer they had so recently left behind. As the small group of bedraggled refugees stood on the rocky shore under leaden skies and thick, unrelenting drizzle, they all wondered what the future would hold. This grey, dreary place did not offer an encouraging promise of things to come. Yet not one of them would have changed their mind, or doubted their original decision to leave behind the dark grip of fear that was day by day spreading over their beloved homeland. Whatever lay ahead could not be as bad as the grasping tentacles of the Dark Ones' influence and tyranny.

They watched until the Edrus disappeared over the barely distinguishable horizon. Then, as one, they turned from the sea and from where they had come to face an uncertain and possibly perilous future. This continent was as alien and unknown to them as the surface of the moon. They had no destination, would simply travel for as long as necessary to find the place where they would make their new home.

The group decided to head south west, inland, they hoped towards a warmer climate. They moved easily and comfortably. There was no need to hurry, no place they had to be, no deadline to meet. No-one knew how long it would be until they found their new home. They could be walking for weeks, months even. They would not exhaust themselves for no reason. This journey would be their life now, so they would make it a good life, travelling in a relaxed and joyful frame of mind for as long as it lasted.

Only Maat-su knew differently. They were here for a definite purpose. She would lead them to the destination that had always been set out for them, and to the destiny they were always meant to fulfil.

34.

'Kua'tzal. Kua'tzal.' The voice whispered in his head as softly as the wind through the leaves on the trees, and as insistently. 'Kua'tzal.'

The priest opened his eyes, shaking the mists of sleep from his mind, listening. It came again. 'Kua'tzal.'

Maat-su. After so many days and weeks of silence when, despite his pleas, she had refused all communication, she had at last returned to him.

'Maat-su.' His own voice rippled through his thoughts in answer. 'Why do you call me?'

'There is much you must know, my dear guardian. I have been waiting for the moment when I may safely speak openly to you. That moment has come.'

'Why now? Why did you not answer me before?' This was the first time she had spoken to him since they had left the Temple.

She did not reply to his question. 'Come,' were her only words, 'I will lead you to a place where we may speak freely.'

Mystified, Kua'tzal scrambled stiffly to his feet. He had still not grown used to sleeping on the hard earth, even cushioned as it was by a thick layer of bracken fronds. He was no longer young, and he missed his soft bed. Unlike his unexpected travelling companion and fellow priest, Jar-Kan, who was never happier than when he was living the outdoor life, Kua'tzal preferred a roof over his head, a chair to sit on and a well-stuffed feather mattress for his bed. Reluctantly, he allowed the skull to guide him from the hollow where his fellow travellers were all sleeping soundly, away from the reassuring glow of the camp fire, and into the woods that bordered it.

* * * * *

They had been ashore only a few days. The dank, uninspiring weather that had greeted them on that momentous morning had cleared soon after; since then they had been accompanied by warm sunshine, blue skies and gentle breezes that carried with them the sweet, delicate scents of blossoming life. The days were filled with light and growing longer, filling the small band with a sense of renewal and joyful hope. The low spirits that had soaked them as deeply as the rain as they had stood on that forlorn, desolate grey beach and watched the Edrus, their only lifeline, sail away over the horizon, had been quickly dissolved by the gentle delights of this new world, so familiar and yet so different from their former home. It was with light and joyful hearts, and a spring in their steps that they embarked upon this journey to none knew where, only that they would recognise the place when they saw it. It would be a place that sang to their hearts and souls and called to them to make it their home. There they would build a new settlement, where the unpolluted essence of the old Atlantis would be reborn.

* * * * *

The refugees had stopped just before the woodland in a grassy hollow situated a little way above a clear, chuckling river that tumbled over a bed of colourful stones on its way down the hillside. It was an idyllic spot and they had been here a few days already to rest and gather supplies. How long they would remain, Kua'tzal wasn't sure. Time had already ceased to have any real meaning for any of them; they were no longer counting the passage of days and nights.

They were in no hurry. They had no deadlines. This journey was their life now for as long as it took, and their enjoyment of its daily unfolding was more important to them than some unknown destination. This was the reality of their day to day existence and they had vowed to live each and every moment joyfully and in the spirit of adventure. They had become nomads who would be travelling for who knew how long – probably many moon cycles, maybe many sun cycles even. For now, this was all they had. Any future was uncertain, unknown... If indeed they had a future.

Perhaps more importantly, every man, woman and child was relishing the fresh breath of freedom after the oppression and menace of an Atlantis held fast in the grip of the Shadow Chasers. It was more than enough. They did not desire anything else. For now at least, food and water was freely available. The land was benign and welcoming. Fresh young leaves and fruits were appearing on the trees, and meat was abundant, as was fish from the many streams and rivers that provided them with fresh sweet water.

The group were mostly town dwellers who had, in their former lives in Atlantis, purchased their food and other needs in richly stocked markets. They had no need, nor any desire, to forage for themselves in the countryside

197

around their homes. Kua'tzal was as ignorant as his companions in this, which meant Jar-Kan's skills were invaluable. His knowledge would ensure the group would remain free of hunger in this abundant land and, if times grew hard and food scarce, would keep them from starvation. Over time, he had promised himself he would teach them all they needed to survive: to find and identify edible plants and fungi; woodcraft; hunting and wild living. For at some point, so Jar-Kan's skull Gor-Kual had informed him, their paths would separate and his companions would have to fend for themselves. They were ignorant of his true identity as they were Kua'tzal's. To them he was a countryman, and a useful addition to the group. That was how it must remain.

Kua'tzal had introduced himself as a merchant from the north. The instructions the senior priest Oolan had given to him, and to those eleven other men and women who were risking all in the service of the skulls, had been absolute: no-one was to know their true identities or purpose. The lure of the skulls and the power they held was too great. Any hint of who he really was and of what he carried with him could put Maat-su in the gravest danger.

All these thoughts drifted through Kua'tzal's mind as he allowed Maat-su to guide him through the forest. Once out of sight of the camp he had taken her from the bag he always carried slung over his shoulder and now cradled her in his hands as he walked.

35.

When Maat-su had roused him from his sleep, Kua'tzal had acted immediately. His trust in her was total. If she had woken from her self-imposed dormancy it was because she had something of great importance to share. Still, he wondered at the wisdom of her request. Inside the wood it was too dark for him to see his footing clearly. He stumbled frequently over roots and fallen branches, staggered as his foot dropped into an unseen burrow entrance. It was impossible to move quickly over the uneven obstacle strewn ground. He sensed Maat-su's impatience but could not increase his speed without risking a twisted ankle or worse.

It was eerie too. The leaves danced constantly in the light breeze, creating shifting patterns that hinted at figures moving through the darkness. More than once he started at a movement caught out of the corner of his eye, or whirled around at a noise behind him. There was never anything there.

Nonetheless, it was pleasantly cool here after the humid night air of the open country and he breathed deeply, filling his nostrils with the sweet scent of pine resin and the sharp pungency of the bracken he trampled underfoot at every step. Above him in the canopy birds fluttered, disturbed by his clumsy passage, accompanied at intervals by the eerie sound of an owl's hoot as it ghosted through the trees in search of its prey. In the lower branches and undergrowth, small nocturnal creatures chirped and scurried for cover at his approach.

Eventually, the trees ahead of him opened up into a moonlit clearing. This had to be where Maat-su was leading him. Hesitantly Kua'tzal walked forward to stop at its boundary, his eyes widening in astonishment. The open area was more or less circular, perhaps fifty paces or so across, he estimated. Its centre was taken up with a small, round grass covered hillock around twenty paces in diameter whose summit pushed up way above his head. At the apex. thrusting into the dark night sky, stood a tall slender pillar of grey granite.

Without the thick canopy of the trees to shield it, the moonlight that shone down into the clearing allowed Kua'tzal to see every detail. He gazed around at the sight that met him, awestruck not only at its unexpectedness in this uninhabited landscape, but also at the potent energies that emanated from the site. It was evident that this place had long been abandoned, yet still the forces surged raw and primal. There was no doubt in the priest's mind that this had once, in the far distant past, been a very powerful and significant place of pilgrimage and ritual. That power was still very much present, undiminished by the passage of time.

Kua'tzal looked more closely. He was standing between two perfectly formed stone spheres. Two others rested at an equal distance on either side. Slowly he walked around the perimeter of the clearing, taking in its form. The stone spheres formed a triangle, four to a side, each side and each angle identical in size. The mound sat in the exact centre of this geometric form. At each of the triangle's points a pair of smaller uprights stood, as if gateways to the inner sanctuary.

Kua'tzal continued to stare in wonder at the carefully constructed monument rising up before him. It was old, the weathering of the stone obelisk bore the evidence of that, but how old he could not begin to guess. He drank deeply of the atmosphere, like he was drinking in a rich, sweet wine, allowing it to fill his lungs and spread through his veins in a warm, tingling glow. Maat-su did not interrupt his reverie as in silence Kua'tzal allowed its significance to crystallise in his mind. Yes, he did understand. He saw the mound and the triangle of stones: a symbol of the feminine essence, enveloping the masculine embrace of the stone phallus to create life. This was a celebration of the sacred masculine and the sacred feminine, coming together in full harmony and balance, the legacy of a culture long vanished.

He was reluctant to step further into this space, unwilling to desecrate its soil, but Maat-su now addressed him again, urging him on. 'Kua'tzal, you may enter without fear. In the beginning, at the time when I first came to your world, this was my home. I have brought you here tonight to hear my words.'

Still unwilling to intrude on this sacred space, nevertheless Kua'tzal put one foot forward, and then the other. As he crossed the boundary of the stone triangle his body began to buzz and tingle.

'Come.' Maat-su guided him to a slight hollow scooped into the far side of the mound. 'Sit,' she requested. When he was settled the skull began to speak once more.

'Kua'tzal, my beloved guardian, you have suffered much in your dedication to protecting your brothers and sisters in the Temple. You have suffered much in your commitment to keeping us, the thirteen Skulls of Light, safe from the scheming and ill-intent of those who would seize us for their own glory. No more. Those years are over. You paid a heavy price, one which no man should be asked to pay, and yet you did it willingly. You hid your true gentle nature and beliefs, becoming virtually an outcast amongst your own brothers and sisters, those whom you loved and cherished the most. That time, that hardship, is now at an end. All deception must be left behind. It is time for the truth to be revealed.

'Kua'tzal, my dearest friend, I ask you to speak the truth now to those with whom you share your life. Tell them of your true identity as a Priest of the Light and guardian of Maat-su, sacred skull of Valkan, who you carry with you. Reveal my presence to those who travel with you on this journey.'

It took a few moments for Maat-su's words to penetrate Kua'tzal's mind, and even when they did, he struggled to accept he had heard her correctly. Speak of his true identity and Maat-su's presence? It went totally against every command he had been given by Oolan and the other Temple elders. And yet... Maat-su had asked it of him. He could not refuse. Her reasons would be sound, even if he did not understand them. What of the consequences though? How would his companions react to his revelations? And then there was Jar-Kan, and the skull he watched over, Gor-Kual. What of them? All these questions flashed through his mind in a split second.

'They will be angry, yes, for a short time. They will fear that you are putting them in danger and that the Dark Ones will come to hunt you down. Afraid of the consequences if they are discovered with you. It is an anger that will soon pass. At last you will be free to walk amongst them as yourself, without dissemblance, and for you that alone will far outweigh any transient discomfort. I will speak directly to them, once and once only, and they will listen to what I say.

'All who accompany you on this path are as true and honourable as yourself. There is not one here who carries any ego or hunger for power and riches that would threaten us. Be reassured that we are as safe amongst these people as we once were in the Pyramid Temple at Yo'tlàn.

'As for Jar-Kan, he must still carry the burden of secrecy, and remain silent. To those who travel with you he must be seen as no different to them, a refugee seeking freedom. His journey, his destination, and that of Gor-Kual, will lead him down a different road.'

36.

Kua'tzal spoke at length to Jar-Kan. The big bear-like man was initially rendered speechless at Maat-su's request, but he accepted its rightness as completely as Kua'tzal himself had done and promised to support his new friend as much as he could without betraying his own cover. It took several days for Kua'tzal to do as the skull had asked, for he was anxious at how he would be received. When finally he did reveal his secret to those who travelled with him, the reaction was as he had predicted. Deep fear and anger rose up in his companions at his deception and at the danger he risked bringing upon them all.

It was only when Maat-su spoke in her tum, as she had promised, that their fears and anger were stilled. They were overwhelmed by her presence amongst them. None had before even seen one of the sacred skulls, let alone been so close that they could touch her. They heard the truth in her words and it embraced them all completely.

She spoke to them of their ultimate destination, far in the future: a lush, green, fertile land where the warm sun shone all year round. She told them how they would be welcomed with open arms by those who lived there, and that she herself would lead them there. In this place they would found a great civilisation that would flourish for hundreds of generations, where the technology and wisdom of Atlantis would rise again, supported by her own energy and knowledge and those of the star races who came there from time to time. They would build great monuments that would strike awe into the hearts of those who came after, far into the future, and at which they would marvel as they wondered what magic had constructed them.

Then she gave them a warning. They would come to be seen by many as gods, worshipped and revered if they allowed it. They must not let that happen, for it would distort their light, and corrupt their hearts and minds, sowing the seeds of the lower energies that had ensnared Atlantis. They must at all times remember who they were and why they had fled that beloved land. They must remain humble, loving and wise, acting always in total harmony with the qualities they all carried in their hearts – the essence of the golden age of Atlantis.

*   *   *   *   *

In even the few days that followed these revelations, Kua'tzal became a different man. Until then he had been constantly on his guard, aware that letting slip some careless word may betray his deception. Freed fully from the necessity to continue living a lie, his face softened even more and his eyes shone. He lost the hunted look that had haunted him for so long, his habitual hunched posture straightened so that he stood taller and stronger, and he felt indescribably lighter in every way. His smile, something that had not brightened his face in all the time since he had first put on his cruel mask, was rarely absent these days. As the tension fell off him, so did the years.

Slowly, slowly, the love, compassion and hunger for life that was his natural character burst out of the prison where he had held it captive for so long, expressing itself in laughter, song and even the occasional impromptu dance that startled his companions with its exuberance. Kua'tzal was making up for lost time.

Jar-Kan, who had only ever known the man in the mask, was amazed, initially unable to believe the change in him. Kua'tzal had appeared to everyone he met to be so cold, distant and lacking in compassion that many of his companions in the Pyramid Temple had wondered often, sometimes aloud, how he had ever been accepted into the priesthood. He had carried a habitual hard, stern edge and impatience, combined with a lack of tolerance that many had found hard to stomach. Now the man revealed himself for who he truly was, emerging from the shadows of his long born deception as the polar opposite, with a huge heart and a sense of humour to rival anyone's. Children were drawn to him as if by a magnet, sitting for hours listening to his tales as a natural ability for story-telling burst into life.

The last remnants of Jar-Kan's suspicion quickly dissolved, his respect for his new friend climbing daily. Only Kua'tzal would know what his dedication had cost him. There was no doubt in Jar-Kan's mind that it had been a high price to pay.

37.

It was with heavy hearts that Kua'tzal and the rest of the now close-knit group said goodbye to Jar-Kan. They would miss him. Miss his kind manner and gentle humour, his reassuring strength and presence. Most of all though they would miss his skills. Over the past months, Jar-Kan had proven his ability to find ample food where everyone else saw only empty stomachs.

Kua'tzal's personal sadness reached even deeper. The two men had forged a strong bond as they travelled together, one born of a common background and a mutual understanding of the role they had to play. More than that though, Kua'tzal was relishing the big man's friendship. Friendship was a blessing he had been sorely deprived of during the painful years of his self-imposed alienation in the Temple of Light.

With Jar-Kan's departure, the final links to Kua'tzal's former life vanished. As the group crested the brow of a low hill, Kua'tzal stopped and looked back across the landscape. A lone figure, appearing no taller than his thumb from this distance, was trudging a solitary path across the wide, flat valley floor. Jar-Kan. The figure paused for a moment; Kua'tzal sensed that his friend had looked back after them one last time, though he could not be certain. It was too far away to tell for sure. He threw his arm up in an exaggerated wave, just in case. The solitary traveller waved back once before he turned and set off once more.

Watching the retreating figure, a brooding sense of foreboding shivered through Kua'tzal's body. Whether it was for his friend or for himself he could not tell. Only time would reveal the cause. His heart heavy, he turned away and started down the far slope of the hill, soon losing sight of the diminutive figure of Jar-Kan as it disappeared behind the brow.

* * * * *

For months they travelled, and the months turned into years. Always they were guided by Maat-su. The gentle slopes where they had said their sad farewells to Jar-Kan had long passed behind them. They had crossed high rolling grassy plains that had in turn evolved into a landscape of barren windswept plateaus and steep gorges, in the depths of which rivers roiled and tumbled, chattering and laughing or angry and ferocious according to the season. Giving way to towering snow-capped mountain ranges and deep, rocky valleys.

Progress had slowed in this less docile terrain but no-one paid it any attention. As far as the travellers were concerned, this nomadic existence was now their life, had become all they knew. All had heard Maat-su speak of their ultimate destination, yet in each day there was no goal in their minds other than where they were in every moment. They went on, understanding that one day, in some place, this wandering would end and they would once more settle. Understanding that Maat-su was leading them forward, trusting her implicitly and following without question.

No-one grew disheartened at the constant wandering, for life was, in general, enjoyable and easy. Food and fresh water always appeared when needed, as if some hidden hand had placed it for them. They did not push themselves, avoiding the high and hostile lands during the winter when they were led to shelter in more benign areas away from the fiercest winds and coldest temperatures; taking more sheltered forest routes during the high heat of summer. She guided them always to the easiest path, the gentlest mountain passes, leading them on a circuitous route that lengthened but lightened their journey.

Over the years that they travelled some, though remarkably few, grew sick or too old, and died. Relationships formed, unions were sealed, children were born. The thirty or so who had disembarked the Edrus came to number nearly forty.

Now and again they chanced across a small settlement or other travellers, some solitary, others in small groups. Always they were welcomed without incident to the surprise of many of the Atlanteans. Maat-su's influence was at constantly at work, protecting her charges, leading them to friendly faces. Her role for now was to watch over and protect this small band of refugees, and to lead them safely to their promised land.

In that place they would create the foundations of a great new civilisation, a new Atlantis. It would be a civilisation that would change the course of human history with its scientific knowledge and advanced technology. One whose legacy would remain long after the civilisation itself had fallen, standing witness to a past that could never be truly understood by those in a far distant future who gazed in wonder on its majestic crumbling stone monuments. It was a legacy that would still be standing when the time came for the thirteen skulls to be reunited for the final time at the point when humankind entered its golden age of understanding.

38.

Early one morning, when nearly ten sun cycles had passed since that grey, damp morning when they had all huddled on a bleak wind-whipped beach and watched their lifeline to the past disappear over the horizon, Kua'tzal woke with a strange feeling in his belly. Excitement and a sense of completion swirled together in a heady cocktail of anticipation. It hadn't been there as he had drifted into sleep the previous evening, but was now surging powerfully through his gut. Although Maat-su was silent he sensed she was behind it.

He sat up and looked around. Their camp, a temporary halt reached only the previous day, was still, his companions slumbering peacefully despite the sun that was already climbing into the sky. They had settled down in the open air, the summer night warm enough to forego the simple shelters they carried. All preferred to sleep under the velvet canopy of the night sky, so filled with pulsing starlight that it seemed to be a living, breathing organism.

That soft, rich darkness had long vanished. An already warm sun blazed down from a cloudless blue. It would be another hot day. They would not travel far in these temperatures, just enough to find shelter from the heat in a cave or wooded grove. There were many dotted along this coastline and they could take their pick of the most suitable.

For well over a moon's cycle now they had been following this same coastline. On one side a deep aquamarine sea lapped gently on the rocky shore, reflecting the sun so fiercely that the glare hurt the eyes of anyone who dared to gaze at it for longer than a moment or two. On the other, pebble and shingle beaches alternated with flat slabs of brown sandstone that jutted out over the water.

They had travelled slowly, taking time to enjoy the pleasures of this place, whether bathing in its calm, balmy waters or gathering dates from the palms that grew abundantly just above the tide line. Nothing had indicated that a change was on the horizon.

This morning though, everything was somehow different. Not outwardly – the sea still caressed the shore with a lover's touch, the sun still bathed the world in its light – but deep inside himself Kua'tzal recognised that from now on, nothing would be the same. The pull in his belly told him so. He wandered down to the water's edge, the sun already pleasantly warm on his shoulders, and allowed the wavelets to nibble at his toes, wondering what was about to unfold.

No, he must not rush to understand. All would reveal itself to him in due course. Kua'tzal pulled off his tunic and trousers and slipped into the sea, allowing its soothing arms to gather him in their embrace, emptying his mind of all impatience. He would find out soon enough.

For a long time he drifted, cradled in the salty womb, until his body had melted into the water and he could no longer tell where one ended and the other began. His thoughts drifted easily through his head, dissipating like wisps of smoke on a breeze, so that his mind too merged into oneness with the ocean. It was with considerable reluctance that he eventually left its sanctuary to dry himself on the sun-warmed rocks of the beach.

* * * * *

He looked down at his naked body, the question that he had up until now pushed aside forcing itself in so strongly that this time he could not ignore it. He was nearly seventy years of age and yet, as his glistening body emerged from the water he could have easily been taken for a man half that. The toll his years of pretence and self-denial had exerted on him had loosened its grip long ago, taking a good decade off his appearance, but this was something more. He had noticed it in himself, and in the men and women who accompanied him, had puzzled over it, only to put it from his mind. This morning however, he could ignore it no longer.

His back was straight, the stoop of his shoulders vanished so that he now stood tall and proud. He felt strong, vital, filled with excitement. The muscles in his arms and legs, once lax and weakened with age, had grown firm again, his eyesight clearer, his hair thicker and darker. Looking into the mirror surface of the water even the lines on his face seemed less pronounced.

'Why now?' he wondered. 'This has been going on for some time. Why do I only really see it and question it now?'

'Because it is now that your real work begins.' Maat-su had awoken. 'The task you are to fulfil will take much longer than your natural lifespan of years and will require

213

you to remain strong, healthy and active for a very long time to come. Your presence will be necessary throughout – yours, and that of many of those who have travelled with you.

'I have been regenerating your cells. It is not hard to do, a simple readjustment of the energy flow through them. You know this process. It was used much by the priests in the Temple for healing, though perhaps you did not understand then its true capacity. For if used in certain ways, and under certain circumstances, aging and death may be delayed permanently.

'We do not inflict immortality on you, that is a burden and a sadness we cast on no-one, but you will live healthily and youthfully for several times your normal count of years, those of you who chose to be part of the work that lies ahead. For those who do not, and it is not necessary for all to do so, they will retain their newfound vigour for some time but as it is not replenished, they will age and die naturally.'

* * * * *

'Kua'tzal!' The boy's voice, calling from the camp, broke the connection with Maat-su. 'Kua'tzal. Look.'

Kua'tzal turned to gaze in the direction of the boy's outstretched arm. A small craft was skimming over the wavelets, heading in their direction. He quickly pulled on his trousers and tunic, slipping his feet back in his sandals.

The camp had woken in his absence; many of the travellers were now watching the craft's approach. Some were apprehensive at this development. Most were simply curious. They hadn't seen another living soul for a very long time. Who now was sailing to meet them?

GEMMA, 5

39.

Over the next couple of weeks, my anxiety faded into the background a little. The release date of my book was imminent and I was getting very excited about seeing my words in print for the first time. Its publication would be marked by a book signing event. It would be low-key, the publishers certainly weren't going to spend a fortune on an unknown, first time author who could prove a total flop, but the fact they were arranging anything was, for me, a major milestone. The signing was to be held in a gift shop in the village of Avebury, only a few miles from my home.

This time of year, mid-August, the school holiday crowds there would mix with numerous new age visitors. On a sunny summer weekend the village would be packed, and the publishers hoped that a good many of them would be attracted to what they had labelled my 'fantasy' writing. Posters had been delivered a couple of weeks in advance and on the day a supply of my books would be turning up, along with their representative, who was charged with holding my hand and making sure I didn't make any major gaffes.

Avebury had long held a magical pull for me and I visited often, so I knew the shop well. Set within the boundaries of the massive stone circle itself, it was a higgledy-piggledy warren of rooms created from several cottages that had long ago been knocked into one. The shop sold everything from woolly hats and walking sticks to dowsing rods and pentagrams. In addition, they stocked a large range of crystal skulls.

I turned up at just after nine thirty in the morning. The day didn't look promising. A dank, grey dreariness of the kind that that only England does so well hung over the landscape in a deadening blanket out of which the massive stones loomed, dejected and miserable. The roads and circle were empty, though I suppose it was perhaps still a bit too early for the tourists to be up and about. As I walked in the door a bright, smiling woman pounced, introducing herself as Tanya, from my publishers.

'You must be Gemma', she beamed, leading me to a small table in a corner of one of the room alcoves. 'Here you are. All set up and ready to go.' Whatever my fantasies may have been, I was immediately brought down to earth with a crash. My career and fame as an author was clearly unlikely to be a meteoric rags-to-riches story. A small round table, perhaps two feet in diameter, was tucked into the corner, a pile of my books teetering on it. Behind it, a large poster blu-tacked to the wall announced 'Meet author Gemma Mason here at 10am today when she will be signing copies of her debut novel, 'Skull Inheritance'.' In the crammed little shop, this was the only space available.

To be honest, it didn't matter. The weather was keeping everyone away. Throughout the morning a few hardy souls ventured out to explore, entering the shop cold and dripping wet in search of shelter from the now heavy rain and to warm their chilled bones. In true British style, this mid-August Saturday was turning out to be more like March.

I quickly realised that I would have to be pro-active and approach the few customers that there were. They weren't just going to come up and start chatting to me. Tanya nudged my arm.

'Go on. Talk to them. They won't bite,' she encouraged. I was totally and utterly out of my comfort zone. I am far from being an extrovert and much prefer to stay out of the spotlight. Clearly, that would have to change. A second nudge indicated I really didn't have much choice.

It turned out to be easier than I expected. The people were friendly, happy to linger chatting in the warmth and dry of the shop, surrounded by shelves of gifts and crystals that sparkled in the artificial light. To my delight I was selling books, signing each one with a deep inner sense of achievement and delight.

As I had told Callum, I had sold 'The Skull Inheritance' to the publishers as a pure work of fiction – after all, who would believe it was true? – and I stuck firmly to that line in all my conversations. Several people came up who were obviously much more knowledgeable about crystal skulls than I was, asking about my sources. I held firm, an inner voice warning me not to deviate from it or give anything away, regardless of the reason. They talked to me about Max, Synergy, the Mitchell-Hedges skull and others, all names I had heard Joe mention, none of which I knew anything about. Unable to answer their questions I felt unjustifiably inadequate, though why I couldn't fathom. After all, wasn't I supposed to be simply a fiction writer, not some learned authority? Maybe I should do some research, I mused during a lull.

'No.' The voice is my head was loud and firm. 'Do your own work and let others do theirs. Their business is not your business.'

I was about to question further when a grinning face peered around the corner. Damp auburn curls were escaping from under a woollen cap shaped like a donkey's head, and hazel eyes sparkled in delight.

'How's it going, superstar?'

'Cathy!' As always I could count on her support. 'Thank you for coming.'

'As if I'd miss your first step on the ladder to fame and fortune. Well?'

'It's good. Tiring, but good.'

She stepped back as a couple approached to ask me about my book. As soon as they had walked away she turned to me. 'It feels wrong that you can't tell them the truth about it.' She kept her voice low.

I glanced around to check that Tanya wasn't in earshot. I couldn't see her anywhere. 'We've been over this, Cathy. This has to be viewed as a story, not reality. I won't say I'm sorry. I'm not sure I'd be comfortable claiming it to be the truth, even if it is.'

'But what about being true to yourself?' We had talked about this countless times and she did fully understand where I was coming from. Which didn't stop it from frustrating her.

'I can't. Not yet anyway. Maybe in the future I'll be able to come clean, but not now. I'm not ready, and with everything else going on, it certainly wouldn't be wise.' I had shared with her the conversation Callum and I had had over lunch.

221

'I know. I do, it's just…' She hugged me. 'We're still on for coffee later, yes?'

I nodded. 'Three o'clock, usual place.'

'Brilliant, you can fill me in then. I have to dash, I'm meeting someone for lunch in Devizes and I want a quick chat with the stones first. Hope you sell the lot,' she winked, cocking her head in the direction of the diminishing pile of books on the table behind me. With a brief wave she was gone.

I grinned. For Cathy, no visit to Avebury was complete without her 'quick chat with the stones', the massive stone slabs that formed the huge mile in circumference stone circle. If she had a problem to resolve, or a question on her mind, she'd ask it out loud as she wandered through them. Invariably she would get her answer by the time she had completed the circle.

I glanced at the clock. Noon. An hour and a half to go. It seemed a long time but my publishers had been banking on the fine weather continuing, bringing a steady flow of people into the shop and to my table. Instead, the weather was worsening. I could hear the rain battering against the windows. The shop was empty and even Tanya, it seemed, had abandoned me.

I started to rearrange the remaining books when I had the uncomfortable feeling that I was being watched. I glanced over my shoulder. A man was standing in the archway between the shop sections, staring at me. I met his gaze and wished I hadn't. I had read something disturbing and unwelcome in those eyes. Or had I? Within a split second he had turned his attention to a book on the

222

shelf beside him, seemingly annoyed at being caught out. I took the opportunity to study him for a moment longer.

He appeared completely out of place. Pretty much everyone who had come into the shop that morning had been dressed for an outdoor expedition; jeans, boots – either hiking or welly – and sturdy waterproofs had been the order of the day. In amongst these casual clothes he struck a discordant note.

The man wasn't tall, maybe five foot eight or nine at the most, but he was well built and looked strong. Not someone you would want to tangle with. He wore a white shirt and dark blue tie under a long grey wool coat that was dripping with moisture, and on his feet what looked like hand-made leather shoes (not that I'm an expert on recognising hand-made shoes, you understand), highly polished but already covered in mud from the lane. The shoes stood out above everything else. I instantly christened him Mr Shiny Shoes. He didn't look at all like he had come into the shop to browse or even just to get out of the rain. There was something much more purposeful in his demeanour than that. The air of enforced casualness he was (not very successfully) attempting to assume only emphasised it.

'Be careful with this one. Watch your step.' The thought flew through my head as once more we locked eyes. This time it was an obviously deliberate act on his part. Again he looked away, poking through the volumes on the bookshelf for a moment or two before wandering, with the same studied indifference, over to the table where I was perched. Shivers of warning coursed up my spine.

'Hi, are you the author?' There was just a faint hint of a foreign accent in his speech, though I couldn't recognise its origins.

'Yes, I'm Gemma Mason.' What did he want? Whatever it was, I was on my guard.

He held out his hand. 'Jürgens Brinkman. I have a deep interest in crystal skulls myself.'

'Dark One.' Unspoken but clear, the certainty lodged in my mind. Where the heck had that come from? And even if he was – my rational brain screamed 'Don't be ridiculous' as my intuitive self trusted the truth of the thought – how could I know that?

The questions started. What did I know about the crystal skulls? Had I ever made contact with them telepathically? Where did I get the ideas for the story from? Why had I decided to write it in the first place? Did I believe any such crystal skulls might really exist? If so, where might I think they would be hidden? And on and on. All polite and seemingly innocent. All with an edge of something harder lurking just below the surface, an ill-concealed arrogance and superiority that sabotaged all appearances of friendly conversation.

My senses on high alert, I couldn't miss that Mr Shiny Shoes Brinkman was watching me like a hawk, noting my reactions and responses as I answered all his questions as lightly and as naturally as I could. For a brief flicker of time the weirdest sensation poured over me, as if someone was trying to peer past my skin right into my thoughts. It lasted only a split second before what felt like a shutter dropped down across my eyes. I can only describe it as a third eyelid. Transparent – I could see as clearly as before

– but a definite shield, as if I was looking through a glass wall. I was being protected, encased in a bubble against whatever was trying to invade my mind. In astonishment I recognised the energy. It was soft, gentle, but incredibly strong. Gal-Athiel. She had intervened. Why? How did she know I needed help?

Strengthened by her protective energy, I stuck firmly to my cover story and gave a very convincing performance, if I say so myself. I suppose I'd practised it so many times, it had become part of me. Plus, and I'm not too sure how proud of myself I should be for this, I was discovering that I was a good liar. A very good liar.

After what felt like an eternity, he appeared to have found out all that he wanted to know. He thanked me courteously for my time, shook my hand and walked out of the shop. Had he believed me? I didn't know, but I hoped so. I really, really hoped so.

Tanya came up as he left, staring after him curiously. 'Wow. He certainly gave you the third degree. Well done. If you can handle that, you'll be able to handle anything that's thrown at you in an interview.'

'Not too often, thanks,' I replied lightly, acting as if it had been nothing. But I had been deeply shaken by the encounter and every muscle ached from the tension I had been holding in. There had been more to it than appeared on the surface, but what? Did this have anything to do with Callum's investigations? Of course it did, though as I was in the dark as to what those investigations were, I could come up with no link. I was deep in thought as I left Avebury to meet Cathy for our coffee date.

* * * * *

There was no way I was going to miss Cathy. And there was no way she was going to let me get off lightly. As I walked into the café the first thing I saw was a big helium balloon sporting the words 'Best-selling author' tied to the back of a chair, with a big blue arrow pointing downwards to where my head was going to be. I hugged her delightedly. Her infectious enthusiasm immediately lifted my dark mood.

Not completely though. I couldn't fool Cathy. She's known me since we were teenagers, which was a few years ago now, and added to her natural psychic gifts, there was nowhere for me to hide. She frowned at me. 'Come on, give. Why aren't you basking in the glory of your unparalleled success?'

I explained about Mr Shiny Shoes and how the experience had completely knocked the edge off the day. Cathy had no answers, I didn't expect that she would, but as always it helped to share my thoughts and anxieties. And as always her grounded common sense prevailed.

'Well, there's absolutely no point in worrying about it. It won't change anything. It seems to me like he was just sounding you out and that you convinced him you didn't know anything.'

'And if I didn't?'

'You have Gal-Athiel on your side, remember?' That was reassuring, even if I wasn't sure what the skull could do to help.

Cathy steered the conversation onto lighter subjects and we were soon lost in a fantasy world of how my life would be once I topped all the best-seller lists, casting the film of the book, and generally letting our imaginations run riot. I considered it simply a bit of fun. Cathy was more focussed.

'If you can see it and feel it happening, you can create it,' she told me with a mock sternness.

By the time we said goodbye I was in a totally different frame of mind. I was even able to consider the possibility that I had overreacted and that Mr Shiny Shoes was nothing but an overenthusiastic skull lover. The good feelings weren't to last.

MAAT-SU: The Lapis Skull

PART 2

A NEW BEGINNING

40.

The boat was light, with a delicate appearance that belied her strength. She was constructed of woven reeds and willow saplings, and carried over the water by four long oars, each wielded by a sturdy-looking man. A fifth man was standing in the stern, and he leapt agilely onto the shore as the craft drew up into the shallows. He was small, standing no taller than Kua'tzal's shoulder, wiry and strong with jet black hair and skin the colour of a polished walnut shell. To the traveller's astonishment, he addressed them in their own tongue, bowing low as he spoke.

'Greetings, my friend. We have long awaited your arrival.'

'You were expecting us? How?' The question came from a thickset man standing at Kua'tzal's shoulder.

'Long ago, it was foretold that two strangers would come to live amongst us. The first arrived many sun cycles ago. Four days since, it was spoken that you had come at last and that we should sail out to meet you and bring you home.' Once more, he bowed low. 'I am DaLim, chief of my people. I welcome you.'

Kua'tzal was curious and intrigued. 'You say there is one like us who is already living with you? What is his name?'

'She calls herself Calista. She carries with her a sacred object like your own.'

Calista. The name was unknown to him. But she carried one of the thirteen skulls. If she had brought it here from

Atlantis, then she had surely to be a priestess of the Pyramid Temple. Which one? To ensure the greatest secrecy, none of those who had taken on this task knew the identity of the others. He wondered what her role would be.

'Which skull does she hold?'

'You will discover that for yourself. She is waiting to meet you. Come, we must leave now or we will not make landfall before night.' DaLim would say no more and Kua'tzal was forced to swallow his impatience. He would find out for himself soon enough.

He looked at the fragile looking boat pulled up on the sand. It was small, very small, able to carry no more than six or seven of them in addition to its crew. No sooner had the thought flashed through his mind than several more sailed into view around the headland.

The crew were gruff, hardy men who spoke little but were helpful and gentle as they helped the passengers aboard. When all the travellers were safely if snugly seated, with a twist of the oars they turned the little craft around and headed back out to sea. None of the passengers, not even Kua'tzal, knew where they were heading; nonetheless each one of them was filled with a sense of completion, a warm certainty that they were almost at the end of their long, long journey. The mention of a second skull had aroused their curiosity and there was plenty of low-voiced discussion at the unexpected turn of events.

Among the murmurs and speculation, Kua'tzal alone was silent. He rested back against the low gunwale and allowed his thoughts to drift, trying to place a face to the

231

name. He had kept his distance from the other men and women of the Temple – or rather, they had kept their distance from him. He had been a pariah to most. Calista? No, no memory came back. No sense of who it may be. Who would he find there?

Like the others who accompanied him, Kua'tzal was filled with a feeling of security and an odd sense of homecoming. It was bizarre to feel this way in a strange land half way across the world from their beloved Atlantis, but the sensation was undeniable.

The crews rowed strongly, the wind was light and the sea calm, and they made good speed. Soon the coast they had just left was nothing more than a low shadow on the horizon. All day they rowed, never seeming to tire. It was sunny, hot, with a light breeze that kept the temperature bearable. All around them the sun-sparkled sea stretched out to the horizon. They were in a tiny craft in an endless expanse of blue, from the almost blindingly vivid azure skies to the deep rich aquamarine of the ocean on which they floated. The craft seemed too fragile and vulnerable to be out here in the middle of nothing. The crew rowed confidently, however, clearly highly skilled and experienced at such expeditions.

As the sun lowered slowly towards the horizon, small, low-lying islands began to appear. Some were no bigger than a small room, barren rocky heaps piled up in the ocean. Others were the size of the Pyramid Temple itself. These larger islands were all alike; from a fringe of narrow sandy beaches, craggy rocks rose towards the centre, which was invariably green and lush with low growing trees and shrubs.

It was on one of these islets that they camped for the night, drawing the boats high above the waterline. They dined on the fish that filled these seas, washed down with fresh water that had been stored under the gunwales and seats of the boats in pouches made of a thin, flexible material that the travellers had never seen before. Neither hide nor fabric, it kept the water cool and sweet even in the heat of the day.

* * * * *

Crimson silhouettes in the firelight, Kua'tzal and DaLim sat talking.

'How far?' the priest asked. Now so close to his goal, he was feeling impatient to arrive.

'Six days at best, seven if the river fights us.' DaLim smiled a slow, easy smile. 'There is no hurry. You have been travelling a very long time, and we have been waiting for you for nearly as long. A few more days will make no difference.'

'Where are you taking us?'

'To our village. It has no name. It is a beautiful place, a very special place. Powerful energy flows through the land there. My people settled there after they were guided to it by the gods who left us with a prophecy that one day a great treasure would be brought to us that would lift us into the light, and that when that day comes, a great civilisation will arise there.' He smiled again. 'That was a very long time ago. We all heard stories of the prophecy from childhood, but, until Calista's arrival, few believed in its truth any more. It didn't matter. It is a special place to live. We are healthy and happy there. We have fresh water

233

and a richness of meat and crops. We need nothing else.'
Kua'tzal remained silent, knowing there was more.

DaLim continued, lost in his thoughts, speaking them aloud as if Kua'tzal wasn't there. 'When I was a child, no more than maybe six sun cycles of age, they returned. The gods came back to us.'

'How did you know they were gods?' Kua'tzal's voice was barely a whisper, unwilling to rouse DaLim from his memories.

'They came from the sky. Descended from the Sky Discs in wreaths of white cloud and golden light. Great silver discs that filled the sky and hid the sun so that our land was darkened all around.

'They spoke with my father – he was head man then as I am now – and told him of your arrival, and that of the other, Calista, although they never shared your names. Merely that two strangers would come amongst us, many sun cycles apart, one woman and one man. They would bring with them treasure unlike any other, treasure beyond price, powerful beyond measure. We were to welcome them, for they were those who the prophecy foretold would stay with us and build that great civilisation.

'I crept out of my bed and hid to listen to them talking, for the men that came from the discs were unlike anyone I had ever seen before. Two, taller than the tallest of your group, golden haired and bright, as if the sun shone through their skin. Two smaller, bronze-skinned with jet black hair and eyes that glowed like amber. I have never seen them since.'

Kua'tzal lay down to sleep that night with his mind racing. What did it all mean?

41.

At daybreak they set out again, the rowers tireless and untiring. The current was stronger now pushing against them, and progress slowed. For the first time, the effort showed in their muscles as they powered through the counter-current. Still they carried on.

The channel was narrowing noticeably, the land on both sides merging into an unbroken, if still distant, shoreline. They were funnelling into the mouth of a mighty river. The current was growing stronger by the stroke, trying to force the little craft away back out into the open sea. Fighting the oarsmen who dug even deeper, sinewed muscles glistening with sweat as they pulled on their oars, straining backs, shoulders and arms, legs taut against the footboards, thigh muscles tight and bulging as they used them to power through the strokes.

They knew these seas intimately, had negotiated them countless times. Their chief kept a calm hand on the rudder, steering them smoothly to the smoothest waters, constantly calling orders to his crew. The boats behind followed in their wake. Progress was slow, at times almost at a standstill. The distance from here to their destination was far less than they had already sailed but it would take them at least another four days to reach it as they battled the river's will all the way.

At night they slept on the bank of the Great River, taking turns to stand watch for the huge reptilian monsters that lived in its depths and stalked them here in search of their next meal. Some of these beasts measured the length of four men, with mighty jaws and teeth as long as a man's finger that would rip his limbs from his body as easily as a child would tear open a ripe peach. There was nowhere else to go. The banks were the only open space between the river, with its deadly fast-flowing currents and flesh hungry inhabitants, and the dense, tangled forest beyond.

The creatures did not give them peace during the day either, following alongside the boats, their monstrous scaly tails sweeping them forward effortlessly against the current with slow powerful strokes as they waited patiently to claim their next meal. Their silent sinister presence and sporadic glimpses of their rough ridged backs just breaking the surface of the water unnerved the newcomers. Those who knew this place had no such fears. They were familiar with these creatures, with their habits and wiles. If one drew too close, threatening to capsize the little craft with a lucky swipe of its tail, a well-aimed rock between the eyes drove it off. The beasts remained empty bellied.

When their passage took them close enough to the bank, they could see a rich, lush, abundant land. Exotic trees and shrubs grew thickly, sometimes right down to the water's edge, bearing colourful blossoms whose rich fragrance hung in the air like incense. Fruits of all shapes and colours dripped from their branches, and the air was filled with the chattering of birdsong and the flash of iridescent wings. Here and there, a scattering of homes lined the banks, along which racks of river fish dried in the sun, next to sweet, plump dates and other luscious fruits.

* * * * *

They arrived at the village in the middle of the afternoon, the boats drawing up on a wide spit of sand from where a well-trodden path led upwards through thick forest. Though it was hot and humid, excitement lightened the travellers' steps. This was where their years of journeying had been leading them. They had reached their destination.

The path opened out onto a flat, rocky platform that was home to the community. The settlement was much larger than Kua'tzal had expected, a town more than a village, with wide streets lined with square squat houses made of bricks formed from the clay of the river bed that had been baked hard in the hot sun. At the foot of the low escarpment the Great River flowed, slow, wide and constant.

Homes had already been prepared for their arrival; they were immediately welcomed with wide smiles and open hearts. After their years of nomadic, solitary life, the newcomers were overwhelmed at being surrounded by so many people and entering proper houses once again. They were both happy that their journey had at last come to an end and uncomfortable at the unfamiliarity. It would take time for them to get used to life in a busy, static community once again. But they would. This had always been their goal. Every one of them recognised it and was happy to have arrived.

Kua'tzal's new home was a simple one-roomed dwelling set a little way from the main square. It was refreshingly cool and dark after the heat and glare of the sun. Still, he did not linger inside. As soon as he had set the small travelling bundle containing Maat-su down on the thin, goat-hair stuffed mattress that covered the floor on one side of the room, he hurried back outside. After so many months and years sleeping in the open air, its confines felt stuffy and claustrophobic.

He wandered through the town, finding his bearings. The streets and buildings looked clean and well-cared for, and the people happy, healthy and prosperous. Everyone he met greeted him with a smile and a heartfelt 'Welcome'. Here, now, his former isolated life in Atlantis seemed a million miles and a million years away.

His feet led him to a low rise at the edge of the settlement from where he could look out over a wide plateau. It was barren, devoid of the wealth of trees and flourishing vegetation that covered the landscape all around it. Patches of sparse grass and low shrubs were dotted here and there, the soil over the bedrock too thin to support anything else. Unsheltered, the wind constantly scoured it bare and today whipped sand painfully into Kua'tzal's face as he stood gazing over this uninspiring grey landscape that appeared so alien to the ocean of green that encompassed it.

The ground in front of him sloped downwards to the rocky plain; ahead of him in the distance he could see a huge construction project underway. It was a hive of activity, tiny figures swarming in and out of a huge hole in the ground. He turned at the sound of a footfall behind him. It was DaLim, who had seen him exploring and had followed.

'Calista's work.' He nodded his head in the direction of the activity. 'It's why she was brought here.'

'What is it?'

'A great monument. More than that she says she doesn't know yet. Apparently Muu-nan gives her only the next step, not the whole plan. Must be difficult to work like that.' The two men stared out over the stony plateau for several minutes, each lost in his own thoughts, before DaLim spoke again. 'I came to tell you that there is to be a feast this evening to celebrate your arrival. Calista will be there. You'll be able to speak with her then.'

Muu-nan. It was the first time Kua'tzal had heard the name of the second skull and he recognised it immediately. The Skull of Arcturus, created from the most delicate pale rose amethyst. Skull of insight and inspiration. Who would Muu-nan have chosen as her guardian? The answer would not come. No matter. He would find out tonight.

42.

A huge yellow moon hung low in the sky, lighting up the night. The travellers were standing together on the edge of the square watching a group of dancers writhing and twisting to the music of flutes and drums.

'Kua'tzal, is it really you?' The voice came from behind him. It was a voice he recognised. No, he had to be mistaken. It couldn't be, could it? He turned slowly to look at the woman standing behind him.

'Cleantha?' Before he could say more, she took a light hold on his arm and led him away from the crowd to a quieter place. He couldn't speak. Cleantha, the only woman he had ever loved. She was here. She was Calista. Though she looked very different from the middle-aged woman only a few years his junior, who he had last seen in the Pyramid Temple the day before he had left for Dendarak. Her skin was firm and soft, its former tracing of lines smoothed and vanished, and her hair fell thick and glossy to her shoulders showing no sign of the grey that had once touched it. She had grown younger, not older, in the intervening years.

His heart lurched. Even though DaLim had told him there was another here from Atlantis, never in his wildest dreams had he expected it to be her. Though why not? She had always been close to the skulls. 'Cleantha?' he repeated.

'Here I am known as Calista. Muu-nan asked it and I had no cause to refuse. I don't know her reasons, but I don't question them.' Her voice was even but the hand that still rested on his arm was trembling and in her eyes he could see the same confusion he was feeling. If he had not expected to find her here, she was even more astounded to see him – the man she had loved so deeply and who had broken her heart when, overnight, he had changed beyond recognition and driven her away. Overwhelming emotion was barely kept in check.

'Kua'tzal…'

He interrupted, unwilling to face his own feelings, hiding them under mundane conversation. 'You look well, Cleanth… Calista. Different. Younger. The way you did all those years ago. How can that be?'

She forced her own voice to normality. 'Don't tell me you haven't noticed the same in yourself, Kua'tzal? I can see it in you. You are stronger, healthier, more youthful than I have seen you in many years. It is the work of the skulls. But you already know that. They are returning us to the perfect blueprint of our form. The patterns of all disease and infirmity have been wiped from our energy fields to leave us at the peak of our condition.'

'I have noticed it in all of us who travelled from Atlantis, only until only a short time ago I refused to acknowledge it,' Kua'tzal conceded.

'Muu-nan tells me that we have much work to do. A massive task lies before us, one that will require many lifetimes of work. It is our role to oversee this task and bring it to fruition.'

'What is this task?' Kua'tzal was talking just to cover his confused feelings. Even as his lips formed the question, he knew the answer. Hadn't Maat-su already shown him,

241

long ago during the early days of their journey? Though she had not clarified the details of what it would entail.

'I don't know.' How could Calista not know? 'I haven't been told. Only that it is of the utmost importance.'

'But you have begun work already.'

'I only see the next step, not the whole scheme. I trust that Muu-nan will tell me at the right time if I am to know.' She looked at him quizzically, her sharp intuition speaking to her. 'You already know the role you are to play, don't you?'

'Not fully. Not the details. Long ago, just after we had left Atlantis, Maat-su told me that we would one day found a new civilisation, a new Atlantis. That we would build great monuments and create a society where people would live together in peace and harmony. As they did before,' he added sadly. 'I didn't realise until today the enormity of the task we were being asked to accomplish, nor the demands it would place upon us.'

Calista put a gentle hand on his shoulder. 'It takes time to accept such things. Come on. Let's go back to the celebrations. After all, they're in your honour. Tomorrow I will take you to see the construction site.'

* * * * *

As Kua'tzal lay down to sleep later that night, a flood of painful and long-buried memories resurfaced uninvited. It had been a very long time ago. They had been so in love and blissfully happy. Until the day that Kua'tzal had been asked to take on his new role. He had refused, resisted, knowing it would spell the death of his relationship with the passionate and dedicated Cleantha. His mission would require total secrecy, hiding the subterfuge even from her. She was fiercely loyal to the temple and her skull charges. She would not accept his change of personality. But the threat facing Atlantis was too great for him to refuse, the penalty for his failure too severe. He had accepted knowing, even as he took his oath of secrecy, that he was sacrificing the happiness of both of them. This was his journey to take. He would be taking it alone.

Cleantha had begged and pleaded with him to step back into his old self. She had reasoned and wept, all to no result. He had to do this, though his heart shattered every time she opened herself to him. Eventually, her despair had turned to anger and she had kept her distance, avoiding him whenever possible, speaking only when she had no choice. He found some relief in that, for it was much easier for him to bear when she was looking at him with condemnation rather than pain. His own hurt he could endure; hers he could not. He did not blame her. In her eyes, as in the eyes of all who shared his life in the Temple, he was betraying his oath. Many times the elders were called on to strip him of his duties and banish him, yet still he remained, all demands for his removal denied. Cleantha's voice had been amongst the loudest.

Now, against all the odds, she was here with him. She had been standing close enough for him to smell the delicate and achingly familiar scent of her skin and her hair. She was so youthful, vibrant and alive. The pain he had buried for so long overwhelmed him. Tears streamed silently down his face in the comfort of the darkness. When at last they stopped, he was cleansed and empty. The final chains to his old life, chains he hadn't even known existed, had been broken. A new life awaited him and maybe, just maybe, Calista would be a part of it.

* * * * *

In the privacy of her own home, Calista too was overwhelmed by feelings, memories and confusion. What was Kua'tzal doing here? How had he been chosen as Maat-su's guardian? All those shadow-filled years when he had become so different to the man she had first fallen in love with, when he had grown cold, distant, hard. Cosying up to the Shadow Chasers, his obvious if unspoken support for their ambitions and actions alienating him from those he shared his life with. She had never stopped loving him but had locked that love away deep in a dark, hidden corner of her heart, never looking at it, for she had no reason to, until she had forgotten it ever existed.

Until this evening. As she had walked up to the stranger, a surge of disbelieving recognition had swelled in her at the figure silhouetted in the torchlight. There was no mistake. It was him. She had scarcely been able to speak his name. He had turned at her voice, clearly as surprised as she was, and Calista had found herself looking into his warm, brown eyes, as soft and open as they had once been; no longer shuttered by the cold, closed stare that had taken them over. Somehow she had kept herself together, remaining composed and neutral in his company throughout the ceremony and feast that followed in the face of the tidal wave of emotion that was constantly threatening to engulf her. She would not be able to resist it for very much longer. She had excused herself early and retired to the privacy and solitude of her dwelling.

The moment Calista closed the door, wave after wave of emotion surged through her, taking all strength from her legs so that she fell to her knees. Shaking her so much that her teeth rattled. Long buried grief and pain. Confusion. Incredulity at the vagaries of destiny. Bitterness, unwanted but undeniable. And anger. So much anger. Anger at his betrayal. Anger that he was here now. Anger that she had to deal with it again. Anger that, after he caused her so much torment, he was again the man she had once known. Anger at the wasted years. Everything she had buried came up to be faced and released. No tears, maybe they would come later, just a violent physical letting go of everything she had used to lock away her love.

That love would no longer be ignored or denied. As the barricades of pain fell away, it engulfed Calista, drowning her in its intensity. She lay on the floor where she had dropped, oblivious to everything but her love for Kua'tzal which, freed from the prison to where it could never return, took possession of her heart and soul once more. When she had looked at him tonight the man she had seen was the man she had fallen in love with. Tender. Gentle. Funny. Kind. Memories came back to her. His lips, warm and hungry on hers. The touch of his hand as he brushed a stray strand of hair from her eyes to tuck it behind her ear, fastening it in place with a scented flower. His warm, dark eyes, through which she could see into the depths of his soul.

All at once she saw the truth. The man he had become was a mask behind which had always been the Kua'tzal she had loved. Why he had done it she could not fathom, but it would have had to have been of great importance for him to have denied his soul all those years. In that moment she felt as her own the pain and loneliness Kua'tzal's sacrifice had caused him. And what had she done? At the time when he had needed her most, she had abandoned him. Stopped believing her heart and listened to her head instead. Refused to look deeply enough to see the truth. She wept then for what she saw as her own betrayal, that of the man she loved.

'Do not blame or punish yourself. You were not meant to see.' The soft voice of Muu-nan whispered through Calista's mind, soothing her soul like a gentle spring breeze lifts the hearts of all who feel its caress, bringing new life and new hope. ''If you had not acted the way you did, the subterfuge would have failed and you would not be here. It could be no other way.'

'But for him to be here, now, after all this time… now that it's too late.' Calista's words carried her sorrow.

'It is never too late. The love you had still burns within you both as strongly as it ever did. Trust, blessed one. Follow your heart in this as you do in all things and let the life that lies before you unfold.' Surrounded by Muu-nan's loving energy, at last Calista slept.

* * * * *

Sleep would not come so easily to Kua'tzal. He lay for a long time going over the evening's events in his mind, contemplating what the future held. It was doing him no good. His mind was a turmoil of jumbled thoughts and memories; he would never sleep while they teased and poked at him. Picking up Maat-su, he went out into the night. The air was warm, sweetly scented by the surrounding forest. Above him the stars glittered with such intensity that he could make out their various hues of blues, reds, whites and yellows. They seemed to be beckoning him onward, so he followed their call until he eventually found himself cresting the same rise he had stood on with DaLim earlier in the day.

Once more he gazed out over the bare expanse of rock, now looking so different in the monochrome light of the fat, slightly squashed yellow ball of the almost full moon that at this moment nestled between the ridges of a distant mountain. Overhead, the Star River swept a twinkling swathe across the sky, the flow of stars echoing that of the Great River beneath it, the one mirroring the course of the other.

In this light the plateau appeared ghostly and ethereal, touched with an otherworldly beauty he would not have been able to put into words. Kua'tzal sat on the still warm ground and lost himself in the view stretched out in front of him. How much time passed while he sat there he didn't know. It could have been mere heartbeats; it could have been hours.

He rubbed his eyes. What was that, out in the darkness? No, it was nothing, just the shadows playing tricks with his eyes. There was nothing there now. And yet... Kua'tzal peered closely at a spot a short distance from where the chasm of the construction site blackened the backdrop. Surely...? Had he imagined it?

He hadn't. There it was again, brighter this time. A haze of pulsing blue light hovered over the ground. Expanding and contracting. Calling to him.

'Go to it.' Maat-su was awake. 'Go to it. This is why you are here.'

Kua'tzal carefully clambered down the rough slope to the flat ground of the plateau and picked his way across the wide empty space to where the light still hung. He moved slowly, cautiously, mindful of the scorpions and other venomous creatures that lurked in ambush, waiting for an unwary footstep to dislodge their stone or tread too close. Kua'tzal's sandals would provide him little protection against a sting or bite.

As he approached the mist, its pull grew stronger. He could no longer resist its power even if he had wanted to. He hesitated momentarily at the edge before stepping into its mystery, allowing it to enfold him.

43.

'Build it here.' The words echoed round and through him, both separate from him and at the same time an unbreakable part of his soul. 'Build it here.'

Build what? Through the soft blue light that encompassed him the ground vanished from beneath Kua'tzal's feet, leaving him with the disconcerting sensation that he was standing in mid-air, high above a circular room. The images, though hazy, were clear enough. The walls were of smoothly polished pale stone instead of amethyst and the chamber was smaller than that in Yo'tlàn's Temple but other than that, its layout was identical. In the centre of this room, Maat-su rested on a square white pillar surrounded by twelve clear crystal skulls on similar pedestals.

Looking up, Kua'tzal saw three massive pyramids forming around him, ethereal but clearly visible, their structure outlined in glowing deep blue light. The central one surrounded him, its shining golden apex far above him reaching up towards the star-scattered night sky. On each side stood another, black sentinels against – what? He didn't know. In the ground, at each corner of these shimmering images, a massive quartz point had been set, plunging downwards into the earth on the same angle as the sides above it climbed skyward.

Gazing deep below his feet, a dizzying distance below, a powerful torrent of water was flowing through the Earth. Superimposed upon it were three whirlpools of light, from which pulsing ribbons of light fanned out into the surrounding rock. These whirlpools were sited exactly beneath the centre of the three structures whose light-drawn silhouettes still glowed around him. Intuitively, Kua'tzal knew what he was seeing; these whirlpools were energy vortices, the stream of light the pathways by which the energy was carried throughout the Earth's natural grid.

Dimensions, angles, depths and calculations downloaded into his mind, crystallising into a thorough knowledge of exactly what was required. Blueprints appeared in the air in front of him, diagrams of shimmering white light dancing in the darkness. As he watched, mesmerised, the images drew together, converging into a dense ball the size of a walnut, increasing in intensity with every second that passed, dazzling his eyes. Still he could not look away, drawn into its spell. Suddenly, the ball flew straight at him, so swiftly that he didn't have time to duck, striking him in the centre of his forehead, just above his eyebrows. The inside of his head exploded in a blinding lightning flash before darkness swamped him and he fell to the ground unconscious.

* * * * *

A woman's voice was calling to him from what seemed a long, long way away, softly, anxiously. Kua'tzal fought his way up through the layers of his consciousness, his head pounding as if it would shatter. The closer he came to the surface, the fiercer the pounding became. A sharp pain in his cheek, a stone digging into the flesh where he had fallen, roused him further.

He opened his eyes slowly, wincing against the daylight. The sun was already high above the far mountain ridges. He was lying on his side on the hard ground. Kneeling in front of him, a worried expression clouding her face, was Calista. Kua'tzal pulled himself carefully to a sitting position, mindful of the pain in his head, and looked around for Maat-su. She had rolled from his hands as he collapsed and was now resting at an angle against a tussock of coarse yellow grass.

'Are you alright? What happened?'

Kua'tzal shook his head slowly to clear the fog that lingered, regretting the move immediately as sharp daggers of pain pierced his skull. 'Yes, I'm fine.' He looked at her, suddenly a little overwhelmed as the enormity of what he had experienced sank in. 'I know what I am here to do, and I know exactly how to do it.' He scrambled clumsily to his feet.

She wanted to return to the town with him, still worried for his wellbeing. 'Are you sure you won't let me walk back with you. You are so pale.'

His hand touched her cheek in a gentle caress as he refused her help, indicating the nearby site, swarming with workmen. It had been one of them who had spotted Kua'tzal lying motionless on the ground. 'I'm fine. Really. You have work to do here.' The love and concern he saw in her eyes gave him hope. 'Will you meet with me later? I'll tell you all about it then.'

She nodded. 'I'll meet you in the square this evening. Please, take care, Kua'tzal. You look very weak.'

He felt weak, but would soon recover. What he needed most now was time alone. He could feel Calista's gaze on his back, watching him with concern as he turned and left her and trudged across the stony ground. Slowly, wearily, he made his way home, falling onto his bed and into a sleep as deep as death as soon as he had closed the door behind him. It was a deep, deep sleep during which everything that had been downloaded into his mind became indelibly fixed. He would from now on have constant access to all the knowledge he needed to fulfil his work.

* * * * *

At first the details were still hazy, Kua'tzal had to learn how to pull them up from his memory store, but day by day the picture became ever clearer. He spoke often with Maat-su for clarification and help. The guidance had been clear. The new skull temple was to be the priority. It would be the focus and inspiration for the peoples' enduring commitment to the lifetimes of work ahead.

He began to plan immediately. There were so many preparations to be dealt with before the actual construction work could begin. Each day he would leave home at daybreak to only return as night fell, when he would speak with Maat-su until the early hours. He saw far too little of Calista, who was busy with her own work. Nonetheless, their once close bonds were rapidly growing strong again. The times they did meet were joyful and fulfilling. As the days and weeks passed, both took care to ensure these meetings became increasingly frequent. It would only be a matter of time.

44.

The world was under threat. The events set in motion through the destruction of the Pyramid Temple, and more crucially its Skull Chamber, were still echoing and grumbling throughout her delicate crust.

When the Shadow Chasers had smashed to splinters the crystal plinths and great central cluster, their death throes had reverberated down into the earth, pummelling into the powerful vortex point that lay there, magnifying and rippling out throughout the entire energy system of the planet. Only a few days later, a huge earthquake had rocked Atlantis, effectively tearing the foundations of that ancient continent in two. It was the tidal wave created by this shock that had nearly swallowed the Edrus in its jaws.

At the time, a series of massive tremors had been the only tangible consequence, and the frightened, battered Atlanteans had gradually settled back into some semblance of their former lives. It was a false security. A chain of events had been launched that could not be stopped; only major intervention could even begin to mitigate the fall-out. Even then, there was no guarantee it would work.

What was this chain of events? The shock waves caused by the destruction had touched every fault line in the Earth's crust, shaking and weakening them so severely that at some point they would have to fail. Not immediately, but the powerful vibrations had created a slow increase in friction that at some point would result in a violent shift to relieve the pressure building up between them. Before long the most vulnerable fault lines were shaken free. Miraculously, their readjustment caused no further severe damage. Sooner or later though the catastrophic would happen. It could not be stopped. When it did, Earth's total destruction, if not inevitable, was highly probable. She would be torn apart at the seams.

The Galactic Federation, an alliance of those star races who had created the crystal skull project and had later been joined by many others who held to similar principles, had long foreseen these events and taken the decision to act when the time came. Whilst non-intervention was their sacred oath, standing by and watching Earth's potential total annihilation, and with it that of the human race, was unthinkable. The repercussions for the rest of the solar system, and even the galaxy itself, would be severe. Even so, there were limits to their involvement. They would not intervene directly. All action had to come through the guidance of the sacred skulls and the will of the human race itself. Humankind had created this disaster. It was up to humankind to avert its worst ravages. They would be given the tools and the knowledge. It would be their choice whether to use them or not.

The solution was the construction of a series of huge pyramid structures sited over major energy vortices across the surface of the planet. They would not all be built at the same time, nor to the same design, for each vortex demanded a unique solution. Some structures would be constructed of stone, others of brick, yet others chalk and earth. Some would be chiselled from natural geological formations, others built from the ground up from materials transported laboriously to the construction site. The work would take several thousands of years to complete.

These pyramids, geometric structures of immense and almost magical inherent power, would absorb the energy of the sun and store it in their fabric. This energy would then be channelled down through integral pathways specifically created in the structure into a second pyramid, the twin of the first but inverted so that the two rested base to base. The second form would be a non-physical structure, created from energy lines forged into the earth. The solar energy gathered would be channelled downwards through the two pyramids into the lower apex and then into the earth to connect with the vortex point far below, strengthening and rebalancing the energy grid and thus relieving the pressure on the fault lines through a form of solar acupuncture.

In addition, a vast library of knowledge would be stored in the building blocks: detailed information on the creation and workings of the universe; human origins and history; medicine, technology and mathematics; the star races who had helped humankind's development; the existence and purpose of the thirteen Skulls of Light. All this information would be energetically imprinted into the stones and available to those who possessed the key to unlock this universal store of knowledge.

It was three of these crucial structures that Kua'tzal had been charged with building. His monuments would be clad in polished black obsidian, which would efficiently absorb the heat and energy of the sun. The capstones would be of the purest gold to insulate against the loss of this gathered power through the upper apex. The skull chamber was to

255

sit beneath the centre point of the centre pyramid. This was unique, for in none of the other structures anywhere on the Earth would one of the sacred skulls be in residence. To protect Maat-su and keep her from detection, a shield would be constructed in the outer skins of these three pyramids; there were many amongst the Shadow Chasers and their descendants who had sworn to track down these skulls and fulfil the ambitions of their ancestors, no matter what the cost.

45.

Kua'tzal was a contented man. The settlement was a friendly and pleasant place to live, its people warm and generous, and they had welcomed the newcomers into their world with open arms and hearts. Work on the new skull temple would begin any day now. The impossibly pure and out of place seam of crystal clear quartz he had found in the cliff side had been carefully extracted and was already in the hands of three highly gifted sculptors who were fashioning twelve skulls to take their place within it. Moreover, he and Calista had spent long hours together talking through their past, healing their rift and the heartache it had caused. They were growing close once more, to his delight, for he had never stopped loving her throughout all the lonely empty years of his life. He believed she felt the same way. He wouldn't push her but maybe, just maybe...

His route this day had taken him down to the river and he was wandering along its sandy banks, deep in thought. The project he was undertaking was immense by any standards. They had been working for months and had barely scratched the surface of what lay ahead. He was starting to realise why the skulls were rejuvenating him. This work would take several lifetimes to complete and already demanded a level of stamina and energy he once thought he had left far behind. He could not say he was sorry. He was enjoying his task, enjoying his new lease of life and the vitality it was bringing him. What was more, the sweet rush of desire and longing he felt every time he looked at Calista was definitely not that of a man nearing the celebration of his seventieth year.

He was paying little attention to where he was heading, so it was with some surprise that he found his feet treading the path above the clear man-made pool that bordered the river. It had been specially built to provide a safe place to bathe, protected from the predators that stalked the dangerous river waters, and was a favourite place for the children of the settlement to congregate. Today however, only one person was swimming languorously through its warm, shallow waters, the sun highlighting her naked limbs. Calista. He should turn away, leave her to her bath. He did not. He stood watching, the deep love and desire he had for so long held in check surging to the surface.

'Now,' his heart whispered. 'Now is the time.' Slowly he walked down the path to the pool.

Calista looked up in surprise at the sound of his footsteps. Love burned in her eyes as she recognised the man standing before her. She did not try to hide her nakedness; there was nothing she needed to hide from Kua'tzal. She stood, unselfconscious in her vulnerability, the water reaching to her hips, trickling down her firm naked breasts and soft belly. She was nearly sixty summers of age and yet she looked barely thirty. She smiled, an enticing, flirting smile, a smile that fanned the flames within him and set his pulse racing.

The heat and hunger rose irresistibly within him. It was time. It had been too long since he had felt Calista's precious skin soft against his own. He would wait no longer. Pulling his tunic over his head, he slid naked into the water to join her.

Calista walked towards him, reaching for him, the unmistakeable dark longing in her eyes telling him she was as hungry for him as he was for her. His desire grew more fervent with every step she took. It had been too many years since he had felt the softness of a woman's caress, tasted the sweetness of her kiss, or been consumed by the fire of her hunger. Even longer since Calista. He had long ago resigned himself to spending the rest of his life alone. All that had changed the moment he had seen her again. His soul, if not his head, had known then it was only a matter of time. All this flashed through his head as he felt the ripples of Calista's approach lapping at his belly. He was standing directly in front of her, his desire obvious and unashamed.

'I love you,' he heard her whisper as her arms wound round his neck and her lips sought his. The fire in his groin, already burning strongly, ignited even more fiercely.

It was as if they had never been apart, as if the intervening years had not existed. The precious softness of her skin and sweet scent of her hair was so familiar to his senses. Any hurt and sorrow that remained dissolved in that moment as time and distance melted away. His hands caressed her gently, lovingly and she opened to him. He wanted her, could wait no longer. Hadn't they waited long enough? As he gazed into her eyes, her lips parted in a silent yes; he felt the urgency in her too, the need that was screaming out to be satisfied.

He lifted her, weightless in the water's embrace, and her legs wrapped around his body, drawing him deep inside her in a warm, yielding and delicious homecoming. He heard her gasp in pleasure as he pulled her even more closely onto him, possessing her as she was possessing him, wanting only to sink ever deeper into that sweet, secret world where nothing mattered but the two of them and the unbearably delicious sensations coursing through his body.

He felt her tense against him, arching her back as the climax burst through her, again and again, shuddering her release so strongly that he too could hold back no longer. His world exploded in a riot of sensation as he thrust deeper and deeper in the throes of his orgasm, wanting to experience every hidden corner of her body, hearing her cry of ecstasy as she felt him give himself to her completely. Holding her against him, soft and relaxed, they slowly returned to the world, still joined, neither willing to separate from the other.

'I love you,' he whispered into her damp-darkened hair. 'Be my wife.' Calista's murmured 'Yes' was all he needed to hear.

* * * * *

Two days later Kua'tzal and Calista exchanged their vows, publicly and joyfully declaring their union. This day had been a long time in coming, and for so many years neither had believed it ever would. There was no reason now for further delay.

The whole town turned out to share their moment. Food was brought and piled onto long trestles in the main square and honey-like wine flowed freely. The celebrations continued until dawn, long after the couple had retired to the seclusion of their home to seal their union privately and intimately. This time their lovemaking was slow and sweet. There was no hurry. They had so much time ahead of them to enjoy one another.

It was a very special night for another reason too, one which only became evident a little later. In those first few hours of this life together, their first child was conceived. For the two future parents it was a joy which they had not dared to hope for; Calista was nearing her seventh decade, well past her normal child-bearing years. Thanks to the rejuvenation of her body, instigated by the sacred Skulls of Light, this miracle was able to take place. In time, seven more children would be born to them who would continue, with the children of the other travellers, the lineage of Atlantis.

46.

The excavations for the skull chamber had begun. It was to be sited deep below the surface, a massive undertaking for their primitive, if effective tools.

Kua'tzal had questioned the guidance he had received time and time again; the spot he was compelled to begin the work was some distance from the original site where he had encountered the blue light. Always the answer returned the same: 'Dig here.' There was no doubt in the message. Trusting in this guidance and that in due course all would reveal its purpose, he obeyed.

His faith was answered. Just below the surface rock, the workers broke through the roof of a narrow passageway. Exploring it, they discovered that after some distance it widened to create a good-sized cave from which the tunnel continued, dropping down through the floor.

Standing in the centre of this cave one morning not long after its discovery, Kua'tzal saw the outline of the great pyramid monument shimmering above him. It had been no accident that he had been told to begin where he had. This cave was to be the skull chamber, the tunnel its entrance corridor. They had been given a helping hand; much of this initial work had already been completed for them by natural forces.

Painstakingly, the walls were carved out to form a perfect circle. There was no amethyst here to line them but it didn't matter. Instead the natural stone was smoothed and polished to a soft sheen. Neither was there available the snow-white opaque quartz that had been used for the skulls' pedestals in Yo'tlàn. In its place, thirteen square pillars of a translucent pure white marble were created, twelve set around the circumference of the chamber, the thirteenth one in the centre where Maat-su would be placed, taking the place of the Master.

47.

They came on the day that the foundations for the first of the three great pyramids were finally completed. It was a little after midday. As usual, virtually the entire settlement was indoors, sheltering from the searing heat of the late summer sun.

Around mid-morning the last shovel of soil had been cleared and the last inches of bedrock in the final quadrant levelled. Work had been declared over for the day. In the quarries, the first immense blocks of stone had been cut and were waiting. Tomorrow, the difficult task of moving them the several miles from their origin to the plateau would begin. It would be back-breaking labour, taking days to transport each one on rollers cut from the trunks of the ironwood trees that grew abundantly here. The male population who were able to undertake such an effort was small, too small in truth for the miracle they were being asked to bring about. Each one was an eager and hard worker; nonetheless, enthusiasm and willingness could not compensate for the lack of man and muscle power.

Kua'tzal was enjoying the cool of his home after the sweltering heat outside, taking pleasure in playing with his young son, Caltas, and watching Calista prepare their meal, his heart as full of love for her as ever. It was a rare joy. His work on the pyramid site kept him from his home and family for long hours. In addition, Calista was always extremely busy, constantly juggling the demands of her own project with those of caring for her family. Somehow,

264

they managed. But time together like this came far too seldom.

His few idyllic moments were rudely disturbed by excited shouts from the street. One voice was rapidly joined by many others. Kua'tzal was getting to his feet to see what was causing the uproar when a knock came on the door and DaLim burst in, his face beaming.

'They're back, Kua'tzal! The gods have returned! Come and see.' Calista followed the two men into the street, Caltas clinging on to her hand.

A huge silver disc-shaped craft hovered high above them, glinting against the deep blue of the sky. It cast a vast shadow that encompassed the entire plateau, swallowing up the two massive construction works that were underway on the far side, and the homes and streets of the village. Those watching stood open-mouthed and silent at the spectacle. Some remembered the stories of those long ago days when the star people were regular visitors, most did not. DaLim was bouncing up and down in excitement, repeating over and over again, 'They're back. They're back.'

A pinprick of brilliant blue-white light appeared on the underside of the disc, then stretched and lengthened until it formed an unbroken shaft of light that connected the craft to the ground below. Slowly it strengthened in intensity and expanded outwards to form a dazzling column several paces in diameter. Tiny black dots appeared in its core, growing in size as they descended until the watching crowd could make out the shape of five figures. No-one spoke as the visitors' feet made contact with the Earth and they stepped out of the light.

DaLim, as head man of the village, stepped forward. 'Greetings strangers, and welcome to our land. Who are you, and why do you come to us?'

'I am Gra-Thar.' A stocky man, though he didn't look like any man Kua'tzal or the others had ever seen before, bowed low. He was short, his face and body covered in a black fur, his only garment a sarong of some shimmering metallic material that he wore swept around his waist. Through the fur on his face, sharp orange eyes glowed, yet for all his menacing appearance he gave off a gentle, steady energy that reassured the Earth people.

The star visitors were communicating telepathically, sharing thoughts rather than words. It was a means of communication that allowed for a universal understanding that reached far beyond the limitations of language. The four others also bowed low in greeting: two more male, two female, all of them obviously not of earthly origin. Five different races in all from five different star systems.

'We have come to help you.' Gra-Thar was communicating again, and all who stood around could hear and understand him clearly. 'We bring you skills and technology to ease the burden of your work. We will not stay long. This is your undertaking. We are here only to teach you so that you may use them for yourselves.'

'Then welcome again, my friends, for we accept with grateful hearts anything you can offer us that will ease our labours.' With those words DaLim led the visitors into his home.

* * * * *

Kua'tzal rose early the next morning, just as the sun was rising. The air was refreshingly cool, though the temperature would rise rapidly as the morning progressed. Gra-Thar had asked that everyone gather at daybreak to accompany him to the quarry. Lessons were to begin immediately. The whole village had turned out and were waiting expectantly for... what?

The trek to the quarry was unusually easy, for the great craft overhead sheltered the land for miles around from the growing heat of the day. Men and women, children and the elderly, trudged together across the unforgiving stones of the plateau.

* * * * *

The five star visitors, Gra-Thar at the centre, stood in front of one of the massive base stones, hewn with punishing effort from the bedrock. It was so huge that twenty men could not lift it. The five did not lay hand on it, standing instead in a semi-circle around ten paces away. Each held out their right hand, palm facing the block, and began to sing.

The purest tones Kua'tzal had ever heard, even from his days in the Pyramid Temple, vibrated through his body, setting every cell shivering. The notes were so sweet and penetrating that it was almost painful to hear them, yet their flawless beauty made them irresistible. Each voice sounded a different note, pouring forth a wave of harmony.

Was this sound affecting him physically? Were his eyes deceiving him? The block seemed to shimmer in front of him, losing its solidity. Appearing hazy, less substantial somehow. The hypnotic sound continued, on and on,

267

holding a pitch no human voice could ever master. No, he wasn't imagining it. The stone was quivering. Fraction by fraction, it began to lift; soon there was a clear gap the width of a man's finger between its base and the ground it had been resting on. Kua'tzal had seen telekinetic expression before, it had been part of his priest's training. But that had been moving a flower, or a feather, and he had once seen someone levitate a mouse, to the poor creature's evident fright. A block this size? He wouldn't have believed it possible.

The chanting lowered in pitch and the great stone settled slowly and soundlessly back down. The five fell silent. After a few moments, one of the females communicated.

'This is how you will move the stones with the people you have.'

'Can we really do this?' Kua'tzal interrupted. 'There is no way our human voices can match those notes with such clarity.'

'No, we recognise that this may not be possible. Which is why more of you will be needed to achieve the same results. We are five. You will need to be ten times that number. This will strengthen the focus. Even so, it will require a great deal of commitment and practice. You must also learn to transmit power through your hands. We know that some of those who travelled here from Atlantis are already skilled in this. The others we will teach. We begin tomorrow.'

48.

Each morning Gra-Thar and his companions gathered the whole village together and taught them to create the sounds that would lift and move the stones. Over and over, they practised the pitches and tones, so difficult for the human voice to reproduce. Men, women and children, all joined in. The women and children in particular, who until now had more often than not been reduced to spectators, wanted to play their full part in the project. In this they could; it was a skill that did not require the raw strength of their menfolk. Everyone persevered with a will. No matter what the hour of the day, the sound of chanting could be heard ringing out from the streets and homes in an overwhelming desire to master the complex notes.

Although Kua'tzal was impatient to get on with the actual construction, he recognised the importance of the time spent on this learning, which would save years of work in the future. So he ruthlessly pushed aside his frustration and joined in with a will. More quickly than he had thought possible, the raggedy band of voices joined together in a heart-stopping harmony of tones that sent thrills through his whole body. They had done it. They had learned to command the power of sound.

Alongside the voice training, the star visitors were teaching the people another skill that they would need to move the stones: to harness and manipulate energy through the power of their focussed mind. Deep meditation and concentration were the keystones of these sessions;

269

those taking part must learn to still their thoughts before calling up that which they wished to accomplish, focussing those thoughts like a laser before sending them out to the target.

* * * * *

Finally the day came when they returned to the quarry. Everyone was present from the youngest babe in arms to the frailest of the old ones. No-one wanted to miss this spectacle. They clustered expectantly on the slope, waiting for instructions.

Gra-Thar wandered through the crowd, selecting fifty of those who had shown most promise in the skill. Most of them were women, together with several men and older children. Forty of the group circled the stone, right arms stretched forward, palms facing it, as Gra-Thar and his companions had done on that first occasion. The other ten stood, five on each side of the huge block, their palms held flat against it. At Gra-Thar's signal, they began to chant.

Nothing was happening. The crowd was holding their breath. The achingly pure sounds continued to fill the air, those creating them standing with eyes closed, as if somewhere else in their minds. Which indeed they were. It seemed an eternity before at last the great stone began to tremble, as if waking up from a deep sleep. Slowly, slowly it lifted. One inch. Two inches. A shout of triumph burst from the watching crowd, followed by delighted laughter… and an ear-splitting thump that rocked the ground as the block crashed back down. Silence.

'Well, now you know that once you have raised the stone, you must continue the sound and the focus until you choose to lower it.' Gra-Thar's amusement was evident, together with a great deal of respect. 'Congratulations, my friends. You have succeeded. From here on it will be much easier, for now you know that you have the ability to do this. Our work here is done. We shall stay for a little while, until you have the confidence to do this without our support, but really, you no longer need us.'

* * * * *

The star visitors were as good as their word. They remained in the village for another moon's cycle and then departed in their disc-like craft, though they did not leave forever. From time to time they returned to check in on progress and meet up with the friends they had made. They were always welcome, for on each visit they brought knowledge and technology that advanced the infant civilisation, carrying it forward in ways and at a speed that would not have otherwise been possible.

49.

Kua'tzal drew in a long, slow breath as he gazed around the skull chamber. He was the last survivor of the Council of Elders, created by the Atlantean refugees, which had guided this land for so very many years. From the snow-white pedestals that surrounded him, only one of the original twelve clear crystal skulls looked back at him. The other eleven were human, glistening ivory; they belonged to his companions and fellow council members. On their deaths, their heads had been taken from their bodies, the flesh and brain ritually and lovingly removed and the empty bone vessel carefully and repeatedly washed until no trace of tissue remained. The skulls had then been preserved with resin and brought here to take their place in the skull chamber.

Kua'tzal sighed again. He was old and tired, ready now to leave this physical body that had served him so well over the six hundred or more years of his lifetime. He had done enough. Calista was already here. His place was by her side and he had been away from her too long. Soon his skull would join the others and he would watch over his cherished Maat-su for eternity.

The next day when they came to wake him, Kua'tzal had left his body. His frail, aged frame, now abandoned by life, resembled a child's lying on the bed, his final expression reflecting the joyful serenity of a life lived well and with love.

* * * * *

Within a moon's cycle a solemn procession left the
settlement for the temple. Kua'tzal had been a well-loved
and highly respected man, and the whole town had turned
out to honour his passage to the light world. In the distance
two huge pyramids loomed skyward; a third, almost
complete, stood alongside them. This was their
destination. Glassy black and imposing against the clear,
deep blue of the early afternoon sky, the capstones
gleamed in vivid contrast. Pure gold reflected the sunlight,
creating the impression of a halo that surrounded the
pyramids' upper heights.

It was a little after noon. Kua'tzal's purified skull was
on its way to the temple to be laid in its final resting place.
The ceremony and accompanying rituals had to be
completed before sunset, when the area would be cleared
and Kua'tzal left alone to make his solitary journey
through the darkness of the night to the light world
beyond.

The procession wound its way slowly towards the
second pyramid, the one to the left of the great Central
Gateway. This was where the entrance to the skull
chamber lay: a wide, exquisitely built passageway that
branched off the pyramid's main corridor. An intricate
mechanism built into its structure allowed a stone wall to
be raised and lowered, designed to seal the passageway
completely should danger threaten Maat-su and her
guardians. From the entrance, the corridor sloped gently
downwards under the ground, past the boundaries of the
second pyramid and across the open ground beyond to end
deep beneath the Central Gateway.

A group of unusual looking people were waiting for them at the entrance portal. These were the representatives of the star people who had helped in this huge project and brought the technology that had assisted in its construction. They had become firm friends with the people and with Kua'tzal. Their part in the project had ended some while ago; they had returned today especially to be present for the ceremony and to pay their final respects. No words were exchanged. None were needed. All recognised that they were sharing a deep grief at the loss of someone dear. In silence they entered the brightly lit passageway and made their way to the skull chamber.

Tomorrow the chamber would once again be open to all, allowing anyone who needed it free access to Maat-su and her guidance. Today however it was strictly controlled. First the temple elders entered, carrying Kua'tzal's skull on a soft cushion that was richly embroidered with gold thread. His closest descendants accompanied them, spreading out around the circumference of the room. To chants of blessing, the last remaining crystal skull was lifted off its pedestal and handed to his family. It was now theirs to care for. With great reverence Kua'tzal's own skull was set in its place, his empty gaze forever watching over Maat-su who sat in the centre of the circle. The ceremony was short but poignant; everyone there recognised that with Kua'tzal's death an era had come to an end. The work would go on. The legacy would continue. But the last of those few Atlanteans who had so long ago stepped bravely into the unknown had left them forever.

One by one, Kua'tzal's friends and family filed through the chamber, circling the now twelve human skulls on their pedestals. They had done this eleven times before, but this time was different. This time was the last. There were no more pedestals to fill, no more crystal skulls to be exchanged.

At the end of the line came the star travellers. They had brought a parting gift. As the last of the humans left, the star people spread out around the perimeter of the room, facing the walls. They lifted their right hands and a beam of blue light flowed from each palm. Slowly, concentrating, they swept the walls from waist height to ceiling, and where the beam passed, images formed on the stone. Not graven or painted, but in shimmering flowing gold. Liquid light. They formed images that related the story of Atlantis, and of Kua'tzal and his companions; of the skulls' desperate flight and the fate of that once great land. Others carried detailed information on the star people who had visited this place and many others like it, becoming friends and allies of the human men and women who lived there. And hidden amongst this, they shared the mystical symbols and language that would unlock the secret of the thirteen skulls. For one day, far in the future, one would come who would be able to read this language and understand its meaning. One who would bring it to the world again.

50.

As those who watched from the far reaches of the galaxy had feared, the Dark Ones' actions had wounded the Earth deeply, and her first agonised writhings would, over time, only grow more violent. The continent of Atlantis had effectively been ripped apart by the first seismic shock caused by the destruction of the Skull Chamber. For nearly a thousand years it clung to itself, barely holding itself together as the crust around it tottered and trembled. Until the day when, after another large tremor close by, the two tectonic plates that bisected the continent finally gave up on their struggle. They slipped, friction jarring the rock above and rupturing the final tenuous links. The southern lands of Atlantis, two thirds of the entire continent including the major cities of Yo'tlàn, Dendarak and Carn'gà, plunged into the sea.

If the aftermath of the Skull Chamber's destruction had been devastating, it was as nothing compared to the repercussions caused by this latest catastrophe. The shock of the collapsing landmass blasted the Earth into an unprecedented twenty degree shift on her axis, displaced her magnetic poles and knocked her entire energetic grid off balance. Tidal wave after tidal wave, each one hundreds of feet high, tore across the oceans, slamming into coastlines, submerging once high-lying lands. The Earth was suffering a potentially mortal blow. Could she recover or would she blast herself apart?

Far above Earth's atmosphere the star races were doing all they could to help, though it was painfully little. Earth would have to undergo her healing process; they could only watch and await the outcome. Would the measures that they had put in place in anticipation of this time be enough?

Earth's rebalancing was creating atmospheric and meteorological mayhem. Volcanoes belched their acrid ash high into the upper levels of the atmosphere, darkening the skies. Thick menacing clouds hid the sun for months and then years on end; endless rain poured down onto a desperate and sorrow-filled world. Floods ravaged the lands. Crops failed in the sodden soil. Cold, borne on winds howling in from the icy polar regions, scoured the Earth as earthquakes ripped her body apart.

The great edifices built for this purpose did indeed mitigate the worst effects of these consequences; nonetheless, life became a living hell for all who endured them. Their suffering was unimaginable. Once thriving populations were decimated by hunger, disease and cold. Whole communities were swept away and lost in raging flood waters that covered the land without respite. When at last it was over, few remained who remembered how it had begun.

In the land of the Great River only a handful survivors remained to carry forward the knowledge that had once been shared by so many. Those few guarded it jealously, all past openness swept away with the deluge. This once vibrant civilisation fell into a time of great darkness, its history and its visitors, as so often happens, passing into legend to be reborn as the stories of the great gods. As Osiris and Isis. Thoth and Anubis. And, of course, Maat.

Those who were strongest, most ruthless and ambitious, hungry to claim power in a world where it was theirs to take, thrived. Those who had been weakened, beaten and cowed by circumstances, did not fight it. Fear – of hunger, death, further loss – sent them to look outside of themselves for solutions and salvation rather than inwards to their own power, which is where those answers always lay. In the kingdom of the Great River this power was handed over to those who were prepared to take advantage of the suffering, claiming to be able to work miracles on the situation. Of course they didn't. They couldn't. But by then it was too late. They had been gifted the reins of authority and would not let them go. Over a very short number of years, this domination was concentrated downwards into the hands of an ever smaller group of people.

The star races who returned to the kingdom to help were quickly banished, painted as perpetrators of the devastation and therefore implacable enemies. Their technology was branded as sorcery and destroyed. All contact with them was forbidden, decreed as an act of treason and punishable by death. With heavy hearts the star visitors stopped coming, not wishing to be the cause of any further suffering.

Eventually, after many years and many generations had passed since those desperate times, power condensed into the hands of just one man, a god in human form, inviolable and unquestioned. Only he, the equal of those ancient gods, was worthy of holding the sacred knowledge. That man was Pharaoh.

Maat-su still rested in the skull chamber, watched over by the remains of those who had brought her here. She was consulted constantly for her guidance, but whereas in happier times she had been available to all who sought wisdom, now she was accessible to Pharaoh alone. In time, even the most trusted of high priests was forbidden from entering her presence.

Successive rulers sought her counsel and used it to rebuild their once ravaged kingdom into a vast and wealthy civilisation. Over time, any knowledge of her origins were lost to all but a small band who kept it alive, in secret and at risk of their lives. Most, including the king himself, no longer knew or cared where she had come from or why. To Pharaoh she was simply the voice of all wisdom, the rock that held him in power, ever present. She was a powerful symbol, an embodiment of the gods, and his spiritual consort. When his time came, she would travel with him in the afterlife to the world beyond the stars where he would rule eternally.

As the power wielded by the dynasties of Pharaohs grew stronger, expressions of past loyalties were gradually erased. The gold capstones on the pyramids were removed, melted down and fashioned into objects of beauty and pleasure. Every physical link to past knowledge was destroyed or mutilated beyond recognition. Even the obsidian cladding of the pyramids was torn down and dumped far out to sea so that the few who did remember – those rebels who held firm to the old ways – could not recover it. It was replaced with polished white limestone to

279

express the purity of Pharaoh's soul, and so became a monument to that omnipotent god in human form. The god who came to Earth.

GEMMA, 6

51.

I frowned. Whose car was that parked in my driveway? I didn't recognise it at all. After Callum's warnings, both before I had left Arizona and only a couple of weeks previously when I had met up with him in Bath, and today's encounter with Mr Shiny Shoes, which had shaken me more than I was prepared to admit even to myself, my nerves were beginning to jangle. I hesitated before pulling up beside it.

Joe? He was sitting on the low wall that bordered the flower bed in front of my cottage. What was he doing here? And what was it with the car? He didn't own a car… My mental meanderings froze abruptly as I caught sight of his face. He was ashen. As soon as I got out of my car, he leapt up and hugged me.

'Gemma. Oh thank God. When you weren't here…'

'What on earth is wrong?' This was strong, dependable, always-got-it-together Joe. Only right at this moment he was anything but. 'I was at my book signing, and afterwards Cathy and I went for coffee and cake to celebrate. Once we started talking, we lost track of the time like we always do. You were going to come along too, remember?'

Joe nodded, sinking back down onto the wall, his strange panic lessening just a touch. 'Yes, of course. I do remember now. But with… Sorry, Gemma. I forgot.'

'Joe, what is it? You look dreadful. What's going on?' I dragged him to his feet and into the house, shoved him down on the sofa and poured him a big glass of red wine. OK, I know it should have been whisky, or brandy or something, like it always is in the movies, but I don't drink spirits so red wine was the strongest form of alcohol I had in the house. It would have to do.

Joe drained the wine and held the glass out for a refill. I duly obliged. He swallowed that back too, then took a deep breath.

'You're scaring me, Joe. What's wrong? What's happened?'

He looked up, steadier now. 'It's Callum.'

My heart pounded. 'What about Callum?' I managed to keep my voice level.

'He's disappeared. No-one knows where he is. I can't find out anything.'

I let out a long, slow breath. 'That's what's got you into such a state? No, Joe. That wouldn't shake you up like this. Callum has a habit of taking off unexpectedly without telling anyone where he is going. You know that. There's more to it. What haven't you told me yet?' Whatever it was, it had to be serious. I had never seen Joe like this in all the years I'd known him. 'What do you mean by disappeared?'

'Vanished. Run away. Gone into hiding. Or even dead, maybe.'

'Oh come on.' Joe was being a bit overdramatic. Wasn't he? But Joe didn't do overdramatic. If he was saying this, he had good reason.

I took a deep breath, not sure what would come next. 'Tell me.'

'It's all extremely muddled. And horrific. Because you'd been out on that expedition with him, and because of what went on there, I was terrified that something had happened to you too. So I borrowed Duncan's car and raced down here to check you were alright. In everything that was going on I clean forgot about your book signing, so when you weren't here...' He slumped back in the sofa, completely drained. His strained eyes met mine. 'I thought they'd got to you too.'

'Who?' I was utterly confused. 'You thought who had got to me?'

'Oh, I don't know.' He buried his head in his hands as if its weight was too much to carry any more. 'Whoever set Callum up.'

I stood in front of him and grabbed his upper arms so firmly that he lifted his head to look at me. 'Joe, will you please tell me what the hell you are going on about. I thought you said Callum had disappeared. Now you tell me someone is after him? Has set him up?'

'He has. They are... have. Oh God, I don't know.' He pulled his thoughts together. 'He may be lying low, but there is a real possibility that he has been kidnapped or murdered.'

I sat down heavily beside Joe, his words sinking in slowly, and stared at him. 'You're telling me that Callum's disappearance might be more than one of his usual taking-off-without-a-word adventures? He might have been kidnapped? Killed? Come on. Why would anybody really be after Callum?' I held up my hand. 'OK, I know what he told me. Even so, it's too far-fetched. He doesn't know anything. Or at least he didn't when I saw him in town a couple of weeks ago.'

I stopped. Was it really so far-fetched? In the 'real' world, maybe, but since I'd started work on the skull stories, far-fetched had become normal, and I had learned what lengths some people would go to in order to get their hands on, or conversely protect these skulls. There was the attack on the university in Norway, and the deaths of Olina Gjerde and Dr Mackintosh. Not to mention the frightening vision of Callum I'd seen while I was sitting in the park... I changed tack.

'You haven't told me what happened yet. Has Callum been involved in some sort of trouble?'

'Big time. They found a dead body in his hotel room. A woman. Hacked to death. I'll spare you the gory details but the descriptions of the crime scene coming off the police reports are decidedly unpleasant to say the least.' He answered my raised eyebrows and unspoken question. 'I found out, OK? Duncan isn't just a font of knowledge on the crystal skulls. His day job is as a computer programmer and he runs an extremely lucrative side-line in high level hacking. When I heard Callum's name mentioned in the initial news report, which was pretty sketchy, I asked him to access the Met's network and pull me up any information and early reports.'

'But why do they think Callum had anything to do with it? He must be able to prove otherwise.'

'There's been no sign of Callum, and his passport and wallet weren't in the room. They did find some of his clothes though, in a plastic bin bag stuffed into one of the hotel dustbins. Soaked in her blood.'

'No.' I couldn't believe what I was hearing. Callum may have been many things, not all of them endearing as I had found out, and if provoked enough, yes, I could see him being tipped over the edge. Certainly Jack had pushed him close on a couple of occasions. As we all could, I suppose, in the right circumstances. But a cold-blooded butcher? No.

'I'm with you on that, Gemma.' Joe was reading my thoughts. 'If we take Callum's innocence as read though, there are a lot of unanswered questions hanging around. Was it just unfortunate coincidence? Wrong time, wrong place? He walked in on the carnage and ran?'

I shook my head. 'No. If that was the case, why bother with his clothes?'

'I agree, in which case who did murder the woman, and why frame Callum? What would the killer get out of it? I suppose it's possible that Callum was simply unlucky, picked out at random as a fall guy, but I don't buy into that.'

I shook my head again. 'Me neither. If we assume Callum has been deliberately set up for this murder, then we have a shedload of possibilities to consider. Like, maybe the real killers wanted him to run for some reason. To keep him so busy saving his own skin that he'd have no time to be any further nuisance to them? Seems a bit complicated though. If they wanted him out of the way, why not just get rid of him? They're clearly not squeamish about that sort of thing.'

'Unless they were planning to. Set it up so that it looked like he'd murdered the woman and then killed himself, only something went wrong. That way, he'd be dead, and discredited as well. No-one would want to touch his work with a barge pole.' Joe sighed. 'Honestly, Gemma? I haven't a clue. He could just have legged it and be keeping his head down while he works out what to do. He could be dead already. And there's still the possibility that he has been kidnapped.'

'Why kidnap him?'

'To find out exactly what he knows. Maybe he was closer to his answers than he realised. Now you understand why I was in such a panic? If they have got to him, you could be next.'

Shivers were running through me so fiercely that I was trembling. 'He must have known, or at least suspected, they were coming after him. That's why he warned me. He tried to make light of it, but it was obvious he was a lot more worried that he was letting on.'

This was crazy. Life had become a bit unreal over the last couple of years since I had become drawn into the world of the crystal skulls (and that was an understatement). This latest situation had suddenly tipped it back into being frighteningly real. Yet at the same time, there was the distinct feeling that I'd just walked onto the set of some Hollywood conspiracy movie. I turned to Joe anxiously.

'I think they are watching me too.' I related the whole episode of Mr Shiny Shoes that had taken place earlier that day. 'I'm sure I convinced him I'm just an eccentric author with a vivid imagination.' I wasn't feeling as confident of that any more. 'At least, I hope so.'

'You won't be putting the Arizona expedition into any of the books, will you?'

I shook my head vigorously. 'No. I write the stories that are shown to me, no more. Real life events have nothing to do with them.'

'That's good. The fewer people who know you were part of that, the better. You didn't mention it to Mr Shiny Shoes? Brinkman?'

'Absolutely not. In fact, I was careful to keep all mention of Callum out of our conversation.' Another thought struck me. 'Frankie and Davey. Might they be in danger? They know so much about Callum's work. And there's Ches too.'

'It depends why these people want Callum. If it's for his research information, then yes, possibly. If it's because he's been poking his nose in where it's not wanted, then I doubt it. It would be wise to give them the heads up in any case, just so they can be on their guard. Can you get hold of them?'

'I've got Frankie's email address.' I rose to fetch my laptop but Joe laid a hand on my arm, holding me back.

'No, don't use your own computer or your email address. If they are watching you, they may have already hacked into it and they'll see you are suspicious. Go to the library tomorrow, create a new email account with a new provider – don't use your real details, make something up – and send it from there. It'll make it hard for them to trace.'

I stared at Joe. 'Can they really do that?'

He shrugged. 'I don't know. If they are serious then yes, they probably could. Better safe than sorry anyway. Meanwhile I'll keep an eye on the police investigation and see what turns up.'

I was still finding it hard to take it all in. After my initial panicky reaction, fed by Joe's unaccustomed disarray, I was questioning the sanity of it all. 'Do you really believe all this, Joe?'

He slumped back on the sofa. 'I don't know. All of a sudden the world has got even crazier than usual. Maybe I am reading more into this than it warrants, but my gut is telling me I'm right to be worried. The murder is real enough.'

I sank deeper into the security of the sofa cushions, my head full of questions that couldn't be answered. What was all this about? What should we do? Should we do anything at all? The whole situation could simply be a huge misunderstanding. Maybe – and here my reason rebelled mercilessly – just maybe Callum was guilty... No, I could never believe that. Volatile and unpredictable he might be. A cold-blooded murderer? Never. OK, let's look at the other options rationally. If, for argument's sake, Joe's intuition was right (and to be honest, mine was in total agreement), what then?

'Oh.' I flicked my eyes across to Joe. 'If they are keeping an eye on me, won't they be on to you as well?'

He considered for a moment. 'It's possible, though there isn't anything to link me to any of the skulls.' His face darkened. 'Not that it'll make a difference if they get it into their heads that I do.' He fell quiet again for a moment. 'Do you really believe you managed to convince Mr Shiny Shoes that you are nothing but an author with a big imagination?'

'I'm sure of it. I told him the book was inspired by the skulls I'd seen in the shop at Avebury and that I simply let my imagination take it from there. Joe, do you really believe this is about the skulls? Couldn't Callum have got himself mixed up in another situation entirely? One that has nothing to do with any of us? His taste for adventure... He's reckless enough, isn't he?'

'Yes, maybe.' Joe wasn't convinced. Several minutes passed without either of us speaking as we brooded over the possibilities.

52.

The phone rang. I was so on edge that its shrill tone tearing through the quiet room nearly sent me into orbit. I stared at Joe, my nerves in overdrive, until it stopped.

Oh, this was ridiculous. I wasn't going to let myself get turned into a nervous wreck by wild speculation. I didn't believe Callum was guilty of murder; there had to be a reasonable explanation for his disappearance. Maybe he just walked in on the carnage, got scared and ran. That would be rational. As for Mr Shiny Shoes, his curiosity and out of place clothes didn't mean anything. Different did not mean bad. Might not my novelist's rampant creativity be building an innocuous situation up into something bigger and more sinister? As far as anyone who read my books was concerned, and that included my publisher, I was a writer of adventure fantasy books, like so many others. Anything else would be inconceivable.

I was using common sense and logic to quell my intuitive knowing, and it was working. I felt myself slowly setting back down into my body, calm spreading through my cells as they took control, pushing out the tension. Joe immediately picked up the shift in me.

'No, Joe. I'm not going to buy into this. I can't. It's too absurd. I don't know what's going on with Callum but there has to be a logical explanation. Everything we're tying ourselves up in knots over is either circumstantial or incidental. We're making mountains out of molehills.' The old head-in-the-sand Gemma was putting in an appearance again.

Joe had opened his mouth to reply when the phone rang again, loudly and urgently. Avoiding the hand he stretched out to stop me, I walked over and picked up the receiver. 'Hello?'

'Gemma?' There was audible relief at the other end of the line as Callum heard my voice.

'Callum?' My eyes flew to Joe in astonishment. I pressed the loudspeaker button so he could listen in too. 'Where the hell are you? What's going on?'

'Fucked if I know!' He sounded angry, scared, and sick to his stomach. 'You've heard?'

'The woman in your hotel room? Yes, Joe's just told me. Who was she? What happened?'

'I have no idea who she was. I didn't recognise her. Then again,' he was clearly fighting to retain his self-control, 'there wasn't much left to recognise.' A long wait. 'Since I met you for lunch – when was that, two weeks ago? – I've been travelling around, meeting up with a few people who might be able to give me a bit of information on the two guys who put up the funding for our expedition. Didn't get very far, mind you. Anyway, I headed back to London on Tuesday. When was that? Three days ago?'

'Four.'

'Well, whatever. Yesterday afternoon I had an appointment at the British Museum to take another look at the crystal skull they've got there. I didn't leave until about nine in the evening and stopped for a bite on the way back so I didn't get to my room until just after eleven. I wish I hadn't.' Another long wait. I could hear him drawing in a laboured, nauseated breath.

'Jesus, Gemma, it was grim. The poor woman was spread-eagled naked on the bed and there was blood everywhere. Everywhere!' Callum repeated, his voice rising dangerously before he succeeded in pulling himself together. 'She had been beaten to a pulp and then stabbed. Or stabbed first and then beaten. How the hell would I know? I was scared and I ran. Yes, it was a fucking stupid thing to do. I should have called the police straight away. But I wasn't exactly thinking clearly.'

'Go to them now. Explain. They'll understand why you panicked.'

'With a bagful of my clothes soaked in her blood in their hands? I have no way of explaining that.'

'You're innocent. Surely you must be able to prove that through a DNA test or what have you?'

'Whoever these people are, they're thorough. They'll have it all covered. Be careful, Gemma. I'm worried about you. When I couldn't get you on your mobile...' My mobile, still at the bottom of my shoulder bag on the kitchen table, where I had dumped it when I'd ushered in the ashen-faced Joe. I hadn't heard it ring. 'Whoever set me up for this wasn't playing games. I'm going to lie low for a while and do some serious digging into the whos and whys.'

'Any ideas?' Joe spoke for the first time.

'Joe? I didn't realise you were there. I'm glad you are. Yes, I have a few possible leads. Nothing solid yet, it's all so insubstantial, but all the indications are leading towards something frighteningly big and powerful. That's all I'm

293

going to say for now. The less you know about it, the safer you'll be. Look after Gemma for me, Joe.'

'Be careful, Callum.' My words drifted into empty space. He had already hung up. I dropped onto a chair and glanced across at Joe. 'Well, at least we know he's not dead or kidnapped. What do you make of it?'

Joe looked like he had a barrelful of questions he wanted to ask me about my relationship with Callum. He didn't. Instead he let his mind turn everything Callum had told us. 'I'm feeling a lot happier now we've actually spoken to Callum,' he said. 'If he'd believed you were in any real, immediate danger he would have said so and told you to make yourself scarce. Now we've heard his side of the story the picture has become clearer. Everything was OK until he started stirring up the wasps' nest. I think Mr Shiny Shoes was sounding you out to see what you know and whether you are involved with Callum's current activities. As long as you stay well out of it, you should be safe. Still, I'd feel happier if I could stay here tonight Gemma, if that's OK with you?'

'Of course you can. I'll appreciate having you in the house after all that's gone on today.' Joe stayed often, usually when we had demolished a bottle or so of wine as we talked the evening away. The spare bed was always made up for him. That evening was no different, except that this time the conversation was more solemn and muted than usual, its sole topic the events that had just unfolded and our speculations on where they might lead. 'Head-in-the-sand Gemma' had been sent well and truly on her way. Callum's phone call had dispelled all illusion that this was just a simple case of 'wrong place, wrong time'.

Much later, as I snuggled down under the bedclothes, all the fears I had set aside flooded back with the darkness. I was extremely grateful for Joe's comforting presence in the next room.

MAAT-SU: The Lapis Skull

PART 3

THE WELL

53.

Long ago, in the land where the pharaohs ruled, a young boy stumbled on a secret. A secret that had been kept for many lifetimes and was now known only to two of the most powerful people in the kingdom: Pharaoh himself and his high priest Hotepi.

The name of this young boy was Lokar and he had just passed the tenth anniversary of his birth. He lived with his family amongst the lush pasturelands, gardens and wooded banks of the Great River from which all life flowed. He often played here in the cool shade of the green branches and soft, sandy earth.

* * * * *

This day he was playing hide and seek with his sister, looking for ever more concealed hiding places where he could escape discovery and spend time alone and quiet with his thoughts and his friends. These friends were not of the flesh and blood kind. Not the same friends he ran and laughed and played with all through these fields and waterways. The friends he spent time with when he was alone were grown up. Wiser and gentler. Friends who simply listened – to his fears and sadnesses, and to his joys and excitement.

As Nekhtari hid her eyes and counted to one hundred, he ran off as quickly as his legs could carry him.

'Coming, ready or not.' He heard her laughing voice as he skirted the bushes that encircled a small, clear pool. Where could he hide? She would be on his trail by now; he would have to find somewhere soon or she would catch him. She could not win this time. She always seemed to find him as easily as if he had left a signpost behind him. No, not this time. He would not lose again to face the teasing of his friends as she recounted her victory. There had to be somewhere she would not even think to look. Somewhere so hidden she would never find it. Where though? There was nowhere here. He could have pushed into the middle of a thick shrub, getting scratched and bloodied in the process, but it wouldn't be good enough. Nekhtari would know to look in those places.

What about…? Lokar's heart pounded in fear as he considered it, even as his head told him it was the perfect place. Somewhere Nekhtari would never look. She would never think he would be brave – or foolish – enough to hide there. Swallowing hard, his pride and desire for a rare victory stronger than his dread, he made up his mind and headed towards it.

The young boy's objective was a now-dry well in the middle of a nearby field. It was not large, surrounded by waist-high stone-built walls as a safeguard against any unwary wanderer stumbling into it. Lokar crouched in the cool shade of its walls and looked around. Nekhtari was nowhere in sight.

He glanced up. Here the trees grew tall and strong. Behind them, towering into the sky and dwarfing them in its shadow, stood a massive stone pyramid. It was the centre one of three that dominated the landscape and partnered the nearby huge stone statue that bore the likeness of a long-dead Pharaoh. The pyramid glistened like an iceberg in the shimmering heat of the mid-afternoon sun, its white limestone façade dazzling in the fierce rays. All three of the pyramids were clad in the same white stone, although he had heard stories that it had not always been the case. That far in the distant past, when they had first been built by hands unknown, they had been clad in glass-like black obsidian, a covering that had long since disappeared. It was even whispered that at its highest level, at the point where the stone kissed the sky, its apex had once been made of pure gold, set with a diamond the size of a man's fist, in honour of the sun god who brought life to everything on Earth.

Although he had grown up in the shadow of these vast structures, Lokar never tired of them. Every time he looked at them, he was filled with a sense of awe and wonder and reverence. There was something magical, something otherworldly, about the pyramids, as if they had been planted here by some giant hand.

'Lokar, I'm coming to get you.' Nekhtari's teasing call roused him from his thoughts. 'You can't hide from me. You know I'm going to find you.'

'Oh no you're not,' Lokar muttered under his breath. His fear was instantly forgotten in his determination to remain undiscovered and to win the game today. He clambered over the low wall and seized the rope to which the bucket had once been tied, tugging hard on it to test its strength. It was sound. It would hold. As quickly as he could, taking care not to slip, Lokar lowered himself hand over hand until he was out of the sunlight that filled the top few feet of the shaft and hidden in the darkness below. He risked a brief glance downwards, wishing immediately that he hadn't. Below him he could see nothing. The shaft plunged downwards into a black void that could have gone on without end, one that would carry him into a stygian oblivion should he fall. Shaking with fear, Lokar gripped the rope more tightly in his hands, his legs twisted around it, pinning it between his feet.

He soon realised his folly. Within a few short minutes, his arms and legs began to ache with the strain of holding onto the rope and its rough fibre scoured the skin from the palms of his hands. He would not be able to stay here much longer. No. Lokar gritted his teeth. He would hold on as long as necessary. Nekhtari would not best him this time. Though Lokar loved his older sister dearly, he was becoming frustrated at always coming off second best to her, and having to listen to her bragging. This time would be different. This time he would show her.

54.

Where was she? The seconds ticked past and he did not hear her pass by. Turned into minutes. Still no sign of her. His hands started to slip and fear touched him more deeply. Gritting his teeth against the pain in his grazed hands, Lokar held on more tightly and gripped more firmly with his legs and feet, but they too were beginning to tire.

He would have to climb out. If he did not go now, he would not have the strength left to haul himself up and over the wall. He was mortified at the thought of losing to Nekhtari yet again, but wise enough, even in his young years, to understand that it would be only a defeat, while to stubbornly remain here would inevitably result in his death.

Lokar had badly misjudged the strain on his arms, however, and they refused to obey his command to pull him up. They did not have the strength left to do so. It was all he could do to retain his grip on the rope. Suddenly his feet slipped and he found himself dangling over the black void, held only by his exhausted arms. His muscles were at breaking point, his legs and feet flailing, scrabbling for a hold.

The movement caused the rope to swing like a pendulum. Somehow, and he did not know how, Lokar held on to the rope, but he could feel his hands slipping more with every swing. He bumped from one side of the narrow well to the other, clinging in desperation to the rope with every last ounce of strength he could call on. On what was perhaps the fifth swing, his foot caught in something protruding from the wall; he allowed his weight to rest on it, easing the strain in his upper body. A wave of relief washed through him as it held. He was still far from safe. Nonetheless it was a respite that hadn't come a moment too soon. As he let out a long breath, Lokar felt a second protuberance nudging into him at chest level, cold against his bare skin. It didn't feel like stone. Taking his weight fully on one foot, he allowed the other to explore its rest, whose detail he had up to now ignored.

The rung of a ladder? It certainly felt like it. But why a ladder, here, in the side of an old, disused well? He was certain nothing like this had existed further up the shaft. He would surely have spotted it. Who would build a ladder into the walls of a well but not take it to the top? Then the thought: if it was a ladder, could whatever was pressing into his chest be another rung? Steadying himself, taking all his weight on his feet and clinging to the rope with just one hand, he allowed the other to reach across his body. It certainly felt like a rung. It was cold, rough, and he could clasp his hand around it. He tugged gently. It seemed solid enough. If it was indeed a ladder, there would be more of these. Cautiously he reached up a little. Yes, there was another. Reached down to below his waist. Another there too. Again questions assailed him. Why was it here? More interestingly, where did it lead?

Common sense told Lokar that now he had found an escape route he should climb back up and not risk his luck any more. But curiosity has a powerful pull, and the young boy fell under its spell, pushing him to explore further. He looped the rope around one of the rungs so that he could retrieve it later – he would need it for the last few feet of the climb – and slowly began to clamber deeper down into the well. Soon he was total darkness, the rim of the well a small bright circle far above his head. He had to feel for each rung, searching around for it with his toes, not knowing how far he had left to go, or whether they would simply peter out to nothing. Neither could he know how far down he had come and would have to return.

Slowly, laboriously, unable to see even his hands in front of him, Lokar climbed on down. And down…

55.

Lokar sat up slowly, shaking the fuzziness from his head, tentatively feeling his arms and legs. They seemed as they should be. He tried moving. Yes, that worked too. He remained still for a moment, catching his breath where it had been knocked from his body, piecing together the last few seconds.

A foot on a rung, reaching for the next... And then he had been falling through the blackness, surrounded by an unearthly scream. His scream.

He remembered. The rung had given way as his full weight sank onto it. He had been transferring his hands from one rung to the next at that same moment; unbalanced and unable to save himself, he had plunged downwards. It was a miracle that he was unharmed. Surely he could not have fallen far? He felt around. The floor beneath him was soft and spongy. Over the years, leaves and other vegetation had fallen in on top of the silt from the well, forming a soft cushion of composted leaf mould. Lokar had fallen onto a natural mattress. He had been lucky, and he knew it.

Enough of pushing his good fortune. It was time to climb back up and get out of here. If he could. If the rungs came all the way to the bottom of the shaft. He would not be so careless from now on. This time he would not take them for granted the way he had on his way down, would test each one before trusting it with his life.

Standing cautiously, he blindly groped around for the first rung. Please the gods that it was here, that it wouldn't be too high for him to reach. No, there it was, just above his head. Lokar let out his breath. He had been holding it without realising. He was eager now to get out of this pitch dark hellhole and back into the sunlight. He no longer cared whether he won or lost the game, only that he would soon be out of here and breathing fresh, clean air.

* * * * *

Lokar stretched up to the first rung of the ladder, wrapping his hands firmly around its rough surface. His shoulder muscles were still tired and protested at his movement, but they had regained enough of their strength to allow the boy to pull himself up and reach for the next, and the next. His feet touched the bottom rung, taking his weight once more, easing the strain. He would be cautious, test the solidity of every hand- and foot-hold, but the hardest part must surely now be behind him. Though the long haul to the surface would be an effort, it would be nothing compared to what he had already gone through.

Lokar began to climb. One hand, one foot. One hand, one foot. Testing. Moving. Testing. Moving. It was slow but steady progress.

He paused, breathing hard, allowing himself to rest for a moment. Looking up, he could just make out the circular rim of the well far above, the sky beyond now velvety black and sprinkled with stars. A crescent moon was just peeking over the stone edge. It was well into the night. His parents would have the whole village out searching for him, beside themselves with worry that he had not

306

returned home. While this was a lush and fertile land, it was not without many dangers. Giant crocodiles cruised the Great River, seizing those foolish or unwary enough to wander blindly too close to the water's edge. Venomous snakes and scorpions basked on the sun-baked ground or sheltered beneath stones and fallen leaves so that a misplaced step could result in a fatal encounter. Guilt-stricken at the thought of his parents' concern, Lokar put aside the grumbles of his weary, aching limbs and began to climb once more.

56.

Lokar halted with a jolt of surprise and fright. Something had brushed against his face. A bat? Surely not a bird this far down? A ghost? Lokar's blood ran cold. Had he disturbed some vengeful spirits or demons in his intrusion of this place? He waited without moving to see what would happen next. Nothing. But as he moved once more, it came again. He put his hand up to his cheek where he had felt the touch. There was nothing there. The sensation had moved to his hand...

Then he realised. It hadn't been a creature at all, not even one from the spirit world. A light but steady draught was blowing directly out of the well wall. As he had moved his head had entered its path.

A draught? How was that possible? Lokar tentatively reached out his hand, wary of any unpleasant crawling creatures that might inhabit a dank, dark place such as this. His fingers came into contact with slimy, icy damp stone. He shuddered but did not take his hand away, feeling slowly across its surface until... The wall had vanished, his fingertips stretching out into empty space. He explored further, blind in the well's blackness, his only guide the touch of his fingers, stepping up to the next rung in an attempt to gauge the opening's height. Leaning precariously from the ladder to search for the other side.

The gap was perhaps as high as from his feet to his shoulder, the base flat and the edges of the curved upper section smooth as if it was worked stone. It didn't feel like the naturally irregular entrance of a cave. A tunnel maybe? Lokar could not understand why anyone would have built a tunnel to come out half way up the side of well shaft. Someone had though. If he could feel a draught, didn't that mean that there had to be an opening at the other end too? Wherever that might be.

Lokar forgot about his parents. Forgot about their worry. Forgot his tiredness, his aching muscles, and the hunger that was rumbling in his belly. Once more his acute curiosity got the better of him and his common sense. He did not stop to consider the folly of heading blindly into a pitch dark passageway carved through the depths of the earth with no idea of where it would take him. Of the possibility that he could lose his way completely and never find his way out again. Instead, his heart racing in excitement at what he might find, he dangled precariously by one hand from the rung, stretched across until his knee was on the floor of the low passageway, launched himself across and tumbled in.

He could see nothing, not even his hand when he held it with his palm no more than an inch or so in front of his nose. The blackness was total, thicker even, if that was possible, than it had been out in the well shaft. It wrapped around him like a cold, impenetrable shroud, claustrophobic and menacing. The gods and spirits who guarded this place were clearly not pleased at Lokar's trespassing, though they did not stop him. In spite of the goosebumps that rippled in waves down his body, and the icy chill that had settled at the base of his spine, Lokar did not think of turning back. He had felt someone at his shoulder, a comforting and familiar presence. His friends were with him, and they were protecting him. He wished they would speak to him, as they so often did, but this time it was not to be. They remained silent. It did not matter. Simply knowing that they were there was enough, and gave Lokar the courage to go on.

*　*　*　*　*

Progress was at a snail's pace. He could see neither the floor nor the walls. After several painful stumbles, and a couple of even more painful knocks to the head where he had walked unseeing into the wall, Lokar was now inching his way along the side of the passageway. He stooped, as the roof was not much higher than even his boy's height, his right hand always in contact with the stone of the wall keeping him at a constant distance, the other stretched out in front of him in case any object reared up in his path. At each step he tested the ground under his foot before he put his weight on it for he had heard terrifying stories of the traps built by the Pharaoh's architects to deter thieves and trespassers. He did not wish to fall victim to one of these deadly defences. He found none. Whoever had built this passageway had either not expected anyone to find it and enter this way, or was of an altogether more benevolent spirit than Pharaoh and his servants.

57.

Suddenly, unexpectedly, Lokar's outstretched fingers bumped into stone. The tunnel had come to an end. He felt around. The barrier reached from one side of the passageway to the other, blocking it completely. A dead end? It couldn't be, not now. Not when he had come so far. But it was. There was no way around it. As if the men that had carved out this tunnel had just stopped. Gone no further.

Lokar sank to the floor, disappointment coursing through his body. He had come all this way, risked his life in the darkness, only to be brought to this abrupt and definitive halt. The thought of retracing his steps did not fill him with enthusiasm, and all the exhaustion that the excitement of a possible discovery had kept at bay returned pitilessly. It didn't make sense. This couldn't be the end of his journey.

It wasn't. As he sat there, an idea trickled into his mind. The draught. It was still there. He could feel it tickling his hair. And if the draught was still there, it had to be coming from somewhere. There had to be an opening of some kind. Reinvigorated, the boy scrambled back to his feet, sought out once more with his hands the source of the air that blew past him, feeling for its direction on his skin.

There. Somewhere above his head. That's where it was coming from. He lifted his arms above his head; the tunnel roof had disappeared. Or at least it was now so far above him he could no longer touch it.

Lokar's fingertips crept across the wall in front of him, searching for another opening. Creeping, seeking, upwards, upwards. Aha. That was it. His fingers had hooked over the lip of another ledge. It was high. Would he be able to get up to it? He had to. He had not come this far only to give up now. At full stretch he could just place his palms flat on the ledge. He could do this. He could.

Lokar took a deep breath and concentrated, bent his knees and sprang, pushing himself up with his palms, his feet scrabbling for purchase on the smooth stone of the wall. He fought to retain his balance and his strength, for some moments uncertain whether he was going to succeed or fail. Finding one toe hold, then another. Hauling himself up over the rim to slump, drained and breathing heavily, on the ledge above the tunnel.

* * * * *

Where did this new passageway lead? Was there a way out at the end or would he have to retrace his steps after all to climb the ladder up the sheer wall of the well?

It took Lokar several moments before he noticed that the blackness in front of him was not quite as dense as it had been in the tunnel he had just left. He could just make out the faint outline of a long, low slit that ran the length of the ledge on which he was lying. It was barely discernible, but it was there. He reached up. The roof here was not much more than one of his ten-year old arm's lengths above him and the virtually imperceptible paler area reached halfway to this ceiling. Rolling onto his stomach, pulling himself carefully to his hands and knees, keeping his head low, he crawled towards it. The air was

312

blowing more strongly here. It had to be his way out; where did it lead?

Lokar wriggled up and through on his stomach, and clambered cautiously to his feet. The blackness that still cloaked him may not have been quite so thick, but it was still dense enough that he could see nothing of the place in which he stood. Was he in another tunnel, or had he come out into a room of some kind? Not wishing to crash his head again, he felt around. He could stand easily; reaching out around himself in all directions, his outstretched arms met only with empty space. Though he was still as good as blind, this place had lost the dank, claustrophobic atmosphere of the cramped confines he had just left behind.

He took a step backwards, feeling the wall above the opening he had just squirmed through. It was smooth, very smooth. Definitely not a natural surface. It was too flat and flawless beneath his probing fingers, which found and traced the straight lines of the joints between the blocks.

Arms straight out in front of him, Lokar walked forward carefully until he reached the opposite wall. Twenty paces. This was a huge passageway. The floor beneath his feet was as smooth as the walls, smoother even, polished and worn by many generations of feet. It was on a gentle incline. To his right, where it sloped upwards, all Lokar could see was black. Dense deep black. When he turned to look to the left, however, he could see a faint glimmer of light far off in the distance. The darkness in that direction was less total, the corridor descending gently down towards it. That was the way he would go.

As he drew nearer, little by little the black shroud around him loosened and he could begin to make out vague details of the corridor he was walking through. The walls were smooth, pale stone, devoid of decoration but skilfully and beautifully crafted, and his curious fingers told him that the joints between the blocks were so fine and perfect that it would have been hard to fit a human hair between them.

58.

Lokar hesitated. He had reached what looked like a small ante-chamber at the end of the corridor. The light was filtering out from a room beyond. What if someone was in there? He could hear no sound; holding his breath and tiptoeing into the first small room, he approached the doorway and peered inside.

After the gloom of the corridor, he was momentarily dazzled by the light shining within. As his eyes adjusted and the interior came into focus, he caught his breath in amazement. Where was he? What was this place?

He was looking into another chamber, not large, perhaps fifteen paces square, lit by over a hundred small lamps. Their light fluttered and danced over the walls, bringing to life the images they carried. It was these walls and these images that stole his attention, drawing him to them as a moth is drawn to a flame. He was aware of nothing else.

Strange and wonderful figures, unlike anything he had ever seen before, danced in the flickering glow. These were not the brightly hued hieroglyphs he was used to seeing in the temples and monuments of the Great City, nor the colourful stylised murals that likewise adorned them. These walls bore depictions of unusual looking men and women with long flowing hair and long flowing robes, so lifelike that Lokar would not have been surprised if they had stepped off the wall and into the room. Around them were pictured outlandish objects of a design and complexity that were beyond the boy's comprehension, their purpose indecipherable.

Lokar walked slowly around the perimeter of the chamber as if in a trance, seeing nothing but the images. More figures – giants who towered above all the others, and small, delicate people from whose bodies beams of light streamed as if from the great sun god himself. Over it all flowed mystical, magical symbols, the like of which he had never encountered. Diagrams of stars, constellations. Each line glittered with fire as if drawn in liquid light. And everywhere, the heady scent of incense, overpowering and intoxicating.

It was much later that Lokar finally dragged his attention away from the walls and turned to investigate the centre of the chamber. His eyes fell on the objects it held and he leapt back in alarm, stifling a cry of fear. He was staring face to face at the blank gaze of a human skull, its flesh long since vanished. He forced himself to take a step back and look around. More skulls watched him back, twelve in all. He sensed rather than saw that their empty eyes were all upon him. He stood frozen, knowing that the spirits of whoever had once inhabited them remained here, locked in this place, and were even now questioning the presence and purpose of this intruder in their midst.

* * * * *

The skulls were arranged in a circle, each set on a square plinth that stood as tall as the boy's shoulder, bringing them level with his face. He could not avoid looking at them and sensing their penetrating, if long dead, enquiry.

In the centre of this circle stood another plinth, also of opaque, pure white stone. On this thirteenth plinth was set another skull. This one, alone of them all, was not of human origin. It was exquisitely carved from the deepest, richest blue lapis lazuli, scattered with star-like golden flakes through which a vein of creamy white brushed across the dome of its crown. It reminded Lokar of the river of stars that streamed across the sphere of the heavens at nightfall.

This skull bewitched and captivated the young boy. Who had carved such a beautiful object? Why was it here? No longer caring about the macabre display of human skulls that surrounded him, Lokar found himself stepping forward, his hands reaching out towards the blue skull.

'No!' The words rang out in his head and Lokar stopped at their forcefulness, unable to disobey. 'You will not touch. You must not.' He recognised the voices of his friends. 'It is not for you to understand the power and purpose of this place.

'One day, in times yet to be, you may be called to return. For now it is enough that you have come here. You must leave, now, and quickly. Others will arrive here soon. You must not be discovered here. Come, little one. Leave now.'

Lokar understood that he should go, that he was trespassing in a sacred area and that the punishment for such a crime, even for a child like himself, would be death, swift and without mercy. Yet still he could not, did not want to tear his gaze from the spell-binding object that lay just a few paces from him. He stood unmoving, staring at it. Felt himself being drawn out of his body… into what?

317

'Lokar!' The voice came again, insistent. 'If you stay here a minute longer they will catch you.' Its urgency finally penetrated the fog of the boy's mind. A distant deep rasping and the murmur of far-off voices reached him. Someone was coming. The sound came from a long way away but was drawing closer with every second.

He darted back through the doorway, praying he would not be noticed silhouetted against the light coming from behind him, and melted back into the darkness of the corridor. He had to get back to the tunnel entrance quickly. Where was it? In the non-light, it was invisible. Panic rising up within him, Lokar spent desperate seconds feeling along the base of the wall until, at last, his hand disappeared into nothingness. It was none too soon. In the distance, from the blackest end of the passageway, the flaming light of a torch had appeared. They were nearly on him.

Crawling hastily back into the opening he had so recently clambered out of, Lokar lay on his back in his tiny sanctuary, his pulse racing at the close call, desperately trying to calm the frightened gasps of his breathing which he feared would give away his presence. He was just in time. Barely a couple of minutes later footsteps approached and the light through the narrow slit brightened considerably. Lokar shrank back as far as he could. From where he lay, he had a good view of the lower limbs of those who passed by.

Two men. The first was a temple priest. Lokar recognised the deep blue robes. The second... The trembling boy pressed himself back even further into the black shadows of his hiding place, not daring to breathe.

Pharaoh. Pharaoh himself! He had just violated one of Pharaoh's own sacred temples and had barely avoided being caught there. If they had discovered him... For a few minutes Lokar shook uncontrollably as comprehension turned into terror and overwhelmed him. Through it all, questions surged around in his head. What did it all mean? What was that place? What was its purpose?

'It is a secret that you must never speak of to anyone, Lokar. What you have seen, where you have been, must stay with you alone. To speak of it, even to one other, would endanger Pharaoh and bring disaster to this land and its people. You were brought here today for a purpose. That purpose must remain unknown to you until the moment comes for you to act. That moment will come. Maybe not tomorrow or next year but it will come, and when it does, you will remember. Now return to your home and put it from your mind. Forget all you have seen here today, little one, until that day arrives.'

59.

Lokar opened his eyes, dizziness swirling in his head. He was lying on his back on stony ground beside the circular stone wall of a well of some kind. In the velvet black sky above him, the stars seemed to be sparkling even more brightly than usual. Low on the horizon, a crescent moon hung suspended from the sky's vault.

Why was it so dark? Why was he lying here on the hard ground? Had he fallen? He had been playing hide and seek with Nekhtari in the heat of mid-afternoon. She had been counting, and he had run off looking for somewhere to hide. More than that he could not remember. That must have been hours ago now though. He had to get home. His parents would be beside themselves with worry, would be out searching for him. He pushed himself to his feet. He was hungry, thirsty, and oh so tired.

'Lokar? Can you hear me? Where are you? Lokar!' It was his father, anxiety and desperation spilling out of each of his words.

'Here, father.'

He was swept up into his father's safe, strong arms, where he gratefully nestled down and allowed his tiredness to claim him as he was carried home. Unable to answer the questions about what had happened to him, because he did not remember.

* * * * *

What Lokar did not know, could not know, was that he had just penetrated the heart of the Great Pyramid itself, the centre edifice of the three that dominated this world and overshadowed even the mighty Great River that flowed past their feet. Three pyramids, carefully placed to echo the three stars of the Osiris constellation that in the summer months reigned over the night skies of this land. Every man, woman and child in this land recognised its importance and power in the cycle of life.

The chamber he had entered was the most secret of the secrets these magnificent monuments held. Only two other living beings were aware of its existence: Pharaoh himself and his high priest, Hotepi. The only known access to it was through a concealed doorway that led from the main ceremonial corridor. When a certain point on the blank passageway wall was pressed, an intricate series of levers, cogs and pulleys slid a wide panel upwards into the ceiling. A simple lever set on the inside wall raised and lowered it from that side. The tunnel Lokar had stumbled upon was unknown to them, ancient and long-forgotten, perhaps a ventilation shaft, escape route, or alternative (if difficult) entrance for those wishing to visit the inner chamber unseen.

Pharaoh's treasure vaults overflowed with gold, jewels, rare spices and ancient knowledge set down on papyrus scrolls, but by far his most precious and priceless treasure was the skull that had gazed at Lokar from across the room. She was both oracle and teacher, guide and mentor, created of inanimate stone yet at the same time vibrantly alive. Long ago, she had been present at the building of these great monuments, companion to the massive stone

321

statue who stood guard before them. Ever since, she had acted as a wise and trusted advisor to those who ruled this land.

Only Pharaoh was entitled to communicate with the skull. Even the high priest, in all his power and sorcery, served merely as the holder of knowledge that he would pass on to Pharaoh's successor on the king's death. This knowledge was immense; not just of the skull's existence, which was a dangerous responsibility in itself, but also of the extent of her power, the means of communicating with her, and of serving her. Pharaoh alone, however, as the living incarnation of the sun god from whom all life sprang, and therefore of divine and equal status, had the right to speak and commune with her, to take on her power as his own when necessary, and to learn her secrets.

Indeed, the high priest was forbidden to even enter the main chamber, waiting in the ante-room with his back to the doorway of the inner sanctum until the audience was over. It had to be so. No-one must watch as Pharaoh abased himself with the menial task of maintaining the temple, tasks to which he would never lower himself outside of this room. Here, under Maat-su's gaze, he would refill and relight the lamps, sweep the floor and clean the skulls, undertaking this work in honour of, and deference to, those whose skulls now adorned the twelve snow white plinths, and the lapis skull who watched over them.

GEMMA, 7

60.

What the...? The front door was wide open. I hadn't forgotten to close it, had I? OK, so my mind was a bit all over the place just now, but I wouldn't have gone out and left it like that. I walked hesitantly through my front gate and stopped, icy claws grabbing at my stomach. One of the small panes of glass had been smashed. Someone had broken into my home.

Were they – whoever they were – still in there, rummaging through my belongings? The thought made me feel sick. Slowly, making as little noise as possible, I backed out through the gate, got back in my car and drove a little way up the road. I called the police, my fingers shaking so much that it took me four attempts to hit the right buttons. Then I rang Joe and told him what had happened.

'Where are you?'

'Sitting in my car in the lay-by just up the road. I didn't want to hang around in case someone was still in the house.'

'OK. I'm on my way.'

'Joe, do you think...' I didn't have to finish my sentence.

'I don't know, Gemma, but it's possible.'

Just at that moment a police car drew up beside mine and a police officer stuck his head out of the window. 'Are you Mrs Mason?' I nodded. 'Are they still in the house?'

'I don't know. I didn't go in. I didn't think it was wise.'

'It wouldn't have been. Alright, we'll go and take a look.'

'Joe?' I turned back to the phone.

'I heard. I'll be with you as soon as I can.' He hung up.

I turned my car around and drove back to my home. One of the policemen was coming out of the front door. He grimaced. 'No-one here, Mrs Mason, but they've made a bit of a mess of it.' He held out his hand. 'Sergeant Michaels.'

I shook it. 'Is it OK for me to go in?'

'Yes, but don't disturb anything until the SOCO boys have gone over it. They may find something that will prove useful.' He pulled a wry face. 'I hate to say it, Mrs Mason, but unless someone saw anything, the chances of catching the culprits are pretty slim.'

A second police officer appeared around the corner of the house. 'Nothing there, Sarge. Looks like they entered and left by the front door.'

I looked at it, not wanting to face what I might find inside. Knowing I had to. Mentally squaring my shoulders I took a deep breath and stepped over the threshold.

No! Oh no, no. My poor, beautiful, devastated home. When Sergeant Michaels had said a 'bit of a mess', he hadn't been totally accurate. The place looked like a series of bombs had hit it. Whoever had broken in here had been thorough and callous. Every drawer had been tipped out onto the floor, every cupboard swept clean. Furniture had been upended. Cushions, pillows, mattresses, even duvets had been ripped apart. As if they had been looking for something? My blood chilled. Was this the handiwork of Mr Shiny Shoes and his cohorts?

If it was, they would have left empty-handed. There was nothing here to find. The safety deposit box key was under a floorboard in Duncan's kitchen. This... This carnage had been for nothing. I wasn't reassured. Silent tears ran down my face as I surveyed what was left of my possessions.

'I'm sorry.' The sympathy was thick in Sergeant Michaels' words. 'It's a bloody nasty situation to come home to. I've seen it far too often and I still don't get used to it.' His tone turned more businesslike. 'I know it might be hard to tell, but do you know if anything is missing?'

I looked around. The television was still there, knocked to the ground. Upstairs in the bedroom, my small collection of jewellery, though scattered callously across the floor, appeared intact. Even the cherished Victorian diamond ring I had inherited from my grandmother, by far the most valuable item I owned, hadn't been taken. It lay forlornly on the carpet under the dressing table. Thankfully, I had taken my laptop with me.

I shook my head. 'I don't think so.'

'Gemma?' Joe's voice was calling aghast from the kitchen.

'In my room.' His feet pounded up the stairs. I turned back to Sergeant Michaels. 'Joe McAllister, a friend of mine,' I explained. 'I rang him straight after I called you.' I looked around the bedroom again. 'As I was saying, as far as I can see nothing's missing. I don't have much in the way of valuable stuff anyway, nothing that would be worth taking.'

Joe appeared in the doorway, his face a mask of anger mixed with disgust. 'Bastards!' One word that said it all.

'Sergeant Michaels, this is Joe McAllister.' The two men shook hands.

'Look Mrs Mason, it'll be a while before we're finished here. Have you somewhere you can stay tonight?'

'Yes,'Joe interrupted. He turned to me. 'I'm still at Duncan's. He's away for a couple of weeks so you can come back there with me. You can have the spare room and I'll sleep on the sofa.' I nodded gratefully. I hadn't at all relished the thought of staying overnight in my raped and ravaged home.

'We'll need to be able to contact you. Someone will be in touch within a day or so to take your statement.' I gave my phone number and Joe gave Duncan's address. 'You should be able to move back in tomorrow. I don't envy you the clean-up though.' He looked around, shaking his head. 'Odd. Seems like they were looking for something specific. Why else leave what valuables there are? Any idea what it might be?'

'Not a clue.' Oh God, here I was, lying to the police! Of course I had an idea, a bloody big idea, but I couldn't share that secret. In any case, whoever had been here hadn't found anything because there was nothing to find. Somehow, that wasn't particularly reassuring.

'Well, we'll do what we can. But like I said earlier, the chances of us picking up anyone for this are slim.'

'Come on. Let's get out of here. Leave them to it.' Joe's arm was round my shoulders, ushering me down the stairs and out of the front door. I was happy to go.

MAAT-SU: The Lapis Skull

PART 3

SANCTUARY

61.

Lokar was tired, hot and hungry. It was harvest and, along with the entire population of the town, he had been up and in the fields since daybreak, toiling under the relentless heat of the late summer sun to bring in the grain. It was at its peak, ripe and plump. To leave it any longer would risk it spoiling.

This was the first break he had taken that day and he welcomed it gladly. He had seized the opportunity to wander away from the sun-baked open fields into an area studded with trees and shrubs, searching for a shady spot to rest. He did not know this place. It was some way from his home and as far as he could remember, he had never had cause to come here before today. Yet, in some unsettling, unfathomable way, it seemed vaguely familiar to him with a hazy recognition that hovered on the edges of his consciousness and refused to come any closer.

Wandering through the small patch of woodland, he came to a clearing in the centre of which was a small, circular structure whose crumbling stone walls stood only a little higher than his knee. He walked over to it and peered inside. It was a well of some kind though it had obviously not been used for years. A frayed rope that had once held its bucket hung limply down as if it no longer had the energy to hold itself firm. Again, a strong and disconcerting sense of recognition swamped Lokar. Did he know this place? He shrugged. Maybe he had seen another place that looked like this. Or perhaps he had been here at some point in the past and didn't remember. Whatever the reason, it wasn't important. He had no intention of wasting thought puzzling over it.

Lokar walked around to the shaded side of the well and leant back against the rough, low wall. Unwrapping his simple meal, he devoured it hungrily. With his appetite appeased, the heat and long hours worked in the fields won Lokar over. His eyes closed and he dozed contentedly.

'Time to remember, Lokar.' The words whispered gently, barely registering on his dreaming consciousness. 'Time to remember.' In his drowsy, half-asleep half-awake state, Lokar watched as a circular room drifted across his vision, surrounded by a structure that mimicked the pyramids that rose up across the river from where he now rested. The image's detail grew sharper, clearer, until he could make out the dazzling gold-white lines that flowed across its walls. In the centre...

Lokar's eyes flew open, as he became instantly wide awake.

'It is time to remember, Lokar,' the voice insisted. And he did remember. Remembered this place. Remembered the time, so many years ago, when he had stumbled on it. Remembered clearly what had happened next. How could he have forgotten all of that? Forgotten his fear, his curiosity, his excitement and bewilderment? All the emotions he had felt back then he felt once more, back in his ten year old body, standing in that mysterious, magical room. In front of him...

Maat-su's image flashed before him, as solid as if she was hanging in the air in front of his face. Beckoning him. She had bewitched him then and she was bewitching him again now, calling to him across the gulf of time and space.

No! He would not be drawn there again. He would not risk his life now as he once had in the recklessness and impetuosity of childhood. He was a husband and a father. His family needed him to protect and provide for them. No, he would not go back to that place again.

'You must, Lokar. It is your destiny. It is why you were called to it then, and it is why you are being called now. Do this. Fulfil your destiny.'

'No, I will not.' Lokar did not know who was speaking to him in this way – it had to be a spirit of some kind, for no living person was in sight – nor did he know what he was being asked to do. Of one thing though he was certain. Whatever it was, it was dangerous. It would put at risk not only his own life but also the freedom, and maybe even the lives, of his family. If he was caught, they would be severely punished too. Resolutely he stood and walked away, back to the fields and the labour of the harvest. He hoped hard work would silence the voice.

It did not. It would not leave him alone for one minute, relentlessly calling to him day and night until he felt he would go mad. It was in his head as he went about his daily work, in his dreams as he tried to sleep at night. His wife noticed his anguish and asked what was troubling him, but he could not speak of it, even to her.

For the tenth night in a row, the tenth night since that day he had dozed in the shade of the well walls, Lokar lay sleepless, tormented by his thoughts and the ceaseless whispering in his mind. He had had enough. This could not go on. It would make him ill. It was already beginning to affect his day to day functioning. Carefully, not wishing to disturb his sleeping wife, he got up. She stirred beside him.

'Where are you going?'

'Shhhh, go back to sleep. I need some air. I won't be long.' Satisfied, she turned over and was instantly asleep once more, reassured by his words. It was a state of mind that Lokar did not share. This had to be resolved. He would not return until it had been.

62.

Slipping his feet into his sandals, Lokar walked out into the warm night. Above him, the sky was ablaze with swathes of twinkling light. In its infinite depths, he immediately recognised the three slightly askew centre stars of the great constellation of Osiris glittering directly overhead. In front of him, suspended high over the distant horizon, swam the delicate slim crescent of the young moon.

His steps carried him to a small, modest shrine set on a raised stone platform that jutted out over the river's edge. Here, more than anywhere else, he always felt at peace, protected by the loving arms of the goddess who watched over this land. Would she hear his prayers and answer him tonight? Would she help him?

He knelt in front of the flower-decked statue and placed his hands together at chest height, closing his eyes as his plea left his lips.

'My lady,' he murmured, 'why am I tormented so? Why do they not let me be?'

'Because you are needed, Lokar. ' Her voice bubbled like the notes of a flute carried on the night breeze. 'That which you are being called to do must be done.'

'Why me, my lady? I'm no hero. I have no status, no worth. I am just a farmer.'

'It is precisely because you have no status and no ambition beyond a contented life that you are being called to this. Because of the qualities that you hold within your heart, the qualities that were seen in you so many years ago when you were still a child. They were the reason you were led to Maat-su. You, and you alone, have the knowledge and the heart that is required to succeed in this task. These times and the events that will soon be upon this land have long been foreseen and planned for. It was no accident that you were led to the skull chamber as a child. It was always part of the plan.

'Lokar, you have free will. No-one can force you to take on this task if you refuse to do so. But it is our fervent wish that you reconsider, that you agree to do as we ask, and to do so willingly. So much depends on it.'

'And if I do refuse? Will I be punished? Will the voices continue to torment me until the end of my days?'

'No, Lokar. If you are firm in your refusal, if that truly is your final decision, then we will accept it and leave you in peace. But you must know this: should you turn away from what is being asked of you, you will find that your future, and that of the people of this land, will be ruled over by the most malevolent of forces.

'This will not be of our doing, nor of our will. It will come by the hand of your own kind. A darkness brought forth by man himself will sink over this world. It is a darkness that you alone can prevent.

'Go now. Think on my words. You will no longer be plagued by the voices, this I promise you. It will be your decision, taken of your own free will. We will honour and abide by it, even if it is not the one we would wish. Should you choose to accept, however, do not delay. Time is not on your side.'

* * * * *

Lokar opened his eyes as the glare of the early morning sun dazzled him through his closed eyelids. He was lying on his back, still on the platform in front of the shrine, having fallen asleep where he sat, the words of the goddess ringing in his ears.

True to her promise, and to his endless relief and gratitude, the voices had gone, his mind clear. Stiffly, for the hard stone surface had not been the most gentle of beds, he stood and thoughtfully made his way home to where his wife was anxiously waiting for his return.

* * * * *

Lokar had made up his mind that he would refuse the task that had been set out before him. He had no wish to be a dead hero. As the day passed, however, he began to question his decision. What if the goddess was speaking the truth? That if he refused, he would be the cause of desperate times and deep sorrow for the whole land? Of course, she could have been saying that simply to get him to comply with her wishes, but the more he thought about it, the more he saw that this was not the case. She had spoken truthfully, of that he was certain. The question now was: what was he going to do about it?

Surely there were others more able, more suited, more worthy, of such an undertaking than he was? True, he had already set foot in the chamber, once, and since the memories of that day had returned to him, they had grown sharper and clearer with each hour that passed. But if he had been deliberately led there, couldn't others be led there too?

As for his other qualities – what other qualities? He was a farmer, not starving or poverty stricken certainly, but neither was he an educated or sophisticated man who had received even the most basic level of education. Wouldn't a priest, or a lawyer, or a scribe, be a better choice?

What Lokar did not see in himself, though many others did, was a man of courage, integrity and honour. A humble man, in the highest sense of the word, who would not let the power of the skull, once he had experienced it, turn him from his path or tempt him to seize it for himself. It was for all these qualities that he had been singled out. He did not even know what he was being asked to do, only that he was being called to step up and take on a potentially life-endangering task with no idea of what it entailed.

Nevertheless, by the time the sun had set that evening, Lokar had made his decision.

* * * * *

Kneeling in front of the shrine once more, Lokar spoke. 'My lady, I have made my decision. I will do your bidding. I will accept that which I have been called to do. Yet I still do not know what this is. Please tell me what it is that you demand of me.'

'As in the sorrowful times of Atlantis, when the dark overran the light and extinguished it completely and forever in that place, so do those who walk in the shadows now seek to overthrow the light of this land.' The

337

melodious song of the goddess could not hide her sadness. 'In those troubled days, knowing of what was to befall their beloved land, twelve priests and priestesses from the Temple of Light were chosen to carry the sacred skulls to safety, to keep them from the hands of those who would abuse their power and, if necessary, to conceal them so well that they would not be found until it was safe for them to return to the light once more.

'Now, as then, these sacred skulls must be protected from those who would abuse their power. Now, as then, when danger threatens, a guardian must be appointed to carry them to safety. That is the role we ask of you.

'For the skull that rests within the chamber deep below the heart of the central great pyramid temple is Maat-su, one of the thirteen sacred skulls that once held power in the Temple of Light in Atlantis. One of the thirteen brought to this world long before that time to watch over and guide humankind in its growth. Her origins lie way back in the beginning of consciousness and the far reaches of the universe. Her power is immense.

'Take this skull, Lokar. Take Maat-su, and carry her to safety. Hide her in a place where she will not be found until, in distant times that are still to come and are as yet undreamed of, she contacts the one who will bring her to the light once more.'

63.

Lokar left his house just as night began to fall, not knowing when – or if – he would ever be returning. He had held his so wife tightly that she began to feel afraid without knowing why. Lokar had not spoken to her of any of this, had not spoken of it to anyone. Nonetheless her intuition sensed that he was about to put himself into danger. With a last lingering kiss he walked through the door without a backwards glance and disappeared into the dusk.

From under some thick vegetation at the junction of the path, he retrieved a sturdy rope and a rough bag that he had hidden there earlier in the day. Now that the memories had been returned to him, every detail was imprinted vividly on his mind. He remembered how insecure and precarious the ladder rungs had been even back then, and that had been almost twenty five years ago. He would not trust his life to them now.

At the well head, Lokar slung the bag around his waist and fastened the rope securely to a nearby tree. He would climb down using a combination of his rope and, as long as they held, the ladder rungs. Tentatively he climbed over the wall of the well and slowly, carefully, began to descend. He had no light – he had no way of holding one – and soon he was out of what moonlight there was and into the unrelenting blackness of the shaft. Down and down he climbed, arms and legs protesting more at each step, feeling for the draught that had first alerted him to the passageway so many years earlier. Would it still be there, or had the tunnel entrance been found and sealed? He had no way of knowing.

There it was. A breath of damp, cold air, faint but definite. Lokar eased his full weight onto the ladder rung, his heart in his mouth. It was holding. And there was the tunnel mouth. He could trace its outline with his fingers. It seemed much smaller than he remembered, but of course he was a full grown man now, no longer a ten year old boy. Back then he had walked, head lowered. Now he was having to crawl on his hands and knees.

* * * * *

The passageway seemed endless, a lot longer than that first time. Where was the end wall? At last his reaching hand brushed against its solid rock surface. The way out should be a little above him. He felt around. Yes, there it was. Where it had been above his head before, now the edge of the ledge rested against his chest. He heaved himself upwards… and misjudged the space completely. With a sickening thud, Lokar's head slammed into the uneven stone of the roof. He crumpled, good fortune keeping him on the ledge instead of rolling off back to the floor of the tunnel below.

He lay, sick and nauseous, as the dark space whirled and danced around him. Stabbing thrusts of pain pierced his head as he fought to stay conscious, vaguely aware of a warm trickle of blood tracing down his cheek, thick and sticky. It took a long time before he felt steady enough to go on.

Lokar traced the outline of the narrow opening with his hand, not wishing to repeat his crack on the head. He did not feel confident. Whereas it had been ample as a child, he was not at all certain that, as a grown man, he would be able to fit through it. He wriggled his shoulders through the gap, his head filled with crashing pain and flashing lights at every movement. It was too tight! For one panic-stricken moment he thought he was stuck fast until, with a determined push that took the skin from his shoulders, he was through and lying on the floor of what he remembered to be the long, wide corridor that led to the chamber that held the lapis skull.

*   *   *   *   *

He rested for a few moments, breathing heavily, once again waiting for his world to stop spinning and the pounding ache in his injured head to subside. Slowly he got to his feet. Unlike on that previous occasion he could see no glimmer of light to guide his way. Left. He had to go left. One hand on the wall to keep his bearings in the pitch blackness, Lokar started out in the direction of the chamber.

As he drew nearer, a faint glow became visible, guiding him to the entrance to the sacred rooms as it had on that previous occasion so many years earlier. Even more cautious this time, he crept towards the doorway. Flattening himself against the corridor wall, he peered around the opening to check there was no-one inside. It was empty. Lokar drew in a long, relieved breath. Quickly he crossed the ante-chamber and entered the main room. It was darker than he remembered, lit this night by only a handful of flickering lamps. The magic, however, remained, as strong as before.

Once more he was instantly mesmerised by the flowing images on the wall, their sweeping lines moving in the lamplight as if they were alive. Once more, he was unsettled by the twelve human skulls that encircled the outer circumference of the space as if standing watch, although now they sat far below his line of vision, level with his heart. And once more it was the skull of the richest, deepest blue lapis lazuli that captivated and bewitched him from the centre of it all. Just as on the previous occasion, over twenty years earlier, he found himself unable to tear his gaze from her, felt his spirit being pulled up and out of his body towards her.

Only this time no voice held him back, and he did not resist the pull. Little by little, he felt himself rising out of his body, upwards, ever upwards. He allowed himself to go. Lifting up into the black void of the night sky, drifting amongst the stars that were glittering with an intensity he had never seen from the surface of the Earth. An Earth that was now so far below him that it resembled a small, richly decorated altar plate. Surrounded by music unlike any he had ever heard before, a music that was coming from the stars themselves, each glittering point of light sounding out its own pure note that merged in total harmony with those of the other stars. So many notes, all unique and yet all as one, a symphony of star song. Floating gently back down. He could see the land, the Great River, the mighty pyramids far below, drawing closer. Slowly, slowly, they were rising to meet him so that he was sinking downwards through the stone of this great monument.

Lokar came to with a start, back in his body once again, the lamplight still flickering around him, the skulls still staring blankly at him from their stands. Waiting. Waiting for him to do what he had come here to do.

* * * * *

The legacy of those whose skulls now watched over Maat-su would last for generations, until the catastrophic events that ravaged the planet and destroyed virtually all memory of what had gone before. Following those years of devastation, authority condensed into the hands of an elite – those powerful and strong enough to seize and retain control of the kingdom. In time, as appears to be a trait in human nature, those outside of that elite came to accept it as the natural state of affairs, giving away their own power and self-determination to those who they were taught to view as different, more worthy, able and powerful, having the divine right to access to knowledge that they, the common man or woman, was not meant to know.

Eventually, as rulers came and went, it had come to this point where only Pharaoh himself had the divine right and status to commune with the gods. Maat-su had been so long hidden from the sight and minds of the ordinary people that they had forgotten her existence and the relationship all had once held with her. Yet somewhere, somehow, the remnants of her memory clung on, taking a new form – that of Maat, goddess and keeper of truth, divine order, harmony, and justice – her true origins lost in the mists of myth, mystery and magic.

That balance of power in the kingdom was under threat though few knew of it, and those who did kept it to themselves. For generations, the priests of the pyramid temples had willingly and loyally served Pharaoh, and in doing so had enjoyed the benefits that accompanied such loyalty. Women, wealth and power were theirs to use as they desired, with little restriction, and their freedom was almost absolute. Now though, the current high priest, Hotepi, had even higher aspirations. He wished to overthrow Pharaoh and take his place. As Pharaoh's half-brother, the high priest saw his claim to the throne as legitimate and had won the support of a large number of followers amongst the priesthood and nobles, followers greedy for the even greater power and riches he had promised them in return for their loyalty.

Hotepi was a cruel and cold-hearted man who carried a bitter grudge against his half-brother that demanded revenge. He should have been the one chosen rule the land; his half-brother was a weakling, ineffective and soft. If he, Hotepi, had the throne, the kingdom would be all-conquering. The plan was set, and everything was ready to go. There was only one step left; Hotepi knew that if he was to succeed in his actions, he would need Maat-su at his side. Without her power, all would be lost. Tonight, after Pharaoh's visit to the chamber, he would return and seize her for himself. By morning Pharaoh would be dead and he, would take his place as unassailable ruler.

This was why Lokar's task was so vital. It was why here was here this night. Pharaoh may not be perfect, but those who would follow would be much, much worse. With Maat-su in their hands, they would be unstoppable.

64.

Pushing down the fear that was now beginning to rise from his belly up into his throat – he could feel it clutching and fluttering as he stood there hesitating – Lokar set his bag on the floor and resolutely stepped forwards, placing his hands firmly on the lapis skull. To his deepest surprise he felt... nothing. It disconcerted him but he wasn't going to let it distract him any further. In one swift movement he lifted the skull from her base and set her in the rough fabric bag. It was time to leave. He had taken far too long already. Every second he stayed here brought him closer to discovery and disaster. Scooping up one of the small oil lamps in his free hand, Lokar moved back into the corridor once more, scanning it for any sound or movement.

* * * * *

He could go no further. The corridor had come to an abrupt end. Yet again Lokar found himself faced with a smooth flat expanse of solid stone. His heart sank. What would he do now? Even as the thought ran through his head, he shook himself in irritation. 'Don't be ridiculous, Lokar,' he scolded himself. 'If this is such a secret place then it's obvious the corridor won't be an open door to anyone who decides to wander in.' There had to be a catch somewhere, some mechanism to reveal an exit.

His tiny oil lamp was spluttering now, its fuel supply low. He was having to feel his way more than see, running his hands over the walls. There, low down on the left hand wall. A small lever. He pulled it upwards. Smoothly, silently, the huge stone panel in front of him started to slide sideways. He squeezed through as soon as it was wide enough for him to do so, and stood taking his bearings.

He was in yet another corridor, this one by contrast brightly lit by closely set flaming torches. To his left, the passageway stretched off into the distance for as far as he could see. Turning to the right he was suddenly and totally blinded by a brilliant white rectangle of light. Sunlight. His way out. He had made it.

His elation was not to last. Before he had taken a dozen strides, the doorway filled with a swarm of men charging towards him. He couldn't discern any details, they were just black shapes against the white. Swords and shields rattled and clashed. Soldiers! How did they know he was here? And where was here? Lokar had no idea. One thing though was clear; it was somewhere important, and he shouldn't be there.

A loud shout echoed in his ears. Lokar did the only thing that seemed sensible to him in that moment – he turned on his heels and ran back the way he had come, pushing down the lever as he shot through the opening to seal the entrance once more. He was only just in time. The final inches closed just as the first soldiers reached it. Lokar leant back against the wall panting, waiting for his heartbeat to return to normal.

Moments later a shuddering thud reverberated through his body. At the same time an echoing crash hit his eardrums. They were trying to break down the wall, and at this rate it would not be long before they succeeded. He turned and ran once more, the hammering and battering echoing down the corridor after him. He would have to go back the way he had come, through the side tunnel and into the well. The prospect filled him with dismay but he could see no other option.

It was some minutes later that a sound like angry thunder cracked behind him, followed by muffled shouts of victory. They had breached the wall. They had seen him come in here, they knew he was in the corridor, and they were on his trail. Lokar began to run faster. His lamp was almost extinguished, he could barely see the floor and he had to take care not to stumble and fall. He risked a glance over his shoulder. He could not see them yet. Pray Isis he would have enough time.

*　*　*　*　*

Lokar skidded to an abrupt halt. The skull room doorway was just ahead of him. In his haste he had missed the side tunnel's entrance and had come too far. He would have to go back. Too late. Turning on his heels, the faint flickering glow of a distant torch was already showing in the blackness. They were too close. There was no time. He was trapped.

In desperation he darted into the skull room, searching for another way out, fingers roaming over the walls in search of hidden recesses or keys. Instinct told him that there had to be another exit, an escape route built in by those who had first constructed this place. Fear was shouting at him that there was not, that all was lost and he

347

would pay the ultimate price for his actions. That he would never see his wife and children again.

'Place me on my pedestal.' The voice was soft in his ears, though no sound had been uttered. Lokar hesitated, confused. 'It is I, Maat-su, sacred skull of the ancients, who speaks to you now. Do as I ask. Place me on my pedestal. There is no time for delay.'

His hand shaking, aware of the soldiers approaching quickly, their footsteps echoing louder at every heartbeat, Lokar did as he was asked, setting Maat-su back onto her base.

'Now press down and turn me half a turn sun-wise,' she commanded. He did so. A shrieking, grating sound filled the room and the pedestal slid aside. It was evident the mechanism had not been used for a very long time; thank the gods it had still worked. Below him, a flight of steps led down into blackness.

Lokar quickly grabbed a good number of the small oil lamps and a flint, which he shoved into his bag, scooped up the lapis skull and started down the steps, tempering his instinctive desire to hurry with a necessary caution. It proved to be a wise strategy. He had descended about a dozen steps when one of them shifted slightly under his foot, unbalancing him. He had triggered a second mechanism that closed the trapdoor above his head, pulling the plinth back into place and sealing it firmly shut. He was immediately enclosed by such a complete and suffocating darkness that he could only feel his way carefully to the foot of the steps.

'Rest, Lokar, we are safe. None alive knows of this passageway. Those who would follow you do not know

348

where you have gone, and even if they did, without me, it would be impossible for them to follow. Rest now, my friend. Much lies ahead of you.' Lokar leaned his head back against the rough wall of the underground passage and allowed himself to sleep.

65.

Lokar woke an hour or so later, stiff and uncomfortable. Now that the immediate danger and fatigue had passed, he was painfully aware of his injured head and raw shoulders. He could see nothing, felt completely disorientated. The oil lamps. If he could manage to light one he would be able to see his way forward. If he couldn't... Lokar didn't want to contemplate that option. As he had descended the first few steps from the chamber, the dim light filtering down had revealed that the walls and roof of this underground room were rough and uneven, natural rather than man-made. If this was a cave system, any number of hidden dangers could be waiting for him as he stumbled blindly on. He held his breath as he struck the flint – he had light. Weak and unsteady maybe, but it was light.

He peered around, taking his bearings. He was sitting on a small square platform, at its rear a wall of rough natural rock. In front of him a further three steps led down into what appeared to be a natural passageway that sloped gently downwards through the bedrock of the plateau on which the town and its monuments stood. He had no need to run. Maat-su had told him he was safe and he believed her. Moreover, it would have been extremely unwise, and probably not possible. The floor here was a ragged bed of stone, and from the walls jagged tongues of rock protruded here and there, ready to punish an inattentive step. This was evidently a natural fissure that had been exploited and enlarged by those who had used this escape route.

* * * * *

It was time to leave. Lokar gathered up Maat-su and placed her in the rough linen bag with the spare oil lamps. There was only one way he could go. He took his time picking his way through the fallen rocks and uneven ground, studying the labyrinth as he went. It was not an easy path. He was forced to clamber over massive boulders and unstable piles of jumbled stone and squeeze through what appeared to be impossibly narrow cracks. Most of it was clearly natural. In places, however, human intervention was evident to see. Obviously man-made tunnels linked the caves, but even though they must have been hand-carved from the bedrock Lokar could feel no sign of tool marks beneath his curious fingers. The surfaces were completely smooth and even, as smooth as those in the great corridor he had so recently walked through; a corridor that he suspected was part of one of the three great sacred pyramids. Had the same people who had built those massive structures also had a hand in this?

Lokar's mind was racing, fear ever eager to seize an opportunity to strike, as he made his way through the tunnels and passageways. How would he ever find his way out of this place? So far the path had been obvious, there had only been one route he could take; surely that wouldn't go on forever. What would happen when he came to a fork in the way, or if he came up against a dead end?

'Don't be afraid, Lokar.' The voice was whispering softly, reassuringly, through his thoughts. 'Look around you. The signposts are there to see. Follow them, and all will be well.'

351

Signposts? He hadn't seen any signposts, although admittedly the light from the small oil lamp he was carrying was weak and barely sufficient to see more than a pace or two ahead.

'The walls, Lokar. Look to the walls.'

He stopped, peering more closely at the rock around him. There WAS something there. He stepped closer, lifting the tiny flame to see more clearly. Images, just like those in the skull room, flowing and moving as the light brushed them, fading back into invisibility as it drew away. Lokar illuminated them again. They flared and danced once more, as if with a life and soul of their own. Their light tickled his skin as it gleamed, like the tingling in the air during a thunderstorm. Were these images the signposts Maat-su was referring to? Her words confirmed his thoughts.

'They will show you the way, Lokar. Trust in them and in yourself. As long as they are with you, you are following the right path.'

His confidence restored, Lokar set off once more, now keeping a close eye on the walls that ran alongside him. The images leapt and glowed, accompanying him at every step.

* * * * *

The tunnels were changing. Here and there small side chambers began to appear, some clearly natural nooks, others just as evidently created by human endeavour. In all of them objects lay scattered over the floor as if carelessly and hastily abandoned, perhaps to be retrieved at some future date. Some of the items – fine linens, papyri – were damaged and rotting, victims perhaps of the floods that regularly swept the banks of the Great River. Others – precious metals and gemstones - were pristine and intact. Reaching one large side chamber, Lokar stepped inside. Statues, plates and plaques were piled up one on another. Gold and jewels gleamed in the weak lamplight. They looked to have lain there a very long time. All of it was covered in a thick layer of dust and cobwebs.

Lying at his feet was a deep red oblong gemstone, beautifully cut and faceted and almost as big as his palm. Garnet maybe? Or ruby? He didn't know. Such a jewel would make him rich beyond his dreams and ensure a comfortable future for himself, his children, and his grandchildren. Maybe even for the generations beyond that. One jewel amongst the many. Surely it wouldn't hurt if he took it. There was no doubt that he had earned it. He was risking his life for Maat-su. This jewel would be just reward for that. He stretched out his hand towards it.

'Leave it, Lokar.' He hesitated. No, why should he? He reached out again. The words repeated more clearly and more firmly. 'No, Lokar. Leave it. It is not yours to take.' The voice was familiar, only this time was not that of Maat-su, who for the moment rested silently in his waist pouch.

'Haven't I earned it?' Lokar replied a little petulantly. 'Don't I deserve some reward for risking everything?'

'What you do, you do for yourself, your family and your people, Lokar. Is their safe future not reward enough?' Memories floated up again from the deep, hidden places within Lokar. Memories of his childhood and of his unseen friends. He remembered then, recognised the voices of those friends, voices that had fallen silent since the day they had urged him to flee the skull room on that first occasion over twenty years previously. Voices that until now had been erased from his mind.

Still he hesitated, the powerful draw of the gemstone and its promise of a life of comfort enticing him to pay no attention to the words filling his head. No. He could not, would not, ignore them. If his friends were speaking to him now, after so long, there was a good reason why they were doing so. He would be foolish to disobey. Regretfully, reluctantly, he withdrew his hand and got to his feet. He must continue on his way. How much further would he have to go?

66.

Much, much later, Lokar was still deep beneath the surface, tired now, stumbling with every step. He had long ago run out of food and water, the small amount he had tucked into his waist pouch quickly exhausted. He needed to rest. His aching legs could not carry him much further. He had no idea of how much time had passed in the eternal subterranean night that surrounded him. There was no way of telling. It felt like he had been travelling for a very long time.

He had to stop. He needed to rest. Lokar slumped down against the wall, setting the last of the oil lamps he had brought from the skull chamber on the floor beside him. It was a miracle they had lasted all this time. How much longer would they guide his way? If he lost their light, he would be abandoned to the unrelieved darkness of this underground world. As if his prayers had been heard, and then scorned, the tiny flame sputtered before his despairing eyes. There was no time left. Perhaps there was one more that he had somehow overlooked? He scrabbled frantically in his pouch, lifting Maat-su free before tipping the remaining contents out onto the floor. No lamp lay there. How could he carry on blindly? In that moment, for the first time since he had set out on this journey, true panic threatened to rise up and overwhelm him.

'Lokar. Lokar!' Eventually the voice broke through his racing, frightened thoughts. 'Get up, Lokar. Look above you in the wall. You will find a small opening, inside which is a lever. Pull the lever downwards.'

Lokar stood and reached his arm above his head, feeling for the opening the voice spoke of. Nothing. He fumbled around to the left and right of where he was standing. He could find no niche in the rock face. Stretched higher, until he was on tiptoes. He was on the verge of giving up when his fingers dipped into a small recess that was at the limit of his reach, explored it and touched a small stone protuberance. Could that be it?

He was at full stretch, his fingertips barely brushing the lever, if indeed that was what it was. Could he reach that fraction more? The walls were flat and smooth here, offering no helping foothold. The oil lamp flickered ominously. He was almost out of time. If he didn't succeed, this would be the end. Gritting his teeth, Lokar reached up again, using the wall to support his weight as he lifted on to the very tips of his toes. Pain shot up his legs. Still he he did not give up. His fingers closed around the projection, struggling to find sufficient force to move it. Yes, there. It had shifted a fraction. Slowly, slowly it yielded, moving through a ninety degree arc before clicking into place.

In an instant the passageway twinkled with light. Every fifty paces or so, from high up on the walls and level with the niche he had just discovered, light beamed out. Lokar sank to the floor, the pain in his toes forgotten, his situation forgotten, the lapis skull forgotten. At least for the moment. He sat and gaped. For the first time since descending the steps from the skull room, he could see beyond the faint pool of the oil lamp's flame. Magic was at work here. He had needed a miracle and he had been granted one.

Of course it was not magic, simply a complex and sophisticated system of crystals and mirrors created thousands of years earlier by the advanced technology of those who had built both these tunnels and the pyramids that stood above them. The system linked to the surface, carrying sunlight (and night light from the moon and stars) from above down into this subterranean world.

High above Lokar, the roof of this tunnel, a natural cleft that had been widened and levelled, disappeared into the shadows, while far ahead the floor seemed to stop in mid-air as the cavity widened out into a huge domed roof. Limping a little from his bruised toes, Lokar moved closer. It was much easier now that the way was illuminated. The view became clearer. The path was leading to a wide, sweeping stairway, as skilfully and elegantly carved as any in the grand monuments and temples of the Great City. The staircase descended to the floor of the cavern, a vast soaring amphitheatre easily two hundred paces across, brightly lit by hundreds of beams of light. Its only contents were a central raised dais with what appeared to be a sarcophagus lying upon it.

Lokar's skin prickled as he stepped down onto the first stair. The whole place was overflowing with a powerfully sacred energy, the air saturated with it. His sandalled feet slapped unnaturally loudly in the stillness, the sound amplified by the great chamber that surrounded him. He was an intruder here, uneasy in his trespass, yet at the same time he was being gently nudged to go on, to investigate further.

The walls were again painted in figures of liquid gold – people, symbols, strange objects. From above them light streamed down, falling onto the floor in waves of soft white. The dais and the sarcophagus resting on it drew him like a magnet, its great stone form dominating the centre of this cavern.

Steps, five of them, led up to the dais itself, which was formed from a slab of smooth white marble supported on nine thick legs, each intricately carved with trailing vines. Hesitantly but determinedly, Lokar crossed the floor and climbed them. The sarcophagus reached to just below his chest. Unsure of what he would find, Lokar gathered his courage, swallowed hard, and peered in.

It was virtually empty. Within the large outer casket lay a second smaller more fragile-looking coffin, its lid missing and the contents exposed and so small that it would have reached no further than Lokar's shoulder. Inside it were a few long fragments of bone, perhaps from an arm or lower leg. Though he couldn't tell, from the delicacy of the bone he felt it had been a woman's body laid to rest there.

At the head of the sarcophagus, a small square chest rested directly on the stone plinth. It measured barely two of his hand spans in any direction and was made of deep blue lapis lazuli, that same mineral as the skull he carried, ornately decorated with intricate gold filigree bands that supported it and came together to form a clasp at the front. It would be the perfect place for Maat-su. Even as he thought it, he could sense her approval. The question still remained however of where to hide it? No-one had set foot in these caves for a very long time, but he could not take the slightest risk that she would be discovered. That had been made clear to him at the shrine. Responsibility rested heavily on his skinned shoulders. He would carry it until he found the right place. If he couldn't hide the skull in these caves, he would find somewhere else.

Lokar knelt and lifted Maat-su from his waist pouch, looking at her properly for the first time. Her deep blue colouring was accentuated by the shafts of light that illuminated the cavern and glittered on the flecks of gold pyrite that drifted through the blue. She was strangely bewitching, calling him deeper even as he gazed into the depths of her rich tones. With difficulty he pulled his gaze away and set her into the casket. She was a perfect fit, as if the chest had been made for her. He stood, lifting the box with both hands. It was heavy. How long would he have the strength to carry it?

67.

Lokar was walking ever downward, accompanied every step of the way by a roar of rushing water that came from far down beneath his feet and was growing louder with every minute that passed. He had lost all sense of time, was exhausted and hungry, and becoming increasingly afraid that he would remain lost, wandering this maze of endless caves and passageways for the rest of his life. Which would not be a long one. The box weighed ever more heavily in his hands, his arm muscles aching and protesting now. Despair threatened to overwhelm him and he fought it down. The skull had shown him this escape route, surely she would guide him the rest of the way.

'Peace, Lokar.' The voice had sensed his distress and was reassuring him. 'I promised you would return safely to your family and you will, once your work here is done. It is not far now, my friend. As soon as I am safe, you will find your way home easily. This is my promise to you.' The promise of the skull. It was all he had. In truth, he had no choice other than to continue. The alternative was to stop where he was and remain here in this underground world forever.

The path was still lit by the unseen lights in the walls, though they were less frequent now, and dimmer. The path had narrowed too, so that at times Lokar had to squeeze through a gap scarcely wide enough for his frame. Until, at last, he crawled around a corner and found himself in a small low-ceilinged cave. From the far wall, a slender waterfall cascaded down into a pool that took up a good half of the floor area. There was only the one way in, the way he had come. This had to be his destination.

Where though could he hide the casket in this tiny place, unless he left it in the open? There were no ledges, no niches in the walls, no piles of stone to act as cover. Nevertheless, he had arrived. Setting the casket containing Maat-su down on the smooth floor Lokar knelt and gazed down into the pool. The water was crystal clear, lit by the few dim lights that still shone. Far below he could see the pebble-strewn bottom. And there, part way down, was a deep ledge. Could he leave her there? A pulse of affirmation gave him the answer. Maat-su was saying 'Yes'.

He had found the place. How though would he get the skull to it? He could not simply drop the casket in. It might tip over as it landed and spill out Maat-su. Or break up if it, when it, hit the ledge. Or drop right to the bottom and shatter both itself and the skull on the pebbles. He had no rope to lower it. There was only one answer. He would have to take it down, place it on the ledge, and swim back up again. It was a prospect Lokar did not relish. Like all those who lived alongside the Great River he was a strong swimmer, but the water here was icy cold and would quickly drain the strength from his muscles. If he was immersed in it too long he would be putting his life in danger.

He slipped off his sandals, waist pouch and tunic, and carefully lowered himself into the water, gasping as its chill took his breath away. It was even colder than he had anticipated. He would have to be quick. Lokar reached across and seized the casket, dragging its heavy weight across the cave floor until it rested on the edge of the pool, then carefully pulled it into the water. Immediately he plummeted like a stone, sinking quickly. Down and down, so far. Too far. Surely he should have touched the ledge ages ago. His lungs were already beginning to protest.

The glass clarity of the water had been deceptive. What had looked like fifty feet was in reality three hundred. The ledge he was making for was much, much deeper than he had believed. He had still not reached it and was beginning to get frightened. He would have to let go or he would not make it back to the surface before he lost consciousness through lack of oxygen.

A moment later, Lokar's feet touched rock and his downward plunge stopped. Hastily he set down his burden and kicked upwards, his chest pounding and painful. The urge to draw in a deep breath was almost irresistible. His world darkened. Unconsciousness was drawing close. He was not going to make it.

With a rush, Lokar's head burst through the surface of the pool into clear air. He thrashed around barely keeping afloat as he gulped in huge wonderful lungfuls. Hauling himself out onto the stone floor he lay gasping and wheezing, trying to replenish his oxygen-starved body, a red cloud of pain descending over him as it regained its balance. He vomited, again and again, the dry barren retching of a stomach long without food, bile burning his throat. Shivering and blue with cold.

A long time later, Lokar stirred, sat up and looked around in confusion until he remembered where he was.

His tortured body felt easier, restored to some extent by his sleep of exhaustion.

'Time to go home, Lokar.' The voice had returned, and was whispering softly to him. He stumbled awkwardly upright and retraced his steps back through the narrow cave entrance, allowing his feet rather than his head to lead the way. Far below, Maat-su rested safe and at peace in the soft cradle of the Earth's waters.

*   *   *   *   *

At last, almost imperceptibly, the path began to rise. Lokar's heart lifted. Could it be taking him back to the surface? Onwards. Upwards. Gradually getting steeper. The rock becoming so smooth and slippery that he had to take care with every step.

He stopped. Ahead was a huge boulder fall, that towered as high as the pyramids themselves. At the top glimmered a tiny chink of daylight. Could that really be his way out, or would it be a false hope, a mere crack in the rock that would merely torment him with its teasing hope of freedom? Even if it was, at least it proved he was now out of the subterranean prison and at or above ground level. Spurred on by its promise he began to climb, hunger and exhaustion forgotten, paying no heed to his bloodied hands and knees which he grazed raw in his haste.

His heart began to pound in excitement. The crack was widening, it looked big enough for him pass through…

Lokar drew in a deep breath of the fresh, sweet, warm desert air that flowed through the fissure in the rock, allowing it to revive him as it surged into his lungs and through his body. He peered out. He was at the edge of a range of hills that overlooked the flat, wide valley of the Great River. Far off in the distance, he could see the three pyramids strung out on their crooked axis and nearby, guarding them as it had done for so many thousands of years, the massive figure of the stone sphinx.

Taking another deep breath, Lokar pushed through the narrow gap. He thought for a moment he wouldn't make it and that he would end his life there, immoveably trapped in its grip. With a huge effort that shredded any remaining skin from his already injured shoulders, still raw and bloodied from where he had shoved himself out of the well tunnel – was it really so short a time ago? It seemed like a lifetime – he was back out in the sunlight, lying panting on the rough, stony ground.

What had happened that night, why the soldiers had been in the tunnel, and where that tunnel had been located, he would never know. It didn't matter. He had fulfilled his promise and he had come through it alive. Wearily he pulled himself to his feet and set out for home, his wife and his children. It would be a long, hot walk.

GEMMA, 8

68.

'Joe and I spent a very subdued evening, lost in our individual worlds of dark and depressing thoughts. The break-in and damage at my house had affected us both deeply, more than anything that had happened up until then with the exception of my experience of Jack's death. This was too close to home. Eventually, I switched on the television and we numbed our anxieties with back to back episodes of 1970s sitcoms until it was time to go to bed.

I dozed fitfully, my mind still full of the break-in and its possible implications. Dawn was already on the horizon when I finally slipped into proper sleep.

* * * * *

This was weird. I was dreaming. OK, maybe that in itself wasn't so weird. I dreamed a lot these days. That's how the skull stories were given to me, like I was watching a DVD or a movie. This was different. Firstly, I wasn't only dreaming, at the same time I knew I was dreaming. Which was a very odd, if not unpleasant, experience. Secondly, unlike the skull dreams, I was actually taking part in this one.

I was walking in a garden. A beautiful garden. Lush and green. All my senses felt awakened and aroused. At every turn, tinkling cool fountains splashed and danced in the sunlight, and countless tiny songbirds serenaded my ears. I was bathed in waves of fragrance from the shrubs and flowers that filled this sanctuary; one moment musky, heady and rich, the next so light and ethereal that it drifted away on the breeze the moment I noticed it.

Someone was walking beside me. Who was it? A man. Tall. My head came just to his shoulders. Well-built. Hmm, that was promising. Deep, rich chestnut hair worn long, several inches below his collar. To my intense frustration though, more than that I couldn't see. I squinted, I peered. Hard as I tried I could not make out his face. Why not? What was I not meant to know?

He, whoever 'he' was, wore sweeping white robes edged with wide bands of what looked to be royal blue satin and gold brocade. I glanced down at my own clothes. I was wearing the same, soft leather sandals on my otherwise bare feet. We were walking on a wide level path of chipped white marble that meandered ahead of us through the borders.

I looked up at my companion again. No use. His face was still indistinct. I felt him rest his eyes on me. Suddenly, unexpectedly, I was flooded with a deep feeling of peace, safety… and love. So much love that tears filled my eyes. Whoever this was, it was evident he was someone very special to me. A lover? Husband? Soul mate? What was going on? I didn't understand.

A flash of recognition. Of course. I did know this place. I had been here before. Or at least, I had seen it. How could I have done, though? This was nowhere that existed on Earth, certainly nowhere I had ever visited. All at once, it clicked. This wasn't on Earth, at least not any more. These were the gardens of the Pyramid Temple. In Yo'tlàn. In Atlantis. This familiarity had been born from

367

the memory of other dreams. What the hell was I doing in Atlantis?

More confused than ever, I glanced at the man walking beside me, even in my dream seeking reassurance in the aura of love in which he held me. In that briefest of moments, fleeting, so elusive that I couldn't be certain of it, I thought I saw Joe's face gazing down at me. Or did I? The image had gone as quickly as it had formed. No, it couldn't have been. I must have imagined it. Why would Joe be here with me in the temple gardens of Yo'tlàn? Even in a dream.

'Haa'nu. Regus.' A chubby, red-faced man interrupted my confusion, puffing up to us on the path, sweat pouring down his face. He looked extremely worried. 'It has happened,' he panted breathlessly. 'Omar has requested that you both join him in the skull chamber immediately.'

What had happened? I had no idea what was going on. But if the bad feeling in the pit of my stomach was anything to go by, whatever it was, it wasn't good!

* * * * *

My eyes blinked open. I had been woken by the wail of an ambulance passing by outside the window. From every angle, blank faces and empty eye sockets peered at me out of the night. Like the other rooms in Duncan's flat, skulls of all sizes, shapes and minerals were crammed onto every available surface of the spare bedroom. The first time I'd set foot in his home, they had made me feel extremely uncomfortable. Now I found myself reassured and protected by their presence.

I lay awake in early morning light, going over and over yet again the events of the past months: the deaths of Olina and Dr Mackintosh; Callum being framed for a brutal murder and his subsequent vanishing act; Mr Shiny Shoes; the burglary. And now this dream, which was still vividly alive in my thoughts. They were all linked. They were all connected to the skulls and the stories I was writing, even if I didn't know exactly how. One thing I was absolutely certain of though – it wasn't over yet. Not by a long way.

OTHER BOOKS IN THE SKULL CHRONICLES SERIES

LOST LEGACY
(Book I)

A beautiful young woman is entombed alive as a sacrifice to angry gods...

A young priest embarks upon a desperate flight across a hostile landscape deep in the heart of Atlantis...

In the possession of each, a sacred crystal skull.

England, 2012. With her life falling apart around her, Gemma Mason's sleep is increasingly disturbed by vivid dreams of crystal skulls, extraterrestrial beings and the ancient temples of Atlantis. Dreams that contain vital messages for us at this point in our history. As they unfold, Gemma realises she has been chosen to share a secret that will have repercussions for the whole of humankind.

Reluctantly she accepts her destiny and finds herself plunged into the forgotten history of an unknown world where myth and legend suddenly become irrefutably real. It is a journey that calls into question everything Gemma has ever believed to be true and demands that she faces her own deepest fears. For she is being asked to share with the world the shocking secret of our hidden past, a secret that will change forever the way we look at ourselves and our place in the universe. But are we ready to hear such a truth?

Travelling from the dense humidity of the rainforest to the desert lands of North America, from frozen Arctic wastelands to the cities and mountain ranges of Atlantis, Lost Legacy weaves past and present together seamlessly in a rollercoaster ride of emotion and adventure.

- *'A compelling page turner'*
- *'Gripping narrative'* ...
- *'Completely blew me away'*

THE RED SKULL OF ALDEBARAN
(Book II)

The adventure continues...

Gor-Kual: the red skull whose origins lie on the distant star worlds of Aldebaran...

Gemma Mason: an ordinary Englishwoman, chosen by these ancient sacred skulls to be their mouthpiece, sharing their stories through her writing...

In this fast-paced sequel to Lost Legacy, the story of Gor-Kual unfolds, from the barren plateau of an ancient land to the fabled continent of Atlantis and, ultimately, the empty deserts of North Africa: a story of loss, heartbreak, courage, sacrifice and love, all to protect this most powerful and sacred of objects.

Meanwhile, in 2013, Gemma is undertaking a quest of her own, travelling to the deserts of the south west USA with a group of maverick archaeologists in search of the blue skull Gal-Athiel, whose story was told in Lost Legacy. As her own journey of self-discovery unfolds further, Gemma is forced once more to step beyond the boundaries of her fears. What will she find there?

'Even better than the first one.'... 'I couldn't put it down'... 'Excellent read.'

OTHER BOOKS BY THIS AUTHOR

FORGOTTEN WINGS
(Dawn Henderson)

Is your life filled with Life? Or do you feel that somehow you're missing the point but don't quite know why?

We are all born with glorious powerful wings that will carry us through life joyfully and effortlessly if we let them. But all too often we forget their existence and they lie dormant and unused.

In Forgotten Wings, Dawn Henderson offers us 10 simple keys to remembering our wings and opening up to the magical and limitless potential of life. Knowledge that seems new but is as old as existence.

Through the insights, wisdom and reawakened knowing she has received on her own on-going voyage of spiritual discovery, Dawn reminds us of who we truly are and why we have chosen to play this game of life. Guiding us gently by the hand, Dawn shows us how, by changing the way we perceive these 10 key areas, we can reawaken our wings and open them once again to the light.

'Uplifting & inspirational'…'An amazingly beautiful book'…'Wonderful self-help book'

'Keep a copy by your bed and take nightly doses to keep you sane' *Kindred Spirit review (5 stars)*

ABOUT D.K. HENDERSON

D.K. Henderson lives in the beautiful county of Wiltshire, surrounded by its mysterious ancient landscape and stone monuments, which are an important source of inspiration for her writing.

She writes several occasional blogs and is passionate about spiritual development and the metaphysical side of life.

BLOGS:
www.soulwhispering.wordpress.com
www.thenakedheartblog.wordpress.com
www.thebigadventureblog.wordpress.com

WEBSITE:
www.dkhenderson.com

FACEBOOK:
www.facebook.com/DKHendersonAuthor

Made in the USA
Charleston, SC
28 June 2014